Christian discovered Lynnette descending the ladder slowly above him.

It was a most intriguing view. One he shouldn't be enjoying. He looked away quickly, but his eyes were drawn upward again. Lynnette's tight pants showed him just exactly how slender her legs were, how rounded her little bottom was. He felt his groin tighten and took a hasty step backward.

Then her toe slipped off the rung, and Christian found his hands had wrapped around her narrow waist.

If she had let go, he could have swung her to the ground...or into his arms. But she didn't let go. She caught her balance and continued down the last few steps. His hands didn't leave her waist until her foot touched the floor. He stepped back and let her turn around.

"Thanks." She was breathless. The climb down, he supposed.

But what was *his* excuse?

Dear Reader,

At the death of her father, a young woman agrees to marry an up-and-coming politician, but when she moves to the family ranch and meets her fiancé's rugged half brother, she realizes she has made a mistake in Cassandra Austin's new ranch story, *Hero of the Flint Hills*. Don't miss this tale from an author whose reputation for emotional depth grows with every new book.

In *A Wish for Nicholas* by Jackie Manning, a young woman who has been draining the income from her profitable land to improve the lives of the crofters must protect her secret, and her heart, from the dashing naval war hero who has been given her estate as a prize. And Margaret Moore's popular WARRIOR SERIES is still going strong, as you will discover with this month's *A Warrior's Bride,* the wonderful tale of a peace-loving knight and a fiery noblewoman who make an unlikely match in a stormy marriage of convenience.

We are very pleased to have *USA Today* bestselling author Merline Lovelace back in our midst with her new Western, *Countess in Buckskin,* the passionate story of a Russian countess who falls in love with the rough-hewn American lieutenant who has been forced to escort her through the untamed mountains of California.

Whatever your tastes in reading, we hope you enjoy all four books this month.

Sincerely,

Tracy Farrell
Senior Editor

HERO OF THE FLINT HILLS

CASSANDRA AUSTIN

Harlequin Books

TORONTO • NEW YORK • LONDON
AMSTERDAM • PARIS • SYDNEY • HAMBURG
STOCKHOLM • ATHENS • TOKYO • MILAN
MADRID • WARSAW • BUDAPEST • AUCKLAND

ISBN 0-373-28997-9

HERO OF THE FLINT HILLS

Books by Cassandra Austin

Harlequin Historicals

Wait for the Sunrise #190
Trusting Sarah #279
Cally and the Sheriff #381
Hero of the Flint Hills #397

CASSANDRA AUSTIN

has always lived in north central Kansas, and was raised on museums and arrowhead hunts; when she began writing, America's Old West seemed the natural setting. A full-time writer, she is involved in her church's activities as well as the activities of her three grown-to-nearly-grown children. Her husband farms, and they live in the house where he grew up.

To Joe, my own special hero

Chapter One

Kansas, 1876

Christian Prescott hurt all over. He longed to soak in a tub of hot water. Instead, he sat on the cold hearth where his dirty clothes wouldn't ruin the furniture and listened to his younger brother extol the virtues of some young woman he had briefly met in Topeka and had evidently promised to marry.

"But you'll both love her, too," Arlen said, aiming the current argument at Christian more than their father, presumably because Hugh needed less convincing. "She's educated and refined. Beautiful like...like a china doll, delicate and pale."

Christian wanted to groan. When his brother's buggy had driven up to the house a few minutes earlier, he had been more than happy to turn the ill-mannered mare over to Jake to rub down. Now he wished he was back at the corral having his joints systematically dislocated. It was damn hard listening to Arlen without saying something he would regret.

"She's educated," Arlen repeated, pacing across the braided rug like an actor on a stage while the kerosene lamp provided limelight. "Cultured. A lot like Mother, actually."

"Your mother left us, Arlen. She hated the ranch." Christian knew he should have bitten his tongue, but if neither Hugh nor Arlen had thought of that, it was time they did. He risked a glance at their father to assess the damage.

"Yes, well," the older man said, straightening slightly in the big leather-covered chair. "She won't be here much, will she? Once Arlen's elected to the legislature, they'll be in Topeka all winter. That's the worst time, Felicia always said."

"Perhaps she'll like the ranch if we make her feel welcome," Arlen said, avoiding eye contact with Christian. "She'll be taking the train to Cottonwood Station next week. I've told her she could be our guest for the summer."

This time Christian did groan. "What's she going to do here all summer? You'll be gone half the time, you know."

"Mother's sending Emily out with her."

Christian tried to imagine Arlen's cultured china doll enjoying the company of their thirteen-year-old sister. Even Emily was increasingly bored by the few social events of the neighborhood. Now they were to have two bored females with them for three months.

Arlen moved to what Christian had begun to think of as center stage. "Her name is Lynnette Sterling," he soliloquized. "Lynnette." His features took on a look of enchantment. "She floated into Mr. Ditmer's office like a spring breeze."

"And it was love at first sight."

It seemed to take Arlen a minute to snap back to the living room. He cast an annoyed glace at Christian. "Mr. Ditmer was helping her settle her father's estate. He introduced us then, and that night I discovered Mother had met her once or twice and knew her situation."

"Which is?" Hugh asked.

"Ira Sterling was one of the early settlers in Topeka. From New York State, I believe. Strong abolitionists."

That had to be worth a few points with Father, Christian thought, tempted to smile for the first time since Arlen had started relating his "wonderful news."

"Her mother's family goes back to the Revolution," Arlen went on.

"That's her pedigree, son, not her situation."

Arlen hesitated. "She's got no place to go." Abruptly he changed from the fast-talking lawyer to the boy who had found another stray. "Her mother died when she was a child, and her father's final illness cost her everything. She's even had to sell her home to pay the debts."

Christian nodded, coming stiffly to his feet. At least now he understood. He still didn't like it, though. "Did you have to promise to marry her, Arlen? Couldn't you simply have helped her find some kind of work?"

"But she's beautiful, Christian. I can't think of her working."

Christian shook his head. No, of course not. Not a fragile china doll. With a sigh, he offered a hand to Arlen; he couldn't quite bring himself to congratulate him. "It's good to have you home, little brother," he said. He wanted to pull Arlen into an embrace, but his brother wore a fancy suit while he was in dirty work clothes. It seemed to describe the distance that had opened between them a few years before and had been widening ever since.

He started out of the room but turned for another look at his brother. Arlen had knelt beside their father's chair and launched into further descriptions of the girl's many talents. Arlen had inherited his mother's fine bone structure. Christian's own rugged features more resembled their father's. In fact, he had often thought of Arlen as his opposite, with big brown eyes to his narrow blue ones, curly brown hair to his straight blond thatch, stringy now from sweat and wind.

They were opposites in more than appearance. Christian supposed that was the secret to their close friendship; they had never wanted the same thing so they were never in competition. Or perhaps the seven-year difference in their age had worked to their advantage. When Felicia had taken the then-five-year-old Emily away, Christian had been a grown man already aware that ranching was what he wanted to do with his life. Arlen had been only seventeen. Christian had helped his younger brother through some difficult times while their father was too hurt and angry at his wife's desertion to notice the boy's need.

And for Christian, Felicia hadn't been the first

mother he had lost. He had been three when his mother died of pneumonia. Neither woman had been strong enough for the solitude and hardships of ranch life. And Lynnette Sterling didn't sound as though she was either.

Christian laughed at himself as he turned toward the washroom. Arlen's wife wouldn't be a ranch wife, as their father had pointed out. He needed a political wife, which was something else altogether. Still, what kind of woman became engaged to a complete stranger? Arlen was handsome and certainly as cultured as his china doll. In all probability, Miss Lynnette Sterling was at this moment singing the praises of her future husband.

"A handsome young attorney! I'm so happy for you, Lynn."

Lynnette Sterling watched her friend do a gleeful little dance around the study. She had interrupted the sorting of her father's books when Amanda Norberg arrived and had thought to continue as she told her friend her plans, but Amanda was in no mood to help.

"The house and all the furniture are sold," Lynnette said, lifting another stack of books from the shelf and placing them on the floor beside the step stool. She sat down before she added, "I have to get my personal belongings out and leave next week. Mr. Prescott was nice enough to offer me a place to stay for the summer."

"Oh, Lynn, I will miss you terribly." Her serious expression didn't last. "My Bill has known your Mr. Prescott forever, you know."

Lynnette grinned at her friend. "Why didn't you fix me up with him instead of Julian?"

Amanda cringed. "I'm sorry about Julian." She took a book from the shelf and read the title before adding it to Lynnette's stack. "And I would have gotten around to Mr. Prescott sooner, but he's in and out of town a great deal."

Instead of going for another book, Amanda sat on the floor in front of her. "I can hardly believe it, Lynn. And to think you told me a hundred times how useless husbands are!"

Lynnette had to laugh at the memory. "That was before I was about to be thrown out on the street. Suddenly one seems very useful."

Amanda leaned away, obviously shocked by her words. "That's cold, Lynn. You should love your husband."

Lynnette watched her friend scowl at her. Relationships came easy to Amanda. Lynnette had always been less confident of her own appeal. When Amanda tossed a brown sausage curl over her shoulder, Lynnette smiled. Her own brown hair would never have held a curl like that and tended to turn red when it was exposed to the sun. Amanda had known since childhood that she would have her pick of men.

"I do love him," Lynnette ventured. "Or I think I do. He's really very sweet."

She meant to be a good wife to Arlen, but she couldn't help wishing something she wrote would sell. She would be bringing something to the marriage that way. It occurred to her that if she could sell her writing she wouldn't need a husband.

She mentioned none of this to Amanda, who considered her ambition to be a writer foolishness. As far as Amanda knew, nothing Lynnette had ever written had earned her a penny. Praise, occasionally, but no money. Lynnette's one success she hadn't shared with anyone. The dime novel, *Passion's Secret,* by Silver Nightingale had paid a great many bills and helped her keep her home nearly a year longer than she would have otherwise.

Lynnette lifted the rest of the stack of books onto her lap, but Amanda took them and moved them back to the floor. "Does his touch make your blood sing? Does his voice speak to your very soul? Do you look into his eyes and feel yourself floating up to heaven?"

Lynnette couldn't resist laughing. "You should be the writer."

Amanda squeezed her hands. "I'm serious, Lynn. If that's not what you feel, you shouldn't marry him. I'm afraid you're going to be miserable."

"You're afraid I'm going to argue with him until *he's* miserable." Amanda didn't laugh. Lynnette rose to her feet pulling her friend up with her. "If that's what you and Bill have, I'm thrilled for you, but I suspect that kind of joy only comes to a lucky few who believe the moon makes plans for young girls."

"I quit believing that years ago," Amanda said, pulling Lynnette into her arms. When she let her go, she continued. "But I still believe in love."

Lynnette stepped away. "I believe in love as well, Amanda, but perhaps most of us have a different kind of love."

Lynnette listened to Amanda's deep sigh and knew

her friend had given up. "Just remember, if there's anything I can do..."

"You're already helping me so much. I can't thank you enough for letting me store some things at your house. Now, you'd better hurry home to Bill before he starts to think you've decided to run away with me."

Lynnette saw her friend to the door, then returned to her father's study. It seemed too soon to be going through his books, deciding what to save, sell or take to the country for the summer. Several volumes had made the rounds to all the piles. If she couldn't decide what to do with a book, how could she decide what to do with her life?

With a sigh, Lynnette sat on the step stool, placing a stack of books in her lap. Her decision had already been made, and she would honor it. And the books had to be sorted. She vowed to be ready when Mrs. Prescott and her daughter came to take her to the train station.

Early Wednesday morning, Lynnette stood in her nearly empty front room beside the large trunk and two small valises that were to make the trip to the ranch. More of her belongings were stored away in Amanda's attic. She tried not to look at the things she was leaving behind forever.

Amanda had come to see her off. "Write me every day like you did when you were in college," she said, pulling the curtain aside to look out the front window.

"I won't be able to post a letter every day," Lynnette reminded her.

Amanda dropped the curtain and turned toward her. The sorrow on her face told Lynnette the carriage had arrived. Amanda gave her a quick hug before letting Mrs. Prescott's servants in and directing them to the trunk.

Amanda sniffed into a white handkerchief as the two women followed the men out the door. Lynnette tried for a brave smile. "I'll send you all my stories."

Amanda's laugh was a choked sob. Lynnette gave her friend a parting hug before climbing into the coach with Mrs. Prescott and her daughter, Emily. One last look at her home and a wave to Amanda, and Lynnette was on her way.

"I'm sure you'll have a lovely summer, both of you," Felicia Prescott said, reaching across to pat Lynnette's hand. "I feel certain that you're perfect for my son. I'm so happy for you, I almost wish I were going, too."

Emily's head snapped up. "Do come, Mama!"

"No, dear."

The older woman's attention turned to the buildings visible through the window. Emily watched her a moment and shrugged. Lynnette smiled sympathetically at the child. Of course she would want her parents together. It must be confusing to shuttle back and forth. From Arlen's conversation she knew the breakup had come a long time before.

At the station, Felicia sent the driver to see to the trunks and turned to say goodbye to her daughter. Lynnette looked away to give them some privacy. In a moment, Emily stepped to Lynnette's side, and they walked to the train together. Just before they boarded,

Felicia called, "Give Christian an extra hug from me."

"I will, Mama." Emily climbed to the platform and turned to blow her mother a kiss.

Lynnette waved as the whistle blared. "We'd better find some seats," she said.

The car wasn't crowded. They were able to find an empty pair of seats, and Lynnette flipped the back of one so they were facing each other. It wasn't until they were settled in and their valises stowed on the floor between the seats, that Lynnette gave any thought to Felicia's last request. She knew that Christian was the older brother, who ran the ranch with their father. Was he so openly the favorite that Felicia didn't care if her other children knew about it? Poor Arlen. It seemed strange, since Lynnette was sure this was the first she had heard Felicia mention him.

She had known Felicia socially since she, at sixteen, had begun attending functions at her father's side, her mother having died when she was a baby. She had, in fact, met Arlen a time or two in the past, though she was sure he didn't remember.

Emily's voice brought her out of her speculation. "Do you like to ride horses, Miss Sterling?"

"I've never ridden." She smiled at the girl. "Please, call me Lynnette."

"Lynnette." Emily seemed pleased. "Riding used to be my favorite thing, but I'd rather go to dances now. They hardly ever have any in the country, though. Do you like games—checkers and cards, I mean?"

"I haven't played much. I suppose because I had no brothers or sisters growing up."

Emily seemed disappointed. "Do you like books?"

"I love books."

The girl's face didn't brighten. "Then you'll love Papa's library. I bet he'll let you read anything you want."

"Are you afraid I won't find enough to keep me busy?"

Emily screwed up her face. "Arlen says I'm supposed to keep you company, but I'm bored often enough myself. I was hoping we could do some things together."

Lynnette laughed. "You can teach me all your favorite games, and we can take turns reading while the other sews."

Emily cringed. "Sews? Like embroidery and needlepoint? You *like* that?"

"Only if there's a good story to listen to." Lynnette reached across to pat the young girl's knee. "Don't worry, Emily. I'm sure we'll have a wonderful summer."

"I know. I didn't mean to make it sound so dreary. I always have fun, especially with Christian."

This was the second time he had been announced as the favorite. Emily didn't seem to notice anything unusual about her statement. Perhaps this was common among siblings.

Emily blithely removed her hat and placed it on the pile of valises, claiming one of her bags to serve as a pillow, and curled up to sleep.

Lynnette closed her eyes and tried to follow Emily's

example, but two young girls across the aisle burst into giggles. Drawn by their merriment, Lynnette turned to watch them. They were about Emily's age and looked very much alike. One clasped her hand over her mouth to quiet herself while the other craned her neck to look over the back of her seat. Their parents, Lynnette guessed, sat behind them with two younger children. The adults gave the girl reproving frowns.

Lynnette smiled to herself. How early the spontaneous pleasures of youth were stifled by convention. She had very few memories of that kind of gaiety from her own youth. She felt a vague sense of loss but dismissed it as grief over her father's death.

The girl who had turned to gauge their parents' reactions settled back into her seat. Her sister leaned toward her and drew a small book from beneath her skirts. They put their heads together and returned to their reading, but not before Lynnette got a glimpse of the cover.

Lynnette started in surprise. She glanced toward Emily to see if she had seen it too. The girl slept peacefully and Lynnette sighed in relief, then wanted to laugh at herself. There was nothing on that dark red cover that anyone would connect with her.

She leaned her head against the seat and tried again to rest. *Passion's Secret* had been so much fun to write and such delicious revenge on an editor who had ignored all her other stories. She wasn't ashamed of the story; it was just that no one would understand. She wasn't prepared for the public censure that would result if her authorship of the story became common knowledge. And so far no one knew, not even Julian Taggart.

Thinking of Julian made her skin crawl. He had seemed nice enough when she first met him. When she had caught him reading through some story notes in her parlor, she had told herself she should be glad he took an interest in her writing, but it bothered her that he hadn't felt he needed permission. When she decided she no longer wanted to see him, she discovered how possessive he could be. Little things that were hard to describe made her wonder if the man was unstable. She was certainly happy to be away from him.

Lynnette forced herself to relax. She should put Julian out of her mind and rest. She had a long day of travel ahead of her. She closed her eyes, but the train stopped every twenty minutes or so and the conductor's calls made sleep impossible. After an hour, she found the book she had packed in her valise and lost herself in it.

Emily alternated between sleep and chatter. At noon she found the lunches her housekeeper had packed for them. Lynnette wasn't particularly hungry, but Emily managed to eat her meal and talk at the same time.

"We're still a couple of hours from Cottonwood Station," she told Lynnette as she packed away the remains of her lunch. She settled back for another nap.

Lynnette tried again to rest, but never gave in to more than a light sleep, fearful of missing their stop. She needn't have worried. Emily roused herself, stretched and began collecting her bags a moment before the conductor called for Cottonwood Station.

"You're quite an alarm clock," Lynnette said, gathering her own things.

"I've done this so often I think I know every curve in the tracks."

Lynnette led the way into the aisle with Emily right behind. They were nearly to the end of the car when Emily turned back. "I'm missing my hat!"

"Shall I help you find it?" Lynnette tried to turn too, but a man had entered the aisle behind her and seemed reluctant to let her pass.

"No, I'll just be a minute," the girl called.

Lynnette stepped into the sunlight and got her first look at Cottonwood Station. She knew the town of Cottonwood Falls was across the river, but perhaps there would be a chance to explore it later.

The porter gave her only a second to study her surroundings before he reached to help her with her bags, tossing them unceremoniously on the platform below. Lynnette thanked him as he helped her down the narrow steps.

Out of the way of other passengers, Lynnette took a better look around. Surely this was a place full of stories. A couple with three small, quiet children and a pile of luggage waited for their turn to climb aboard. A young woman in provocative finery watched the passengers disembark. Was she waiting for someone in particular or for a potential customer? An elderly man in a top hat leaned on a cane, ignoring a woman's chatter. His wife?

As Lynnette's eyes roved the area, they lit on the most interesting person of all. A young man with blond hair to his shoulders lounged against an open wagon. His long slender legs and hips were encased in dusty denim. His blue shirt was open at the throat, its sleeves rolled nearly to his elbows. He thrust his hands into his pockets, pulling the black suspenders taut. His chest and shoulders looked far more muscular than the men's she saw in the city. Were theirs simply hidden by their dress jackets?

She felt the curl of excitement in her stomach that meant she smelled a story. My, but he was interesting, she thought, then realized he was watching her just as intently. She turned away, but not before she noticed that his expression was more than slightly unpleasant. She glanced at the train and considered going back after Emily, but realized it had only been a couple of minutes since she had disembarked and there was still a steady stream of travelers exiting the car.

What could she represent that would make the young man scowl at her? Sure, her dress was slightly out of style and well-worn, but it was tasteful and clean, or had been this morning. It must have been her imagination. She looked back at him to see. No, he was scowling. Well, frowning at least. His hat was pulled down too far to see his brows so she couldn't say he was actually scowling.

But I'm definitely staring. She turned away but movement brought her eyes back again. He straightened, pulled his hands from his pockets, and broke into a dimpled smile. Lynnette was astounded. It was several seconds before she could turn to see what had caught his attention.

Emily, overloaded with bags, had emerged from the car, her hat held precariously between two fingers.

Lynnette hurried to help the porter lighten her load. Emily suddenly seemed like a vulnerable child. That strange man looked at her as if he wanted to devour her. Lynnette considered asking the porter to stay with them until Arlen arrived.

When Emily jumped to the platform, Lynnette drew her close, keeping herself between Emily and the stranger. "That man," she started, giving the barest nod in his direction.

Emily leaned around Lynnette, then squealed. "Christian!"

Emily flew across the platform, down the steps and into Christian's open arms. He lifted her off the ground as if she were a small child and spun her around. The wind finished what the nap had started, and Emily's hair fell down her back. Christian's hat hit the ground and for a moment their faces were blurred by straight blond hair and dark brown curls.

Lynnette was too stunned to follow. She stood beside their collection of bags watching the brother and sister. It had never occurred to her that family would actually greet each other this way. She had expected a warm smile, a handshake, perhaps a kiss on the cheek. She was envious.

Christian finally let the girl go, and they walked together toward her. They still had their arms around each other, and Lynnette wondered how his long legs kept from becoming entangled in Emily's flowing skirts.

"Lynnette," Emily said when they reached her. "This is my brother, Christian. Christian, meet Miss Lynnette Sterling."

"Hey! Good job, Muffin," Christian said, unwrapping his arm from his sister's shoulder to stretch it out toward Lynnette. "Pleasure to meet you, Miss Lynnette Sterling."

Lynnette took the hand, hoping her face no longer registered her surprise. "How do you do," she murmured. She couldn't quite forget that this same man had been scowling at her only moments before. Frowning at least. It seemed a little hard to believe now, he was so obviously happy.

She realized they had both looked at each other a little too long, measuring, she decided. She pulled her hand free and reached for one of the bags.

"Mama said to give you an extra hug for her."

A hesitant quality in the girl's voice made Lynnette straighten to see his reaction. For a moment he was completely still. She thought she saw pain in his eyes, then it was gone and the dimpled smile was back. "Well, let's have it," he said.

Emily giggled and jumped into his arms. He swung her around again. Up close, Lynnette could see how tightly they held each other, how their cheeks pressed together. The envy she had felt before was replaced with a longing not quite so sisterly. She was staring again. Even as she turned to reach for the bags she had a feeling he had noticed her interest.

A moment later, Emily was on her feet and all three were gathering up the bags, with Christian taking the largest share.

"You ladies ever hear of traveling light?" he asked, leading the way to the wagon.

"Not me," said Emily. "We each have a trunk besides."

Christian let out an exaggerated groan as he set the bags down beside the wagon and retrieved his hat. "Come show them to me, Em." He tugged on one of Emily's curls. As they walked away, Lynnette heard his teasing. "I better braid your hair before we head home. Wouldn't you like that? Two nice little pigtails like you used to wear?" Emily squealed and tried to pull her hair out of his reach.

Lynnette watched them as they found the trunks in front of the luggage car. She tried to think of a word to describe the way he moved. Lithe, she decided, and wondered if he knew how to dance. When Christian hoisted Emily's trunk to his shoulder and started across the platform, Lynnette turned away, pretending to study her surroundings. She didn't want him to look at her and guess she had been imagining herself dancing in his arms.

He dropped the trunk to the wagon bed and pushed it forward, then turned to lean against the wagon while he caught his breath. "Real tight pigtails," he said to Emily, as if carrying the trunk had only been a momentary interruption in his teasing. "So you always look surprised." He raised his eyebrows to demonstrate, and Emily hit him in the stomach.

He merely grinned and headed back for Lynnette's trunk. Lynnette hadn't been certain what she would need on the ranch and, along with every imaginable type of clothing, she had packed several books and lots of writing supplies. It hadn't occurred to her until she watched Christian try to lift the trunk just how big and heavy it was.

He didn't waste time struggling with it but got the porter to help. When the two men had shoved the trunk into the back of the wagon, Christian gave the man a coin. "Thanks for the help," he said. "You know how it is. You go away for the summer, you just have to take your favorite anvil."

Lynnette tried to swallow her embarrassment. She felt a need to apologize, but before she could, Emily applied another blow to Christian's stomach. "Quit teasing!" The girl walked demurely to the front of the wagon and waited, one hand out limply, for Christian to help her in. Christian tossed Lynnette a persecuted look before following obediently. He reached for the hand as if to assist the girl, but grabbed her waist and lifted her instead. Emily giggled.

He held a hand toward Lynnette, indicating she was next. She was almost afraid to approach him. He grinned a challenge. She stepped forward with no small amount of trepidation, but he merely steadied her as she climbed aboard.

The seat seemed rather narrow, and Lynnette was uncertain how to make room for Christian. The wagon rocked as he sprang into the bed behind them. She retreated to the side, pulling her skirts out of the way, as he climbed over the seat to sit between her and Emily.

Emily seemed less concerned about her skirts. "Why didn't you bring the buggy?"

"And do what with the trunks?" He reached across Lynnette to untie the reins from the hand brake and release it. Lynnette tried to shrink out of his way and wasn't entirely successful. It somehow embarrassed her to be this close to a man she had just met. Doubly so when he seemed capable of ignoring the contact.

"You could have taken our trunks in the wagon, and Arlen could have driven us in the buggy." Emily emphasized Arlen, making it sound like a preferable arrangement.

"Arlen's off shaking hands and kissing babies."

Lynnette felt a twinge of guilt. It hadn't occurred to her to question why Arlen hadn't met the train. In fact at that moment she could barely call up an image of Arlen's face. She wished she could see Emily; she and Arlen looked so much alike. When she tried, she ended up studying Christian's profile.

He looked nothing like either of them. One sandy-brown eyebrow arched above an incredibly blue eye. Well, she knew there was a matched set, but she could only see one. She knew also that the tanned cheek could crease into a charming dimple. His strong, lean jaw contrasted with his full lips. Exactly what color were those lips? Carnation? No, not quite so bright. Rose, then? Perhaps. A pink rose at dusk.

The lips curved up into a grin that revealed white even teeth. Lynnette jumped, her attention quickly shifting to his eyes—both of them. When had he caught her staring? She couldn't have been more mortified if he had winked. The humor in his eyes made her think he would do it. She pretended to look beyond him toward Emily, but he had to know she couldn't see her. Emily was talking, she realized, but she couldn't concentrate enough to make any intelligent response. After a moment, she turned away.

Lynnette thanked God she wasn't prone to blushing. *He* could be debating between scarlet and crimson. She resolutely turned her attention to the countryside. Their route wandered a little through rocky hills, climbing ever higher, and Christian's leg pressed against her own. She was sure she felt its heat soak through her heavy skirt. She tried to scoot farther away, noticing how the trees seemed greener and fresher here than in the city.

She took in a deep breath of the summer-ripe air. She identified the scent of wind-tossed dust, growing vegetation, a faint hint of horse, soap and sun-dried clothes. She wanted to groan. She had never been so preoccupied with a man before.

She only noticed everything about him because she was a writer, she told herself. She looked for details. She liked to try to describe what she saw and touched. Possible descriptions of the man sitting next to her made her fingers tremble.

She would block him out. It was much more useful to describe the countryside. The...hills...grass...

Christian cleared his throat.

Lynnette closed her eyes for a moment. She had to get her imagination under control. It was fatigue, of course, that made it so difficult.

"Arlen should be back sometime tomorrow," he said.

Lynnette turned toward him; she really had no choice without being rude. My, but he was attractive.

After she'd gazed for a moment into sky-blue eyes,

his words found their way to her brain. Arlen. Tomorrow. He expected a response. She wasn't sure
what she should say. That she was dying to see Arlen
again? When she couldn't remember what he looked
like except he *didn't* have full lips or dimples or blue-
blue eyes? Besides it didn't sound quite proper.

"I'm grateful to your family for letting me visit this
summer," she ventured.

He eyed her oddly for a moment then turned his
attention back to the team. Lynnette supposed it hadn't
sounded particularly romantic.

"How's Papa?" Emily asked. "Catch me up on
everything."

"Well," Christian began, "Papa's fine. Nothing
much slows him down. Perry broke his leg last winter,
but he's healing." He turned to Lynette. "Perry's our
hired man."

Lynnette nodded, too rattled by their earlier
exchange to think clearly. He must have taken her lack
of response as lack of interest. He made no further
effort to include her as he described the health and
activities of several people whom she did not know.
She hung on every word, trying to associate each name
with each situation. She wasn't merely captivated by
his voice.

When Christian mentioned Elayne was due to foal
in a few weeks, Emily leaned forward to inform Lynnette, "I named her. Elayne was Sir Lancelot's
mother."

Christian turned to Lynnette. "You know what she
was reading the summer we got the mare."

"It's a great name," Emily said, scowling at her brother.

"I suppose if the foal's male we'll have to name it Lancelot."

Lynnette thought he spoke to Emily, but his eyes were still on her. It was easy to gaze into those blue pools and forget to speak. She thought of a mouse hypnotized by a snake. Emily rescued her by mentioning Tyrant, pulling Christian's attention away from Lynnette. Tyrant turned out to be a cat who had the run of the house.

They had been steadily climbing into the rocky hills and at the top of one, Christian stopped the wagon. "I thought you might like to stretch your legs." He reached across Lynnette to set the brake and tie the reins. He stood and, placing one foot on the dashboard in front of Lynnette, leaped to the ground.

Emily didn't seem particularly surprised by this rather athletic feat. "You're the one with the stretched legs. Lynnette and I are fine."

Christian grinned and offered his hand to Lynnette. She knew she hesitated a moment before taking it and hoped he thought it was because of his sister's words. He held her hand no longer than necessary and stepped away. Still in that one moment she had felt his strength and warmth. And his calluses, she reminded herself, as if that would make a difference.

The wind played with Lynnette's heavy skirts as she turned and stared. "You can see forever up here."

The green hills tiered below them to the valley and the cottonwood trees that hid the river. Hazy hills were visible beyond, complementing the pale blue sky.

"This is the worst part of coming to the ranch," Emily said.

Lynnette turned toward her, laughing in surprise, then realized what Emily was talking about. The girl had pulled her hair together and held it at her shoulder in one fist while tendrils whirled around her face. Lynnette could feel her own small hat being tugged loose from its numerous pins. "We have wind in the city, too," she offered.

"Not if you don't go outside."

Lynnette turned to Christian and caught his playful grin. "She should have let me braid her hair."

Christian's conspiratorial tone disconcerted her. "Perhaps we should go," she suggested. Christian pulled a basket out from under the seat and handed it to Emily who balanced it on her lap. After one last look across the valley Lynnette let Christian help her aboard and waited as he resumed his former place.

As soon as the wagon was moving again, Emily opened the basket. It contained three pint jars packed in straw. "Tea," Christian said, handing one to Lynnette. "It isn't hot, but it's wet."

"Why didn't she send lemonade?" Emily was clearly disappointed.

"Martha seemed to think tea would be more proper."

Emily snorted her disagreement but soon began plying Christian with questions about the summer activities planned for the neighborhood. Lynnette opened the jar, grateful it wasn't full. She was afraid she would spill it on her dress and look a fright when she met Arlen's father.

Perhaps Emily was used to drinking from a jar in a moving wagon. Her conversation never faltered. Lynnette was only half-listening when a tall rock house became visible. It dropped from sight as the wagon dipped into a valley then reappeared, looming over the countryside.

"Thank goodness." Emily sighed. "We're almost home. I'm so-o-o tired of traveling."

"Poor little Em," soothed Christian. "Didn't you get to nap on the train?"

Emily's elbow landed firmly in Christian's ribs, causing him to jolt into Lynnette. He gave her an apologetic smile, but he didn't exactly look repentant.

"I slept some," Emily said, "but there were two little girls giggling the whole way."

Lynnette felt a twinge of apprehension. She hoped Emily didn't relate the source of the girls' giggles. Even if Emily had seen the book, even if she remembered the title and author, no one would guess it was hers.

She stole a glance at Christian and found his eyes on her. Had he sensed her unease? She concentrated on breathing slowly, willing her hands to remain still in her lap. She didn't want her reaction to make him curious enough to ask Emily why the girls had been giggling.

Another glance told her he still watched her. Perhaps he was vain enough to take credit for her nervousness, to believe his leg pressing against hers made her heart beat loudly enough for him to hear, to believe his arm against her shoulder made her fingers tremble.

And of course, that wasn't it at all.

Chapter Two

The wagon was almost even with the house before Lynnette was able to relax. And it wasn't because of the man sitting so close beside her. Or at least it wouldn't have been if she wasn't certain that *he* watched *her.*

"Mostly we live in the top two floors," Emily said. She seemed to take Lynnette's effort to keep her face turned away from Christian as interest in the house and leaned around Christian to talk as the wagon jostled up the slope. "The bottom floor's for entertaining, which we don't ever do." She scowled at her brother.

Lynnette stole a glance at Christian. He was smiling fondly at Emily. Deep dimples in his cheeks made her long to test the texture of the fine blond stubble visible where the sun struck his face. Shocked by her thoughts, Lynnette turned her attention back to the house.

It had been built into a hillside, allowing ground-level entrances to the bottom floor in front and the middle floor in back. The first floor sported corner bay windows and a porch at the front door. These became three balconies for the rooms above. The top floor consisted of a mansard roof with two large dormers, each with its own smaller balcony.

Christian drove the wagon past the house and turned up a graveled path that led between it and the barn. Lynnette had been so enthralled by the house that she had scarcely noticed the barn. It too had ground-level entrances on two floors and a ramp that led to the third. She looked forward to a chance to explore the massive structure.

The wagon turned again, and Lynnette got a glimpse of a wide valley below before her view was blocked by the house itself. The back had the same quiet grandeur as the front, though it was less imposing with only two stories visible.

The two gables had the same small balconies, and she turned to see what their view might be. The ground sloped upward gradually from the house for barely twenty yards then rose sharply. A trail meandered up a hill that dwarfed the house, and Lynnette could only guess what the view would be from there.

"Welcome to the Prescott Ranch."

Lynnette turned to find Christian regarding her quizzically. Was she acting like a city girl, studying her surroundings so intently? There was no need for her to feel defensive. She *was* a city girl. Besides, she had no reason to impress this man.

"Thank you," she murmured, hearing the chill in her voice.

Emily had already climbed down from the wagon and run around it. Christian jumped down from the dashboard and turned to offer Lynnette a hand. She was about to grasp it when Emily's shout caught their attention.

"Papa!"

A tall thin man with fine gray hair had come through the door. Emily flung herself into his arms, and he swung her around much as Christian had done. "It's good to have you home, Em," he said once she was back on her feet. He sounded slightly out of breath. "Help the lady down, Christian."

In a moment she was on the ground, and Christian's calloused hand was slipped out of hers. Instead of stepping away, he took her arm lightly and led her forward. "Miss Sterling, let me introduce Hugh Prescott. Pa, Lynnette Sterling."

"We're happy to have you, Miss Sterling," Hugh said, his arm still around his daughter. "I'm sorry Arlen isn't here to make you feel welcome. The rest of us will do the best we can."

Lynnette smiled. "That's most kind of you." He looked so much like Christian she had to turn and compare their faces. But Christian wasn't smiling. She turned back to the elder Prescott quickly. "Please, call me Lynnette."

"Christian, get Jake to help you with the trunks. I'm sure the ladies would like to get out of the sun." He turned and walked Emily to the house, releasing her only as they came to the door. He held a hand toward Lynnette, encouraging her forward.

She resisted taking a backward glance at Christian. Why had he been watching her so seriously? Was he judging her suitability to marry his brother?

She decided to put Arlen's strange brother out of

her mind and walked resolutely through the door. Emily had crossed a small room lined with benches. Hooks on the wall held coats and rain gear. Several pair of boots were shoved under the benches. At the end of the room, the door stood open.

"That way's the washroom and the kitchen." Emily pointed to the left when Lynnette had caught up with her. "This is Pa's study," she said, indicating the room to the right of the entry.

Lynnette followed Emily through a door across the hall and stepped into the living room. There was a rock fireplace, groups of comfortable-looking chairs, small tables, shelves and an open stairway leading to the top floor.

Across the room stood double glass doors. The view of the valley beyond was breathtaking. Lynnette walked toward the doors trying to think of words to describe the shades of green in the grasses and trees, the sheer distance that one was able to see.

She opened the doors and stepped out. The round balcony was larger than it had appeared from below. With the breeze on her face and nothing in sight to ground her on the hillside, Lynnette felt as if she were floating over the valley. Her fingers and toes tingled with adrenaline, and she gripped the rail.

"I'll tell Martha to bring some lemonade." Hugh had spoken softly, and Lynnette turned in time to see him leave his daughter's side. As she walked back inside, he disappeared around the stairway. A large black and white cat entered from the same direction and sat inspecting the new arrivals.

"That's Tyrant," Emily said, motioning Lynnette

into a chair. "Don't try to be his friend." At Lynnette's raised eyebrows, she continued, "He'll make up his own mind, and you're better off ignoring him. He loves Arlen and Papa, but barely tolerates the rest of us. Martha despises him, but I think he loves her the best, maybe because she smells like the kitchen."

Tyrant walked past them as if they were unimportant and sprang into a brocade-covered chair, making himself comfortable. "Come here, Tyrant," Emily coaxed. "Don't you remember me?" Tyrant gazed at her, blinked and proceeded to wash his paws.

Christian came through the door backward, carrying one side of Lynnette's trunk. The other end was supported by a boy only slightly older than Emily. "Welcome home, Miss Emily," he said, giving her a smile that could only be described as teasing.

"That's Jake," Emily said to Lynnette. "He works in the barn and does *simple* tasks around the place."

Lynnette bit her lip and tried for a pleasant smile. "It's nice to meet you, Jake."

Christian gave an exaggerated sigh. Jake, of course, had stopped walking as soon as he saw Emily. Christian set his end of the trunk on the floor, causing Jake to drop his, then seated himself on the trunk, crossed his arms and watched his younger sister. Her hair was a most unsophisticated mess around her shoulders, making her look younger than her thirteen years. In contrast, she sat demurely on a wingback chair, modeling her pose after Lynnette's. Miss Sterling, he corrected himself. *He* hadn't been invited to call her Lynnette.

Emily cast poor Jake a twinkling smile. "Miss Lynnette doesn't really mean it, Jake. She's just being polite.''

Christian turned his attention to Lynnette as the young people continued their teasing. Her eyes traveled from one to the other, amusement evident in the soft curve of her mouth. If he wasn't mistaken she deliberately avoided looking at him. Fine. It gave him time to study her.

Arlen's "china doll" came to mind, but it didn't quite fit. There was too much life under those porcelain features. That, more than her beauty, made her attractive. She had perfect manners, as Arlen had said, was quiet and reserved—reserved to the point of being embarrassed by his display of affection for his little sister, a sister whom he hadn't seen in nearly a year.

Once or twice he had found himself trying to measure her reaction to this land, his home. What did he care whether she liked it here or looked down her nose at their way of life? *He* wasn't looking for a wife. And if he was, a woman like Lynnette wouldn't even be in the running.

But that wasn't why he studied her. He felt a need to protect his brother. Arlen was young and could be easily taken in by promises from those pretty lips. And she didn't love Arlen. He was sure of it. She hadn't asked about him once, not when Arlen had failed to meet them at the station, not during the long ride to the ranch.

Had she committed herself to Arlen out of desperation? Arlen had indicated that she was practically destitute. Was that the truth? Her dress certainly seemed older than the latest fashion, but had she chosen it carefully for effect?

Christian gave himself a mental shake. Her actual situation wasn't the point. What kind of a wife would she make Arlen? His eyes narrowed as he watched her laugh softly at one of Emily's quips. She was a beauty, all right, just as Arlen had said. What was inside, however, remained to be seen.

He stood abruptly. "Are you two done bickering?"

"I believe so, sir," Jake replied. "The poor girl's starting to repeat herself."

"Only because it's so hard for you to understand things," Emily replied airily.

Christian and Jake lifted the trunk as one and headed for the stairs. Christian stepped aside at the bottom, allowing Jake to back up the stairs, taking most of the weight himself. Jake was strong, but he was seventeen, a boy yet.

A grinning boy, at present. The grin didn't leave Jake's face all the way up the stairs. They put the trunk down and Jake opened the door to the room Lynnette would be using. "This is one heavy trunk." The boy grunted as he lifted it again.

"I think the lady plans to stay awhile."

"You reckon she's got a different outfit for every day?"

Christian chuckled. They walked down the stairs and met Martha at the bottom with a tray of lemonade. Christian reached for a tall glass. "Why thank you, Martha. You read my mind."

She carefully swung the tray out of reach. "These are for the young ladies."

Christian threw his arm around Jake's shoulder as they walked through the living room. "Fine thing, Jake. We do all the work, and they get the refreshment."

"It's the way it always is, boss. The way it'll always be." Christian noticed he cast a sidelong look at Emily as they passed. These two had been teasing each other since they were babies. Eventually, one of them would outgrow it. He hoped.

By the time they came back with Emily's lighter trunk she, Lynnette and Hugh had taken their drinks out on the balcony. Christian noticed Jake's disappointment and wondered if an end to their childish relationship was a good thing after all.

"You know, Jake," he began as they set the trunk on the landing and opened Emily's door, "you can tease my sister all you want, but remember she's a child. And remember whose child. I'm afraid if you lay a hand on her, your father and mine will take turns making you wish you hadn't."

Jake shuddered. "Not to mention what *she* would do."

Christian laughed. "Let's get those bags up here, then find our lemonade."

A few minutes later Christian, lemonade in hand, stepped out onto the balcony. Martha had insisted Jake stay in the kitchen and not "interfere with the family."

Emily and Lynnette were sitting on folding chairs while Hugh leaned against the rail. Christian took a place on the far side, not wanting to block the ladies' view of the valley.

"In spite of all that, school isn't too bad, Papa," Emily said, smiling an acknowledgment of Christian's arrival. "I have lots of friends there. None so nice as Rose, of course. Will Rose be able to stay sometime this summer?"

"I'm sure she's planning on it, dear." Hugh had nodded a greeting to Christian but hadn't interrupted his daughter's chatter. She was evidently catching him up on the past year.

As he sipped the lemonade, Christian reflected on his family. They had remained close in spite of Felicia. Did she ever miss this sense of belonging or had she found something she valued more? Of course, Felicia had Emily nine months out of twelve. And Arlen nearly half the time. What Christian really wondered was if she ever missed her husband or stepson.

He shook off the thoughts and studied their guest, Arlen's addition to the family. She appeared to relax, dividing her attention between Emily, Hugh and the view below.

Perhaps sensing his scrutiny, her eyes turned in his direction. He knew he should give her a friendly smile and turn his eyes elsewhere, but it wasn't that easy. She was lovely to look at. Small perfect features were surrounded by shining chestnut hair, upswept and anchored so securely only a few stray wisps had come loose during the wagon ride. Hazel eyes, almost green in the sunlight, watched him questioningly, as if she tried to read his thoughts and failed. If she was after Arlen for his money, he was the one she needed to worry about. Had she recognized that already?

"Did you put Lynnette's trunk in my room, Christian?"

Christian pulled his gaze from Lynnette to Emily. "Arlen's room," he answered.

"Arlen will be gone a great deal," Hugh interjected. "When he's home, he'll share his brother's room."

"I didn't know which bags were whose so they're all on the landing," Christian said.

"Thank you," Lynnette said. "For moving my things and for making room for me."

Christian caught himself gazing at her again. He drank the rest of the lemonade quickly, setting his glass beside Emily's chair. "Great to have you home, little sister," he whispered, bending close to her ear. He kissed her temple, stealing a glance at Lynnette over the top of her head. As he expected, she averted her eyes, embarrassed that he would kiss his sister. Poor Arlen, he thought, as he left the balcony.

Lynnette chewed on her lower lip, trying to quash her reaction to Christian's presence. The atmosphere had changed the moment he entered the balcony. He was different from the businessmen she was used to. His manner of dress, his long hair, these made the writer in her curious.

She had been trying to explain away her interest in him when he kissed his sister. The sight of those full lips as he bent toward Emily sent butterflies loose in her stomach. She couldn't remember when she had ever had such a reaction. Surely it was the long trip, the upsetting change in her situation.

"Are you ready to see your room and unpack?" Emily asked.

"I believe so," she answered gratefully. "Just let me return my glass to the kitchen and thank Martha." She stood and turned toward Hugh. "I can't thank you enough for letting me stay the summer."

"That's quite all right. Leave your glasses on the tray. I'll take care of them. You two run along and rest before dinner."

"Thanks, Papa." Emily ran to give him a hug before leading Lynnette into the house. The stairs were all that separated the living room from the dining room, and, as they started up, Lynnette looked over the banister at a lovely simple table with six straight-back chairs.

"The stairs are in the center of the house," Emily explained. "There are four rooms upstairs, one in each corner."

The stairs emerged onto a narrow landing. A railing that matched the banisters circled the stairwell. "That's your room." Emily pointed to a door to the right. "Papa and I get the great view. I hope you don't mind."

"I'm sure it's fine," Lynnette said.

Emily paused by the collection of valises, picking one to take to her room. "I'm over here," she said. "If you need anything, just knock."

"Thank you, Emily. Have a good rest." She watched the girl go into her room. If Christian and Arlen's rooms were to the back of the house, that must be Christian's door. She quickly turned and noted

Hugh's door as well. She didn't care which room was Christian's.

She turned the knob to Arlen's door and pushed it open. Her trunk stood just inside. She gathered up her valises and brought them in with her, plunking them down on top of her trunk before she turned to look around.

The room was large, as she had expected. A star quilt in shades of pink and green covered the four-poster bed, giving the room its only color. The tops of the dresser and writing desk were bare except for oil lamps. The drapes that could be drawn across the balcony doors were an eggshell white. Only two pictures were on the wall, one a family portrait, the other a garden scene in hazy, subdued colors.

Did this colorless room reflect Arlen's tastes? She was sure the pink and green quilt wasn't his. She decided she shouldn't make too much of it. Perhaps the quilt replaced one of even brighter hues. She crossed to the writing desk, opening the top drawer. It was stuffed with items that normally would have cluttered a desktop. Lynnette smiled to herself as she closed the drawer. He had cleared the top for her.

A quick check of the dresser revealed that he had emptied more than half of the drawers for her belongings, evidently moving his necessities to Christian's room. She went to work, unpacking her bags and the trunk. She tried to conjure up some feeling of intimacy with Arlen as she put her undergarments away where his had recently been stored, but she didn't feel any different than she would moving into a hotel room. She brushed it off as a result of his items having been

removed before her arrival. There was very little here
to remind her of Arlen.

She left a few of her things in the trunk for storage
and shoved it against the wall. Once everything else
was put away, she went to the balcony. It was smaller
than the one downstairs, probably no more than five
feet square. She stepped to the railing and let her eyes
follow the twisting trail to the top of the hill.

To her left and right was the roof itself, with Christian's balcony rails visible beyond. She looked quickly
in the other direction. She could see the corrals where
the ledge, upon which most of the house was built,
widened to accommodate them. Nearest the house was
a square pen with a lone post of mysterious purpose
in the middle. She could see part of the barn. Fascinated, she considered going down to explore but knew
dinner would be served shortly.

Turning back into her room, she eyed the quilt-
covered bed. She should lie down and rest before dinner as Hugh had suggested, but it didn't sound attractive. Closing her eyes would bring forth images of her
father dying, her lost home, her friend, Amanda, so
far away. She felt a need to stay busy.

A china basin with matching pitcher sat on a shav-
ing stand. Relieved to find the pitcher full, she quickly
washed her face and fixed her hair.

Coming down the stairs was a marvelous experience. She could look down on the rustic living room
or the simple dining room or out the tall glass door a
few feet from the base of the stairs onto the valley
below. The latter commanded most of Lynnette's attention. She couldn't resist stepping out on this center,

square balcony and looking across the valley again. She wasn't sure if it was the colors, the feeling of flight, or the sheer openness that most attracted her. If she would be allowed to spend all summer on one of these balconies, she knew she would be happy here.

"It's quite a view, isn't it?" Hugh's voice startled her, and she turned to find him on the corner balcony off the dining room.

"It's lovely," she said.

"That's precisely why I chose the back of the house for my study. I'd never get any work done as long as I could see this."

"To me this seems like a lovely place to work. I can imagine bringing paper and ink here and writing to my heart's content."

Hugh laughed. "You might watch all your papers fly across the valley with a sudden gust of wind."

Lynnette looked out, trying to picture it. It was so lovely and peaceful. She shook her head. "I'd take my chances."

"Be my guest. I'll have Jake move a desk out for you, if you'd like."

"I'm sure I'll manage something simple." She heard footsteps in the dining room. Martha setting the table, she guessed. "I should leave you to your contemplation," she said.

"Shirking," he corrected. "Merely shirking, my dear."

She smiled. "Whatever. I leave you to it."

Lynnette closed the balcony doors behind her and moved toward the table. She returned Martha's shy greeting. "May I help with dinner?" she asked.

"That's not necessary, miss," Martha said, unfolding a crisp white cloth on the long table.

Lynnette caught one corner of the cloth and helped her spread it evenly. "I'm not used to being waited on. I'd really like to help. That is, if you don't mind."

"Of course not, but you're supposed to be resting like Miss Emily."

Lynnette followed Martha to a beautiful china cupboard. "I won't tell if you don't," she whispered.

Martha showed Lynnette where the dishes and silver were and which four places to set, then returned to the kitchen. In a few minutes, the table set, Lynnette followed. A man, several years older than Martha, was laying plates out on a long plank table. He worked effectively in spite of a crutch under one arm.

"You must be Perry," she said.

"You must be Arlen's Miss Sterling."

Lynnette shook the callused hand he offered, pleased by the friendly greeting. Martha was at the stove and seemed surprised to see Lynnette actually in the kitchen. "What can I do now?" Lynnette asked her.

"There's a bowl of wildflowers on the counter that can go on the table." She nodded toward them.

Lynnette smiled, taking the hint. Martha was efficient and there were no jobs left this late in the preparations. She took up the bowl of flowers, sniffing their pungent odor. "It was nice meeting you," she told Perry on her way past. He nodded in response.

The flowers on the table contrasted well with the fine bone china and crystal. Refined, yet simple. She cocked her head to one side, studying the table, searching for better words to describe it. Comfortably elegant, she thought.

"Do you approve?"

Lynnette's hand flew to her heart as she jumped. Christian stood at the base of the stairs, one hand on the banister. His hair was damp around his face. He looked comfortable enough to have stood there for several minutes.

"I didn't hear you come in," she said, when she found her voice.

He smiled, but it wasn't the unrestrained smile she had seen him give his sister. "That's because I was here first."

Lynnette laughed, hoping to break some of the tension that seemed to exist whenever he looked at her. "I was too intent on the flowers, I suppose."

He nodded. "Is Emily down yet?"

She shook her head. "I could get her, if you'd like."

"I'll do it." He turned and went up the stairs two at a time. Lynnette realized she watched him until his legs disappeared.

"Whom shall I annoy next?" she mumbled.

Not wanting to bother Hugh on the balcony and feeling unwanted in the kitchen, she moved into the living room. The room contained none of the decorative finery that cluttered Felicia's home in Topeka. She had discovered a shelf of Indian artifacts when she heard Christian's boots on the stairs.

"Is Emily ready?" she asked, turning to greet him.

"She's fixing her hair."

He walked into the room, studying her much as

though she were some strange artifact herself. She was relieved when Hugh, donning his suit coat, ambled into the room.

"Ah, you've found my treasures," he said, moving to her side. "These were all found on our ranch at one time or another." He pointed out several arrowheads, inviting her to hold them and examine them up close. There was also a piece of a clay pipe.

"This is my favorite." He lifted a large stone ax head and handed it to her. Lynnette rubbed the cold smooth surface, surprised at how heavy it was. She set it carefully back in its place.

They heard a door upstairs open and close. "Well," Hugh said, offering her his arm. "Bad enough to bore you with my hobbies without keeping you from dinner in the process."

They met Emily at the bottom of the stairs, and Hugh directed everyone to their seats. Lynnette and Emily were on either side of Hugh at the head of the table, and Christian took the seat beside Emily.

Emily had changed out of her traveling clothes into a simple gown of pale green lawn. She looked refreshed and lovely with her hair piled on her head and tumbling down the back in natural curls.

It occurred to Lynnette that both Emily and Hugh had dressed for dinner. It was a custom she had forgotten since her father's illness. She would have felt out of place in her traveling dress if it hadn't been for Christian, at ease in his open shirt with the rolled-up sleeves.

Hugh asked a brief blessing and Martha, evidently

waiting for their arrival, entered, carrying a platter piled with thick steaming steaks.

"I told Martha Miss Sterling's—Lynnette's—first meal at the ranch had to be our own beef." He took the platter from Martha who returned to the kitchen. He speared a huge slab of meat and held the platter for Lynnette. She was grateful that a few pieces were cut more to her appetite. She stabbed the juicy steak with her fork as he had done and put it on her plate.

Martha returned with potatoes and gravy and then with corn and bread, all of which she set near Hugh's place. He served the women, then passed them to Christian. "Holler if you want more," Christian said, taking up his knife and fork.

"When's Arlen coming home?" Emily asked.

"Tomorrow, I believe," her father said. "I'm sure he'll return as soon as possible." He gave Lynnette a warm smile.

Lynnette returned the smile shyly. She almost dreaded Arlen's return. That was foolish; he was the reason she was here.

"I think we should have a party," Emily suggested, evidently feeling her numerous hints had failed in their purpose.

"Did you and Arlen discuss any activities for the summer?"

It took Lynnette a moment to realize Hugh had spoken to her. "No. Nothing specific." All eyes were on her, and she added, "I'll be content to enjoy the country air. You needn't make plans for me."

Christian and Hugh went back to their steaks. Emily frowned, evidently hoping Lynnette's plans would be taken more seriously than her own. Lynnette cast the girl an apologetic look.

Emily's frown didn't last. She soon launched into a story of one of her classmates' extracurricular activities, keeping the men entertained and Lynnette free to enjoy the dinner.

Occasionally Lynnette cast furtive glances at Christian. He was an extremely handsome man. In town, a man with his looks would be out to charm all the ladies. Perhaps Christian was like that in other settings; he didn't flirt with her because of her relationship with his brother.

The disappointment she felt was most inappropriate! She turned her attention to Emily's story, looking for an opportunity to join the conversation. Emily left her none. Besides, the girl's story was hard to follow since she knew none of the principals. Her next glance at Christian revealed him watching her. She met his gaze. *Let him turn away,* she thought.

Instead he let the hint of a smile touch his lips. Deliberately, he placed an elbow on the table, planted his chin on his fist and turned toward his sister, pretending to hang on her every word.

Emily's voice faltered. She must have caught sight of him out of the corner of her eye. She glanced at him, did a double take and slapped at his arm, slowing, but not stopping, her story.

Christian's laughter finally silenced her. She turned to scowl at him. "Eat, little sister," he said. "I want dessert."

"I'm done," Emily said. Whether she referred to her dinner or her story wasn't clear to Lynnette.

Christian rose from the table and headed for the kitchen. Emily scowled after him. "At home we ring a bell so the servants serve dessert," she said.

"Martha and her family are having their own dinner," Hugh said quietly. "It doesn't hurt us to wait on ourselves."

Emily looked unconvinced but didn't argue. She quickly thought of another story to share with her father and was well into it when Christian returned. He carried a tray of soup bowls heaped with ice cream.

Lynnette laughed when he traded one for her plate. "If all meals are like this, I'll be fat long before summer's over."

"Perry cranked all afternoon," Christian said. "We can't hurt his feelings."

"Where did he get the ice?"

"From the icehouse," Emily offered, digging in without concern for the rarity of the treat.

"We cut ice from the streams in winter," Hugh explained. After a moment he broke the silence left by Emily's preoccupation with the dessert. "Christian, did you know our guest here wants to take over one of the balconies so she can write?"

"Really?" Lynnette felt Christian's scrutiny. "What do you write?"

"Fiction," she said, trying to include everyone in her answer to avoid looking directly at Christian.

"Have you had anything published?"

Chapter Three

Christian's question hung in the air, repeating itself in Lynnette's mind until it became an accusation. "Have you had anything published?"

She opened her mouth to speak. Should she lie, keep them in the dark the way she had everyone else, even Amanda, or tell them about the book and risk their censure? The notion that Arlen might not wish to marry the author of one of those scandalous novels occurred to her for the first time. Her heart beat hard enough for the others to hear, a ringing beat like boot heels on a wooden floor. Boot heels that grew closer.

Christian's attention turned away from her, toward the living room. It *was* boot heels she had heard. She almost wilted with relief.

"I believe Arlen's home," Hugh said.

Lynnette's relief quickly turned to a different kind of dread. How should she greet the stranger who had asked her to marry him?

There was no time to decide, however. Arlen strode into the room. Hugh stood and extended his hand. Emily barely looked up from her ice cream.

Arlen bent to kiss Lynnette's cheek before reaching past her to shake his father's hand. He slipped into the chair next to her. "I'm so sorry I couldn't meet your train, darling. I hope you had a good trip."

"Of course," she murmured. "And you?" He was really quite handsome with a dark curl caressing his forehead. And charming. It felt nice to have someone's undivided attention.

"Fine. Just fine." His gaze was almost worshipful. "It's wonderful to see you again. I hurried away as soon as I could."

"You eaten?" Christian asked.

"All I've done for two days is eat." He seemed to notice his siblings for the first time. "I might have some of that ice cream, though."

Christian slowly savored a spoonful, swallowed it and smacked his lips. "You know where it is," he said. "You might want to hurry before Jake finishes it off."

Hugh laughed. "We're about ready to move to the living room, Arlen. Why don't you get a bowl and join us. Bring yours along, Lynnette." He rose from the table and a moment latter Emily and Christian followed.

Arlen detained Lynnette with a hand on her arm. "I'm truly sorry I couldn't be here when you arrived," he whispered once they were alone.

"That's quite all right, Arlen. I understand. Your family's made me feel welcome."

"I don't want you to think this campaign is more important than you are," he said, still in a hushed tone.

"You're everything to me." He lifted her hand to his lips.

Lynnette fought the urge to squirm. She wasn't sure if it was his kiss or his words that made her the more uncomfortable. She gave him a wavering smile when he finally lifted his head. They could hear voices from the next room, and Arlen stood, helping her to her feet. "I've kept you alone long enough," he said softly. "Join the others. I'll be along in a moment."

He headed toward the kitchen, and Lynnette gazed after him. She should be flattered by his words. She should be falling head over heels in love with him. Instead she felt uneasy. She didn't think she wanted to be "everything" to anyone. *At least not to Arlen.* She felt guilty for that thought. Why not Arlen? They just needed time.

She glanced down at the half-finished dessert and decided against bringing it. In the living room, she found Hugh setting up a chessboard while Christian built a fire. Emily stood over Christian, her hands on her hips.

"Do you have to tonight?" she asked.

"You don't break a horse by working with it once in a while."

"But tonight? I just got home."

Christian rose to his feet, brushing his hands on his pants. "Go on up now," he said. "I'll wait for you."

Emily turned and ran toward the stairs. She met Arlen coming with his bowl of ice cream but barely acknowledged him as she grabbed the banister and scurried up the stairs.

"What's she up to?" Arlen asked. He urged Lynnette into a love seat and sat down beside her.

Hugh answered his question. "She wants to change for bed before Christian goes out to work with the stallion."

"One would think she would have outgrown that by now," Arlen said.

"Let her be a little girl when she's home." Christian took a seat near the fire, almost hidden from Lynnette's view by Hugh and his chessboard.

"Do I have any takers?" Hugh asked. "Lynnette, do you play?"

Lynnette smiled. "I have played. I don't know if I'll be much of a challenge to you, though."

"He doesn't want a challenge," Arlen said. "He plays chess at night for the same reason Christian waits until evening to break his horses. They want to catch their opponents when they're tired."

"In that case," Lynnette said, coming to her feet. "I'm the perfect opponent." She crossed to the table, and Christian stepped forward, moving a big leather-covered chair into position. She took the seat, nodding her thanks as he returned to his place. She thought she should have felt some loss at leaving Arlen's side, but actually she was more comfortable across from his father.

He offered her the first move, which she took. This prompted him to spend a long moment studying the board as if this were a most unusual first move.

"He's waiting for you to fall asleep," Christian whispered into the silence.

Hugh promptly moved.

Lynnette knew only three basic strategies. She found them thwarted easily by Hugh and was soon on the defensive. "Do I have any hope of winning?" she asked at one point.

"None," said Christian.

"Oh, I wouldn't give up yet," Hugh encouraged. "You have several good pieces left."

"But I can't seem to do anything but sacrifice them."

"Take charge," Christian said, leaning closer. "Make him do what you want."

Lynnette's eyes met Christian's, blue and deep. She felt oddly touched that he would offer her encouragement. She tried her best to do as he said. In three moves she was able to call check instead of always hearing it. But four moves later it was over.

"I'm afraid your advice came too late," she told Christian.

"Another?" Hugh asked.

"I think I should quit while I can still salvage my pride." She glanced at Arlen, thinking she should return to his side. The comfort of the chair was her excuse for not wanting to move.

"Arlen?" Hugh asked. His son declined, and he waved Lynnette back into the chair, settling deeper into his own. "Tell us how your trip went, Arlen."

As Arlen started to speak, Emily came down the stairs. She was dressed in a pale blue robe, the hem of a white nightgown and her bare toes visible as she walked. Her hair was down around her shoulders again. She went straight to Christian and handed him a brush. He moved to the edge of his seat, and Emily, turning away from him, knelt on the floor.

Lynnette heard very little of what Arlen said. The wing of the chair hid him from her view, anyway. It was much more pleasant to watch Emily's profile as Christian dragged the brush through her hair. An occasional glance at Hugh told her he was engrossed in Arlen's conversation.

With skillful movements, Christian began to plait his sister's hair. He drew up lock after lock, working them into the braid. Never once did Emily's expression suggest that he had snagged a hair or tugged too hard. Christian's face bore a wistful expression that brought a lump to Lynnette's throat.

It was all over in a few minutes. Over her shoulder Emily handed him a ribbon, and he tied it around the end of the braid. She stood, and he gave her the brush. When she whispered something to him and hugged him, Lynnette forced her eyes away.

Arlen seemed to be coming to the end of his narrative, and she had heard none of it. She hoped he wouldn't expect her to remember something later. Perhaps she could claim she had fallen asleep.

"I'll play you, Papa."

"Have my seat," Lynnette offered. "I believe I'll turn in."

"I'll see you to your room." Arlen was at her side in a moment, offering his arm. From the corner of her eye, she saw Christian turn and look at her before stepping out the door.

Arlen walked her slowly up the stairs and, outside the bedroom door, he wished her good-night. He bent to kiss her lips, and Lynnette felt she shouldn't flinch away. At the same time, she didn't return the kiss, and it all felt very awkward.

Lynnette wondered if he even noticed. He gazed at her adoringly, and she needed to break the spell. "It's kind of you to give up your room," she said, placing a hand on the doorknob.

"I'll dream of the night I can share it with you," he murmured softly. Lynnette saw his cheeks blush faintly.

She opened the door, her thoughts on escape. A cool breeze greeted her. The balcony door was open, and the temperature had dropped quickly after sundown. Arlen brushed past her and latched the door. For a moment she thought her quick move into the room had been interpreted as an invitation.

"Is there anything you need?" he asked, striking a match and lighting the lamp on the dresser. "I could start a fire to ward off the chill."

"No thanks, I'm fine," she said, praying that she had been wrong. How would she gently discourage him?

"Then good night," he said, and started out of the room, only to stop short once he was past her. Lynnette held her breath. "Tyrant," he said.

Lynnette turned to the bed to find the big black and white cat sitting disdainfully in the middle of the quilt. "How did he get in here?"

"From the balcony, I imagine. Come on out, now." He waved the cat toward the door.

Lynnette tried to picture the view from the balcony. "I don't remember any large trees near the house."

The cat hopped off the bed and rubbed himself against Arlen's legs. "He climbs the chimneys," Arlen explained. Lifting the cat in his arms, he bade her good-night once again. Lynnette followed him to the door and closed it behind him.

Picturing the cat's athletic feats brought a smile to her lips. It wasn't until she was ready for bed that she allowed herself to remember the things Arlen had said. He seemed to be actively wooing her. He would make a kind and caring husband, and she was unusually lucky.

She blew out the lamp, and twilight spilled into the room through the balcony door. She went to pull the curtains, but found herself stepping onto the balcony instead. What she could see of the barn was a black silhouette against the orange remains of the sunset.

She stepped to the railing to see more. A whinny brought her attention downward. A black horse was barely visible in the small corral. It was tied close to the center post. Christian slowly rubbed the long neck. Her ears, more in tune to the distance now, heard his soothing voice.

She remembered Arlen's comment about catching opponents while they were tired, but Christian didn't look at odds with the horse. In fact, his movements reminded her more of the way he had braided his sister's hair. It was beautiful to watch. As he moved around the horse, it tossed its head and tried to shy away. In moments it was still again as Christian rubbed it neck, its back, its sides.

Something warm unexpectedly curled inside her. She had begun to imagine those hands running over

her own body. What wicked thoughts! She quickly
turned back into the room, latching the door and drawing the curtain.

Christian spoke softly to the stallion, stroking the
silky coat. He had seen the light go out in Arlen's
room, the one Lynnette was using. It hadn't helped
him get his mind off the woman. This morning he had
determined to spend as much time with her as possible
to learn her true feelings for Arlen. Now, he was reluctant to do so and wasn't sure why.

Some tiny sound or sixth sense told him he was
being watched. He moved toward the stallion's head
and without breaking the rhythm of his strokes,
glanced toward the house. In the twilight, he could
make out a white-gowned, almost ghostly, figure on
the balcony.

He closed his eyes, willing the figure out of his
mind. The horse, sensing his inattention, whinnied and
tried to pull free.

"Whoa now," he murmured. "You can't go till I
say. You might as well relax. That's a good boy."

He wasn't going to look up. He turned his back on
the house to avoid the temptation. The stallion tossed
his head, testing the rope. Christian calmed him again.

Hell, why should an audience ruin his concentration, especially when that audience was a little slip of
a city girl he didn't even like. No, that wasn't true.
He had decided not to like her and found it harder to
do than he had expected.

He heard the click of the balcony door closing. He
should be able to put her out of his mind now. Who

was she, anyway, to dominate his thoughts? She was pretty, sure. Polite and pleasant. Still, she was nothing like the woman he wanted for a helpmate. She should be easy to forget.

But she wanted Arlen, he reminded himself. And he wasn't going to let his little brother ruin his life by marrying a gold digger. It had all happened too fast to be anything else. He would watch her and expose her for what she was. If her circumstances were truly dire, his family was in a position to help her find some kind of work.

The thought brought a smile to his lips. Imagine her as a teacher or governess! The suggestion would probably make her faint dead away. Especially compared to marriage to a wealthy politician.

The stallion tossed his head and danced around the snubbing post, tightening the rope. "All right," Christian said. "I get the message." The animal sensed his master's tension. Trying to continue would cause more harm than good. He untied the rope and led the nervous stallion into the barn.

Lynnette awoke disoriented. Pale light seemed to be coming from the wrong direction, and she wondered if she had turned sideways in her bed. The room righted itself quickly when she remembered she was no longer in her own bed and never would be again. She tried to toss aside the melancholy with the covers and rose to greet the day.

She washed in the basin and put on one of her favorite dresses. It was a soft rose color trimmed in deep green. The colors suited her and normally made her feel confident. It wasn't working today. The dress was designed to be worn with hoops, which had gone out of style to be replaced by tight skirts and bustles. She had shortened the dress and substituted four petticoats. It gave it a rather casual appearance.

Until now she hadn't regretted the lack of funds that prevented her from buying any of the new dresses; they looked immensely uncomfortable. But today she wondered if Arlen would be embarrassed by her appearance. She tried to shrug off her unease. It was still a lovely dress, quite serviceable, and Arlen knew her situation.

She gathered up the basin of used wash water and left the room. There was no one in either the living room or dining room when she came down the stairs. The table was bare, and she wondered if she had missed breakfast. It seemed quite early, but she had heard that country folk rose before dawn.

She went into the kitchen and found Martha kneading bread. The woman looked up from her work and seemed flustered to find their guest in the kitchen again. She came forward, wiping her floured hands on her apron. "Miss Sterling. I'm so sorry. I would have sent Jake after that."

"That's quite all right," Lynnette said. "I was coming down anyway. Have I missed breakfast?"

Martha carried the basin to a table near a screen door. She was startled to discover Lynnette had followed her. "I can fix you whatever you would like if you care to wait in the dining room. I could bring it up to your bedroom if you prefer."

Lynnette stood for a moment before the screen door,

letting the cool breeze touch her. It was just a little too cold to eat on the balcony. "Am I the last?" she asked.

"Emily and Arlen are still asleep."

Lynnette walked toward the counter where Martha's dough sat, hoping she would return to her work. "I could wait and eat with them," she suggested.

"Neither will want breakfast, I'm sure. And Emily might not be down for hours."

"Please," Lynnette said, indicating the dough. "If you don't mind, I'll fix myself an egg and toast some bread."

"I can do that for you," Martha said, hurrying toward the stove.

She had the skillet on the stove and was greasing it when Lynnette caught up with her. "I'm used to fixing my own breakfast, and my father's. I really don't mind. In fact, I'd enjoy it." When Martha hesitated, Lynnette added, "If you don't mind someone in your kitchen."

"It's not my kitchen," Martha said, stepping away from the stove. She helped Lynnette find what she would need and set out a tray with dishes and finally, when the egg was nearly cooked, returned to her dough.

Lynnette glanced at Martha's back as she checked on the toast. She hadn't meant to force her way into Martha's kitchen. In her effort to avoid being an extra burden she had made herself a nuisance instead. At the earliest possible moment she filled the tray and left the kitchen.

The dining room table looked too large for her

alone, and she walked through to the living room. Finding an end table near the glass doors, she set her tray down and moved a chair into position.

What would Arlen want to do today, she wondered as she sat down. She hoped he would want to take her riding. Their surroundings were so beautiful, it seemed like a perfect way to spend the day. It couldn't be too hard to learn to ride.

She bit into the toast and frowned. She had nothing appropriate to wear riding. Perhaps she could borrow something from Emily. Though the girl was shorter they weren't so very different in size.

She was thus deep in thought when she heard heavy steps on the stairs. She turned her smile toward them, expecting to see Arlen. Denim jeans and a loose brown shirt descended through the gap in the ceiling. She hadn't realized how muscular Arlen was. But as she watched, it wasn't Arlen's face that emerged above them. It was Christian's.

He saw her immediately—before she had time to wipe the look of surprise off her face. She decided it was better to explain. "I thought you were up already."

"I was," he answered, coming toward her. His smile was friendly if a little cautious. "I had to roust your boyfriend out. Jake and I need his help repairing the hay wagon." He hesitated a moment, then took a seat near her. "Don't let me keep you from your breakfast."

Lynnette took a sip of coffee and watched him self-consciously. She should ask him something, perhaps something about the ranch, or about Arlen. It seemed awkward for them to sit watching each other. "I'm hoping to learn to ride while I'm here," she blurted.

His dimples deepened. "You've come to the right place. Plenty of horses and plenty of trails."

They stared at each other for a long moment. His eyes were incredibly blue, like the sky beyond the glass doors. It took an effort to turn her attention back to her cooling breakfast. She deliberately began eating again.

After another long moment, he spoke. "I'm sorry to take Arlen away from you this morning, but with Perry's leg still mending, Pa's out checking water levels in the pastures. And I need the wagon fixed before the first cutting of hay."

"I understand. I certainly don't need to be constantly entertained."

He looked as if he didn't believe her. It occurred to her then that he might not like the idea of a city girl staying here. She resolved to stay completely out of his way. *For more than one reason.* She tried to dismiss the thought. She wasn't attracted to Arlen's brother!

They were still gazing at each other when she heard more footsteps on the stairs. She was glad for the excuse to turn away. Arlen was dressed in what looked like discarded dress pants and shirt. He rolled up the sleeves as he descended.

"Lynnette!" He took the last steps much faster and hurrying to her side. "What are you doing up so early?"

"Flirting with me," Christian said with a grin.

Arlen brushed a kiss across her cheek, ignoring his

brother. "There's really no need to be up and around so early, dear. Emily won't be up till nearly noon."

"It's what I'm used to, Arlen," she said, hoping her voice didn't show her irritation.

Christian stood, giving her a polite smile. "Come on, brother, let's get to work."

Arlen didn't seem inclined to leave. "This shouldn't take long. Make use of Father's library. Have you seen it yet?"

"Come on, brother. Tear yourself away."

Lynnette couldn't help but laugh. They were both watching her, one so serious, one with a teasing grin. "Don't worry about me. Go fix the wagon."

"It shouldn't take long," Arlen repeated, as Christian began dragging him from the room.

"It'll take all morning," Christian called over his shoulder, waving with his free hand. They were nearly across the living room before Arlen actually turned and followed his brother.

Lynnette went back to her breakfast, hardly caring that it had grown cold. She loved the teasing relationship between the brothers and the obvious affection between Christian and Emily. It would be wonderful to be part of a family like this.

And if she married Arlen she would be. Christian and Emily would be her brother and sister. She smiled at the thought, though it didn't seem quite real.

It wasn't until she had finished eating and took her tray back to the kitchen that she began to consider what she would do during the morning. She could go to her room and write, but the thought held little interest for her just now.

The kitchen was empty when she arrived, and she washed her dishes quickly in the soapy water still in the sink. She headed for her room feeling she had put one over on Martha who would surely have stopped her from cleaning up after herself.

In her room, she stared at the small writing desk. She considered taking a notebook to one of the balconies but felt certain that she wouldn't get anything done. She stepped out on the balcony and looked across at the barnyard. The small corral was empty this morning. There was no sign of the men, probably working inside the barn.

As she leaned over the railing to see more of the yard, she noticed a narrow path that disappeared around the barn. Instantly she decided to follow the path. She wanted to explore her surroundings, and she didn't need a guide to do so.

She turned back into the room, carefully closing the doors against the invasion of the cat. She slipped out of two of the petticoats to make walking easier, changed to her sturdiest shoes and grabbed her broadest-brimmed hat. She adjusted the pin through the hat and hair as she left the room.

Christian caught a glimpse of pink through the open barn door. He couldn't help watching the trim figure as long as she was in sight. The moment he returned to work, he realized he had been caught.

"She's lovely, isn't she?" Arlen's tone said, I told you so.

"She certainly is." Christian grinned at his brother. "You'll forgive me for staring."

"Of course. I rather enjoyed it. Stare all you want. Just remember I saw her first."

Christian laughed. "You won't mind having men stare at your wife?"

Arlen seemed surprised but not offended. "That's part of the idea," he said. "If they don't remember me, they'll at least remember her and think I have extremely good judgment. Or good luck. Either way, I'm sure to get their votes."

Christian tried not to show his shock at his brother's words. "She's a campaign strategy, then?"

Arlen laughed. "She's more than that, of course."

They heard Jake coming, and Arlen changed the subject. "This really will take all morning, won't it?"

"That's what I said." Christian placed another board between the sawhorses and measured it.

"You said we were fixing the wagon," Arlen hollered above the sound of the saw, "not rebuilding it."

"It's all in how you look at things," Christian hollered back.

Lynnette followed the path past the barn and along the side of the hill. A stone bench under a huge tree caught her eye, but she was determined to walk and turned her attention back to the path. It seemed to follow a natural terrace that narrowed to barely four feet as it turned sharply with the hillside. Around the corner, the terrace widened out again. She fell into a comfortably brisk pace.

She had walked often at home, her neighborhood being only a few blocks from the capitol building and the business district. Her trips had been fewer and more rushed the past few years because of her reluctance to leave her father alone for too long.

Lost in thoughts about her father and her home, Lynnette paid little attention to where the path led. Abruptly it forked. She wondered fleetingly if it had branched out before and she hadn't noticed. To her left the path wandered along the hillside much as it had before. To the right it dropped into the valley. Part of the path was hidden, but she could see where it crossed a little stream below. Looking back she discovered that all sign of the ranch yard had disappeared.

The stream looked inviting. The day had warmed considerably since she left the house and her only shade was the insubstantial brim of her hat. Studying the slope between her and the stream, she decided against it. Her legs ached at the thought of climbing back up the hill. She considered going back, but the sun wasn't close to its zenith yet. She had a couple hours, she was sure, before noon. She would walk on a little farther then make her way back.

A few minutes later the path abruptly disappeared. She stood on the edge of a large grassy prairie. This, she decided, was where the path had been leading. From here a rider would turn in any number of directions to check cattle, or water levels, as Christian had said his father was doing. Or whatever else ranchers did.

Lynnette realized she had been picturing Christian on horseback riding across the pasture. She tried to change the image to Arlen, but it was too late.

She brushed the thoughts aside as an outcrop of

limestone caught her attention. It wasn't far away, and she decided to take a closer look before turning back. The ground was uneven and littered with rocks and clumps of coarse grasses. She hadn't realized how smooth the path was until she left it. Lifting her skirts, she walked on.

The rocks were farther away than she had realized and much larger. As she approached, she wondered if Christian and Arlen had climbed them as children, perhaps Emily too, though it was hard to imagine.

Lynnette walked around the outcrop, searching for toeholds and found instead the letters *C* and *P* scratched deeply into the gray stone. She ran her fingers over the letters, trying to imagine the young boy carving his initials here. Arlen's were probably around someplace. How different their childhoods had been from her own.

She continued around the outcrop more slowly, studying the surfaces of the irregular rock. A movement at her feet made her jump and gasp. A huge gray-and-brown-mottled snake slithered away from her. There was no rattle on its tail, she noted with relief. Still, she hadn't even considered snakes.

"Time to go," she muttered to herself. She made her way back around the rock and started across the prairie. The sun was high overhead now and she re-pinned her hat to better protect her face. She hadn't thought about any possible dangers involved in walking alone. She hadn't even told anyone where she was going. She tried to walk faster and nearly stumbled into a hole.

She was well across the pasture when she realized

that she couldn't see the path. The hill, viewed from this direction, didn't look at all the way she remembered it. She looked back toward the outcrop. How had it appeared from the edge of the path? She couldn't remember. With the sun directly overhead, she couldn't even use it to orient herself.

She walked on in the direction she had, until recently, considered the right way, thinking—hoping—the path would be just up ahead. But it wasn't.

She had felt warm a moment before, but now she felt uncomfortably hot and dragged down by her heavy skirts. She had noticed a mild thirst before that now seemed unbearable. This was panic, she decided, deliberately shaking it off. She loosened a button at her throat and wiped her face on her sleeve. She had been fine a moment ago; she was still fine—only lost.

She had always prided herself in her powers of observation. She should have noticed the terrain; she should have remembered landmarks. "I should have dropped crumbs."

Hearing her own voice made her feel better. "I *will* find my way back," she announced. "But how?" She looked around again, noting a definite slope to the land. "I'll head for the highest point," she said, starting out. "From there I should be able to see something familiar."

Chapter Four

Christian stepped into the sunlight and stretched. Arlen started past him on his way to the house, but Christian caught his arm. "Did you see Lynnette come back?"

"No." Arlen turned. "Were you watching for her?"

Christian cast his brother a careless grin that he hoped was convincing. "You said you enjoyed it."

Arlen threw a mock punch toward Christian's face. "I think I changed my mind."

"Fine," Christian said, unable to keep the annoyance out of his voice. "But I don't think she's back."

"Don't be silly. She wouldn't have walked far. I'm sure she slipped past us." Arlen clapped him on the shoulder. "Let's get cleaned up for lunch."

Inside the house, Arlen headed for the washroom, but Christian went in search of Emily. He found her curled up in one of the big overstuffed chairs, a book in her lap. She put the book aside when he entered the room.

"Where has everybody been?" she asked as she stretched.

"Lynnette isn't back?"

"Back from where? I haven't seen her all morning."

All morning probably meant the past hour. Christian started for the stairs as he asked, "Have you checked her room?"

"She isn't there. And she isn't in the kitchen with Martha. And she isn't in Papa's study."

Christian paused, one foot on the bottom step. She could be exploring the rest of the house or somewhere around the yard, but he doubted it. Somehow he knew he would have seen her come back.

"Tell Martha to hold lunch for a little while, will you?" he asked as he started across the room. Arlen opened the washroom door just before Christian could pound on it. "She isn't back," he said, already turning toward the back door.

"What do you mean, she isn't back?" Arlen at least followed as he asked the question. "Surely she's around someplace."

In the barn, Christian began saddling a horse. Arlen hesitated before he did the same. "Maybe she got tired and is waiting for someone to come get her."

Christian cast his brother a skeptical look. If that was the case, he sure hoped Arlen was the one who found her. He would have no patience for such foolishness.

"Do you think she fell or something?" Arlen asked a moment later.

"That or got lost," Christian suggested. His horse

was nearly saddled. He was eager to be about the search, but this was Arlen's girl, and he should be in charge.

"I don't think she'd go far enough to get lost. That trail she took is pretty well defined for more than a mile. If we follow it, we'll find her."

Christian nodded. "You go ahead. I'll head for the bluff and see if I can spot her, just in case she did get lost."

They swung into their saddles and left the barn. Christian told himself his brother was right. A city girl would have tired after half a mile. She might have sat down to rest and fallen asleep. But he didn't think so. He wasn't sure why, but he had a feeling she would have gone beyond the trail. He remembered the purposeful way in which she had walked past the barn.

Or maybe he was unwilling to think about her being hurt. And that was really the most likely explanation. It would be easy enough to fall and sprain an ankle, or worse. Especially for a city girl.

Christian leaned forward in the saddle as he urged the horse up the steep trail that snaked to the top of the hill behind the ranch yard. He reached the top of the bluff in a matter of minutes. He patted the horse's neck as he looked around and spotted her immediately.

She was a pink figure in the distance walking toward him. Not stumbling, not running, but walking. She raised a hand but it seemed more a greeting than a hail. "Maybe she doesn't know she's lost," he muttered before riding toward her.

It seemed odd that she would continue walking even

as he came to her rescue. He expected her to collapse at any moment, but she didn't stop until he drew up beside her. She squinted against the sun as she smiled up at him. "I'm lost, I'm afraid. Will I be able to see the ranch house from the top of this hill?"

She pointed, and he turned to see how far he had come from the bluff. "Yes, ma'am," he said.

"Thank you." She started on.

He watched her for a moment before reining the horse around. "Want a ride?" he asked, as he drew up beside her.

She eyed the horse a moment as if she were tempted. "No, thank you," she said instead. "I'm sure you're busy."

Christian laughed, and she cast him a curious smile. "I'm busy looking for you."

"Oh dear," she murmured. She turned a little pale, showing off a touch of sunburn on her nose. "Are there others looking for me as well?"

"Only Arlen." He thought of Arlen expecting to find a helpless heap no more than half a mile from the house. Instead she had walked for miles and still wasn't complaining.

"I'm terribly sorry," she said.

He kicked his left foot out of the stirrup and reached an arm toward her. She hesitated only a moment before climbing up behind him. When she had wrapped her arms around his waist he started toward the bluff.

She felt very warm pressed against his back. He told himself he was going slowly because she wasn't an experienced rider. At the bluff he stopped. "You might want to brace your hands behind you and lean back as we go down.''

He felt her peer cautiously around him. "We're going to ride down that? I think I'll walk.''

"I think you've walked enough for one day.''

"I'm afraid to let go,'' she whispered.

"Then don't let go,'' he said gently. "Just be prepared for me to lean back a little. All right?''

He felt her nod against his back. She really clung to him now. He wished he knew how to make her feel more secure. "We could ride the long way around,'' he suggested.

She shook her head. "No. I'm fine. I don't want to cause any more trouble than I have already.''

"You haven't caused much trouble,'' he said, starting the horse slowly down the steep trail. "In fact, you were close to finding your own way back.''

"I feel foolish for getting lost on my very first day.'' Her voice sounded strained as if she would rather hold her breath than talk.

"Would tomorrow have been better?''

"I suppose not,'' she murmured against his back.

"That was a joke,'' he said gently. He wanted to turn and look at her. He wished he had put her in front of him where he could wrap his arms around her and make her feel safe. He tried to dismiss the image.

"I know. I'm laughing on the inside.''

"Yeah,'' Christian said, feeling her arms loosen slightly. "I think I hear the vibrations in your voice.''

She did laugh then, nervously. "What you hear is terror.''

"Really?'' Christian eased the horse around the last

hairpin turn. "I never would have guessed. Course, I do kinda feel like there's a vise around my rib cage, but I just figured that was sisterly affection. Emily does the same from time to time."

Behind him, Lynnette tried to think of a clever retort. The truth was she felt more embarrassed than frightened now. She really had been clinging to this near-stranger as though her life depended on it. Which it did, or at least seemed to.

She forced her eyes open and found they had nearly reached the bottom of the hill. When they leveled off and Christian sat upright again, she let out a sigh of relief. She wasn't sure but she thought she heard him chuckle. Well, what difference did it make if he thought she was a frightened little ninny? His opinion hardly mattered. Still she loosened her grip around his waist and tried to sit up straighter.

As the horse walked toward the house, Lynnette became more aware of the ride itself. It was rather fun feeling the horse's movement beneath her, seeing the world from about eight feet off the ground instead of five and a half. What would it be like to actually sit in the saddle and control the horse herself? She would have to ask Arlen to take her the next time he wasn't busy.

Emily came out the back door to meet them as Christian drew the horse to a stop. He helped her down the same way he had helped her up, though she was sure she was even more awkward the second time. With her feet on the ground again she removed her hat, which was hopelessly askew, and looked up at him. She would have loved to retreat to the house without speaking, but good manners forced her to smile. "Thank you for finding me and bringing me back," she said.

His smile brought out his dimples. "I'll tell Arlen that the lost is found." He touched his heels to the horse and headed toward the trail beyond the barn at a pace that made her realize how slowly the horse had walked while she was aboard.

She stared after him until Emily touched her arm. "Your nose is sunburned. Come inside and get cleaned up. Martha will know what to put on the burn."

In the washroom, Emily pointed out the pump and showed her where clean towels were stored. "You can have a bath, if you like. It won't take long to heat some water."

"No, thanks," Lynnette said, pumping a basin full of water. "I've delayed lunch long enough. Besides, the cold water will feel good."

When Emily had left to find Martha, Lynnette slipped out of her dress and washed. She had loosened her hair and was running her fingers through the tangles when she heard a knock on the door. "It's me," Emily said.

Lynnette kept herself hidden by the door as she let the girl in. "Are the men back yet?"

"I heard them ride in while I was in the kitchen. They have the horses to unsaddle. You want to make a dash for the stairs?"

"I don't think so," Lynnette said with a grin. "But I am afraid I'll have to change my dress before lunch.

It's terribly wrinkled, and I seem to have torn the hem in a couple places.''

"I can bring what you need down here," Emily suggested.

"Thanks for the offer," Lynnette said, pulling the wrinkled dress on again. "But I'll go up myself. The men might want the washroom.''

Emily shrugged. "Oh. Here's the ointment Martha sent for the sunburn. If it's really bad, she said she'd make a baking soda paste.''

Lynnette sniffed the ointment and drew back.

Emily laughed at her reaction. "It's punishment for staying out in the sun.''

Lynnette screwed the lid back on the jar. "My nose is barely pink," she said. "I'll see if a little cold cream doesn't take care of it.''

"Good thinking," said Emily.

They left the washroom laughing and nearly ran into Arlen. His stern expression made Lynnette sober immediately.

"Lynnette, darling, I've been so worried. Whatever possessed you to wander off like that?''

"I didn't mean to—''

"I thought you had fallen or been bitten by a snake." Arlen took her arm and drew her into the living room. At the nearest chair he took both her shoulders, and Lynnette wondered if he would have pushed her into the chair if she hadn't sat down. "I want you to promise not to walk alone again.''

"But Arlen—''

"I suppose you were upset that I was busy.''

Lynnette shook her head, too stunned to speak, but

Arlen was pacing across the room and didn't notice. "If it was possible, I would spend every minute with you, but the ranch and the campaign are going to take some of my time." He paced in the other direction, barely looking at her. "You will have to find some other way to amuse yourself. I had hoped Emily would prove a suitable companion."

A glance toward the doorway revealed Emily with her hands on her hips, glaring in Arlen's direction.

"Arlen." Lynnette was only partially successful at getting his attention. He turned in her direction, but he kept talking.

"Look at what happened to you. Your dress is torn and wrinkled, your shoes are dirty, and your face is burned. And it could have been much worse. What if Christian hadn't found you so quickly? You might have been wandering around on the bluff for hours." He came to kneel beside the chair. "Promise me you won't do it again, Lynnette."

Lynnette took in the concerned face. She knew he meant well, even though he had managed to make her feel stupid and helpless. Christian had said she had nearly found her own way back. Perhaps he was just being kind. Still, until she had gotten lost, she had really enjoyed the walk. She gave Arlen a contrite smile. "I promise I won't get lost again," she said, hoping that would satisfy him.

"Good girl," he said, coming to his feet and offering her a hand. "Now, we both need to get cleaned up for lunch. Run along to your room to change."

He walked toward the washroom, and Lynnette, uncertain how to take his little lecture, watched him go.

Christian stood beside Emily. How long he had been there, she could only guess. Lynnette spun quickly and hurried for the stairs. She wasn't sure which humiliated her more, being scolded by Arlen, or knowing Christian, as well as Emily, heard.

Lynnette changed her dress and fixed her hair as quickly as she could, determined that she wouldn't be the last one ready for lunch. When she came down the stairs a few minutes later, she was pleased to see that only Christian and Emily were in the dining room and had not yet taken their places at the table.

"Do we have to wait for Papa, too?" Emily asked. "I'm starving."

"You should eat breakfast, Muffin. But no, Pa took a lunch. And I'm only giving the other two about three more minutes."

"Then I'm just in time," Lynnette said, stepping off the bottom stair and turning into the dining room. She knew Christian watched her. Too embarrassed to look him in the eye, she walked to the balcony doors and looked out on the valley.

"Go tell Martha we're ready," she heard Christian say.

"*You* tell her," was Emily's response.

"No, *you* tell her," Christian repeated, but she heard his footsteps as he moved toward the kitchen and knew it was safe to turn around.

"I feel like I've messed up everyone's day," Lynnette said to Emily.

"Don't be silly. It's barely twelve-thirty. We're not

that punctual around here, believe me. Especially at noon. Sometimes we don't even try to eat together."

Lynnette smiled her thanks. Before she could speak, Christian came out of the kitchen. He tried to run softly in his boots. "Quick. Act like we've been waiting forever."

They could hear Arlen on the stairs and both women slid into their chairs as Christian rounded the table to take his place. He immediately rested an elbow on the table and his chin on his hand and began toying with his fork. He looked completely bored. It was all Lynnette could do not to laugh. Emily visibly bit her lip, and her shoulders shook with suppressed laughter.

Christian looked up, startled, when Arlen entered the room. "Oh, there you are Arlen. We thought you had gotten lost."

"Very funny." Arlen was dressed impeccably, as Lynnette had always seen him in the city. It seemed a trifle overdone for the circumstances, but perhaps he had a business call to make during the afternoon. "Why don't you return thanks, Christian?" he suggested, taking his place beside Lynnette.

"It's Emily's turn. I remember from last summer."

Lynnette heard a thump and guessed Emily had just kicked her brother. He showed no reaction other than to grin at her before bowing his head.

Emily sighed. "Bless this family and Papa who's gone and Martha who made the food and—"

They heard the kitchen door open, and Christian pronounced a loud "Amen."

Emily echoed him quickly and slid her napkin into her lap.

Lynnette gave her and Christian no more than a quick glance, afraid she would laugh aloud if either of them so much as grinned at her. Instead she turned to Arlen beside her. The urge to laugh quickly fled.

Arlen's expression wasn't quite sour. Embarrassed perhaps, or disgusted, better described it. He appeared to watch Martha set the plates of thinly sliced beef and thick slabs of bread on the table. Christian and Arlen reached for the plate of meat at the same time. Christian held on with both hands, and Arlen gave it up, rolling his eyes.

The moment they heard the kitchen door close behind Martha, Arlen spoke softly. "Quit acting like children." He looked from Christian to Emily and back. "Our guest isn't used to such foolishness."

"I don't mind, really," Lynnette said, then realized she probably shouldn't be arguing with Arlen. "That is, they were just having some fun."

"You're too forgiving," Arlen murmured. He gave her an adoring look that disconcerted her more than his earlier irritation. She turned away to take the plate Emily passed her.

Martha returned with a tray full of assorted pickles and relishes. The family quietly made their sandwiches until this last tray reached Lynnette. Arlen held the tray and told her what each was and recommended a mild relish and a sweet cucumber pickle. A few he dismissed with a warning that they were spicy. Lynnette wanted to try a little of each one, but with Arlen holding the tray, it seemed to take too long. Instead she took a sample of three and hoped the tray would come around again.

The atmosphere seemed strained after Arlen's scolding, and Lynnette was relieved when Emily asked her brothers what their plans were for the afternoon.

Arlen explained that he had a few letters to write, and Christian said he was going to ride out and meet their father.

"How will you find him?" Lynnette asked. From Arlen's startled look, she decided it must have been a stupid question.

"He's checking the water levels on all the ponds and streams," Christian said. "We talked about his route before he left. I'll circle around the opposite direction, and we'll meet wherever we meet."

"Will it take all afternoon?" Emily asked.

"I doubt it. Pa could probably make the rounds himself before dark. It's just that he's not used to spending the day in the saddle anymore."

Emily grinned. "Did he just say Papa is old and decrepit? I think that's what he said."

"I'll deny it if you tell him," Christian said.

"Perry would normally do it, but he broke his leg last fall," Arlen said.

Lynnette nodded, feeling it wasn't necessary to tell him that Christian had already explained about Perry's leg.

"So," Emily asked Christian, "how long do you think it'll take before you meet Papa?"

Christian grinned at his sister. "Did you need me for something this afternoon?"

"No," she said quickly. "I just wanted to know what everyone was planning. Lynnette, what are you doing this afternoon?"

Before Lynnette could chew and swallow the bite of sandwich she had just taken, Arlen answered for her. "I'm sure she will want to rest after her ordeal this morning."

Lynnette wanted to protest that while she might feel tired later, she would surely be able to spend some time with Emily. Emily, however, didn't seem disappointed that everyone would be busy. She announced that she would spend the afternoon in her room reading. A few minutes later she excused herself and scampered up the stairs. Christian looked after her with narrowed eyes.

Arlen didn't notice anything amiss with his sister. He turned to Lynnette. "As soon as you're finished, you should go up and lie down. I'll get what I need out of my desk now and do my writing in Father's study." He stood and bent closer to Lynnette. "Will you need help up the stairs?"

Lynnette took a deep breath before she answered. "I don't believe so, Arlen."

Arlen nodded and left the room.

Lynnette told herself not to be irritated. Arlen was trying to be kind. She lifted her sandwich to her mouth, and her eyes came in contact with Christian's. Her hands stilled for a moment before she forced herself to take a small bite.

Christian studied her, and she found it impossible to turn away. Finally he spoke. "If you need any help chewing that sandwich, be sure to let Arlen know."

The giggle that bubbled up inside her almost made her choke.

"If you want to keep up with this family," he said

as he stood, ''you're going to have to learn to gobble your food.'' He pushed the tray of relishes toward her. ''Of course you may enjoy your lunch more with the rest of us gone.'' He stacked his and Emily's plates and cast her a dimpled grin before he headed for the kitchen.

Christian wasn't sure why he had stayed to tease her. Perhaps he just wanted her to finish the meal with a smile. Arlen meant well, but he treated her like...well, like a china doll. And she wasn't made of china. The soft press of her body against his back flashed in his mind, and he brushed it away. He could have no such thoughts about his future sister-in-law.

In the kitchen he put the dishes in the sink. Martha and her family were still eating, and he slid onto the bench beside Perry. ''That bread was even better than usual,'' he told Martha.

Martha blushed at the compliment and offered him another slice. He took it, broke off a piece and popped it into his mouth. He groaned in ecstasy.

''He wants something, Ma,'' Jake said.

''You could end up mucking out the barn by yourself today, boy,'' Christian warned. ''But I do have a favor to ask.''

Martha and Jake nodded knowingly, and Perry laughed.

Christian ignored them. ''Our guest has been abandoned for the afternoon,'' he began.

''And I should entertain your guest?'' Martha didn't sound pleased with the prospect.

Christian flashed her his biggest smile, knowing she

couldn't resist. "All I'm suggesting is if she comes moping around this afternoon, find something for her to do."

A slow smile spread across Martha's lips. "You mean, put her to work?"

"If you can make her think it's her idea, sure." He clapped Perry on the shoulder as he slipped off the bench. "Don't overwork that leg."

"Maybe I should put the little gal to work mending the chicken pen."

"There you go," Christian said. He was grinning when he left the kitchen. Miss Sterling in her pretty pink dress struggling with a roll of mesh wire was quite a picture.

In any circumstances, she was quite a picture. The image of her walking across the prairie would stay with him forever. Damn, Arlen should have been the one to find her. They could have had a romantic ride home.

Maybe not so romantic, he thought, remembering Arlen's overreaction. Arlen was simply concerned for her, of course. Why did he let it bother him?

He slid open the barn door and stepped inside, letting his eyes adjust to the dim light. His earlier resolution to expose Miss Sterling as a gold digger seemed somehow dangerous, now. He shook off the odd thought and went to saddle his horse.

He was leading the gelding out of the barn when he heard Emily call. He turned to watch her run toward him. She wore a reworked pair of men's pants that were decidedly tighter than they had been last summer. One of his own shirts was tucked into them, the sleeve rolled three or four times. Her hair was in a braid down her back, a braid she had managed to make herself. She wore one of Arlen's hats.

She came to a stop beside him. "I want to go with you," she said as she gasped for breath. "Please, can't I go?" She didn't wait for an answer before hurrying into the barn.

Christian shook his head as he looked after her. He tied the gelding in the shade and followed his sister. She had gone to the tack room and was struggling with her saddle. Christian took it from her and headed toward a stall. "You remember Trooper?" he asked her as he threw the blanket over the gray's back. "He's Jake's favorite."

He glanced at Emily in time to see her wrinkle her nose. When the horse was saddled he led him toward his sister. "You almost missed me, Muffin. Why didn't you ask to go at lunch?"

Emily shrugged and stepped forward, ready to mount. Christian made no move to help her, waiting for her answer. Finally she turned toward him, stomping a foot. "If you must know, I didn't want *her* to ask to go, too."

Christian keep his face straight. "So you lied and then abandoned her."

"She's Arlen's guest not mine."

Christian decided he needed to remind himself of the same thing—hourly. "And why didn't you want her to come with us?" He was afraid his voice caught on the words. He was already imagining it, imagining her in a pair of tight jeans.

"She's all right, I guess, but I just got home, and I

want some time with you. Besides, she doesn't know how to ride. You'd have to spend all your time helping her. She'd slow us down, and you'd probably have to bring her back early. No. *I'd* have to bring her back so you could get your work done.''

Christian tried not to grin. He bent to give Emily a leg up. ''You convinced me,'' he said.

Lynnette had just opened the balcony door when she heard Emily shout. It took a moment for her eyes to reconcile what she was sure she had heard. She would have believed the person hurrying into the barn was a boy if she hadn't heard Emily's voice, and seen the bobbing braid.

Christian had gone into the barn, leaving his horse tied outside. Lynnette stepped onto the balcony. She had intended to move the desk chair to the balcony and bring her notebook outside. She stood for a moment considering. She shouldn't let the appearance of Christian and Emily change her plans. Besides, wouldn't it be better for them to look up and see her happily engaged than to catch her lurking about in the doorway?

In a moment, she was seated with her notebook on her lap and her ink bottle and rag on a step stool beside her. She would write a story about a young rancher, something she would never have dreamed of doing back in Topeka. Her rancher would fight off rustlers and gunmen to save his ranch and the woman he loved. Maybe his beloved could dress in men's clothes at some point in her story. No, that would be too shocking to accept. She must be sweet and demure with maybe a touch of independence.

Lynnette was busily scribbling notes when the pair emerged from the barn, Emily already mounted. She was so engrossed in her work that she was surprised she noticed their return. She watched Christian walk the few strides to his horse and swing gracefully aboard. The slightest touch controlled the horse and soon he moved across the yard, Emily close beside him. She gazed at the long leg and booted foot resting easily in the stirrup. She noticed the way the breeze billowed the loose shirt and ruffled the ends of his long hair...but only because she needed to describe him.

Chapter Five

It was all going very well. Lynnette had scratched pages and pages of notes and had plotted out her entire story. She had most of the first scene down on paper and the next two fairly well in mind.

A movement in the corner of her vision broke her concentration, and, as she lifted her head, her stiff shoulders screamed in protest. She had been hunched over the notebook in her lap for far too long. She flexed her shoulders as she looked up to see what had caught her attention. Three riders were making their way down the winding trail from the bluff.

The shadows had grown long while she sat absorbed in her work. It must have been the fresh air or the rustic surroundings that had her so inspired she was able to work for hours.

She wiped her pen on the rag and carefully put the glass stopper on the ink bottle. She set the notebook on the step stool and stood, stretching her arms over her head, then stepped forward to lean on the rail and watch the riders come in.

Hugh was in the lead followed by Emily, with

Christian a short distance behind. She couldn't see if the horses were soaked with sweat as she had described the horses in her story. It was easy to imagine, though.

Hugh and Emily reached the bottom and headed for the barn. Lynnette found her eyes falling on Christian more than the other two. His horse was a dark brown (she would have to ask if that color had a special name) and he rode as though he and the horse could read each other's minds. She grinned. She would have to remember that.

He rode toward the sinking sun, his hat pulled low over his eyes. She could imagine any expression she liked on that handsome face. Her favorite, of course, was the dimpled grin. She wondered just how far away a person could be and still make out those dimples.

When Christian had ridden past her window he shifted slightly in the saddle. Lynnette realized he had been watching her as intently as she watched him. For a moment she felt embarrassed, feeling she had broken a social mandate. But surely if she hadn't known exactly where his eyes were, he couldn't have known she watched him specifically. Still she should have waved to make it seem less improper.

She turned to gather her things from the step stool. "*He* could have waved," she muttered.

Downstairs a few minutes later, Lynnette found Arlen in one of the huge stuffed chairs, reading from a stack of papers. He set them aside and stood. "Lynnette, darling," he said, coming forward to kiss her cheek. "Did you have a good rest?"

Rest? She had forgotten that she was expected to spend the afternoon in bed. "I feel quite refreshed, thank you," she said, trying not to grin at the truth of that statement. "I had a very pleasant afternoon."

"Wonderful, darling." He waited until she had taken a chair then returned to his own. "I finished my letters about an hour ago and didn't want to disturb you. Is Emily still in her room?"

"No." Lynnette hesitated. Should she admit that she saw Emily ride out with Christian and therefore admit that she hadn't slept all afternoon? She didn't like this pattern of dishonesty she saw forming. Why was it easier to let Arlen think she did as he said?

"She went with Christian," Lynnette said, feeling better already. "They just rode in with your father. I was on the balcony."

"Then dinner might be on time after all," Arlen said.

Lynnette wasn't sure why that response irritated her. Perhaps she had expected him to take more interest in his family's activities. She was certainly fascinated— because of her story. She felt a contented smile settle on her lips at the thought of the story. Her sensitive story about the hardships and loneliness of ranch life had changed subtly as she plotted. She had to admit it was developing into something Silver Nightingale would write. She hadn't intended to ever write one of those novels again, but it all fell into place so perfectly.

"I'll be taking my letters into town to post them tomorrow, would you like to go along?"

"What? Oh, I'm sorry, I was woolgathering. Yes,

a trip to town would be nice." Actually she wanted to stay here and write, but she *should* want to spend the day with Arlen.

"You have some letters to post, too, I see." He pointed toward her hands, resting in her lap.

She glanced down at her ink-stained fingers. "Oh." She laughed. "I did make rather a mess of myself, didn't I?" She rubbed at the stains, knowing they would simply have to wear off. "I'm writing a story."

Arlen looked incredulous. "A story? Whatever for?"

"I enjoy writing," she said. "I always have."

"Well, once we're married, you'll be too busy entertaining important men and their wives to care about that kind of nonsense."

"Arlen—"

"Besides, we won't want you meeting voters with unsightly ink stains all over your hands."

"Arlen."

"Ah, here we are."

Emily nearly bounded into the room. "Hi, Arlen. Lynnette."

Lynnette smiled at the girl. "Hello, Emily. Did you have a nice ride?"

"It was great fun." She crossed the room and turned to walk backward toward the stairs as she finished speaking. "I'm going to get my things and take a bath before dinner."

Lynnette laughed as the girl scampered up the steps. Arlen chuckled too, but more with resignation than humor.

"I don't understand Father letting her dress like that."

"I imagine it's very practical for riding," Lynnette said, feeling too piqued at Arlen to resist the urge to argue no matter how unladylike it was.

"Perhaps. But it's not necessary for her to ride." Arlen came to his feet and stepped in front of Lynnette, offering her his hand. She noticed that his fingers were as ink-stained as her own. "We should go and dress for dinner," he said, as she took his hand and stood.

"But if she enjoys it," Lynnette said hesitantly. Here she was, arguing again. "Shouldn't Emily dress in a fashion that makes riding as pleasurable and safe as possible?"

Arlen tucked her hand in the crook of his arm and led her toward the stairs. "There are so many other things to give a young lady pleasure. She needs to be taught to enjoy them. It's difficult for Father to take a firm hand with her when she is only here for a short time. As a result, she's a bit spoiled."

Lynnette wasn't sure how to respond to Arlen. Emily and her father's rearing of her were none of her business. She shouldn't argue with Arlen, especially within Emily's hearing, and the girl came out of her room at that moment, her arms loaded with clothing, and passed them on the stairs.

Arlen walked Lynnette to her door where he took her hands and gazed into her eyes. "You are truly the most beautiful of women. You need to be careful not to let anything mar that beauty." He touched his finger to her nose where the sun had left its mark that morning.

She should be flattered by his words but coming after his announcement that her writing was nonsense, they only stung. "Beauty will fade eventually, Arlen. What we are is more important."

"Of course," he said, bringing her hands to his lips. "And what you are is my beloved. When we're married I'll take good care of you." He reached behind Lynnette and opened the door for her, holding it as she went inside. "I'll meet you downstairs in about an hour."

Inside her room, Lynnette sat on the bed and stared at the writing notebook and ink she had left on the desk. Perhaps Arlen was right, writing stories wasn't a proper pastime for a woman. Especially stories like this one. She found a smile creeping across her face and shook it away.

Amanda had often told her she wasn't proper, and Amanda didn't even know about *Passion's Secret*. She had been referring to Lynnette's penchant for making her own decisions and, sin of sins, arguing. Amanda had once predicted she would never marry because of them. Here she was, already chafing under Arlen's admittedly light hand.

With a deep breath she stood and walked to the wardrobe to choose a dress for dinner. If she wasn't cut out for matrimony, she thought, it would be better to find out now than after the ceremony. It was only fair to Arlen to let him see what she was really like. Perhaps, as her father had predicted, he would love her the more for her independence. She was even more skeptical now than she had been when her father had suggested it.

"What do you think of Arlen's lady?" Hugh rubbed down his horse while Christian took care of Emily's and his own. Christian wished he could avoid the question entirely. He didn't like how his answer seemed to change with each encounter.

"She seems nice enough," he said.

"Yes, yes. But not very sure of herself or perhaps of Arlen. Didn't she seem hesitant around him? Almost nervous?"

"I don't know." Christian wished he had some excuse to leave until his father went into the house, but the saddles were already in the tack room and the horses needed his attention.

"I was only with her last evening, you understand. How were things this morning? Did she sleep as late as Emily?"

"No." What had happened this morning was hardly his business. He didn't care to share it with his father.

Hugh had other questions about Lynnette, and Christian answered them as briefly as possible. If he gave his father the impression that he didn't like the girl, all the better. The questions forced him to recall her expressions, her words, her smiles until he could no longer deny his attraction to her.

He sighed with relief when his father left the barn. His brother's future wife! He felt disgusted with himself. How had he let this happen? He didn't even like her type, these city girls who only cared about the latest fashion and expected life to be a parlor game.

Only he already knew Lynnette wasn't like that. Now he wished to God she was.

He washed his hands and face at the well before he went into the house. He still debated whether he should spend as much time as possible with Lynnette, hoping this foolish attraction would go away with familiarity, or avoid her entirely. The first seemed too dangerous and the second impractical.

He walked into the living room and decided he would save that second idea as a last resort. She looked gorgeous. She was on a balcony again, and the sunlight on her hair formed a halo around her head. Her narrow-waisted dress was the color of wine, and he felt almost drunk just looking at her. He stifled a groan as he turned away.

Arlen and Emily were in the room as well, though he had nearly missed seeing them. Arlen, engrossed in his reading, couldn't have noticed his interest in Lynnette. He wondered what Emily might have read on his face.

"My, my, little sister, I hardly recognized you. You look almost civilized."

"I look lovely, and you know it." She sat in the love seat, her skirt spread around her as if she were posing for a picture. She cast a glance toward Lynnette.

Christian cursed himself as he did it, but he turned to look at her as well. She had left the balcony and walked toward them. Her dress wasn't nearly as elegant as Emily's but it showed off a figure that made his mouth go dry. She smiled. He had no idea what he was doing, gaping probably.

"Lynnette fixed my hair," Emily said, drawing his attention again. He was immensely grateful.

He cocked his head to one side, studying the elaborate style. "What keeps it from falling down?" he asked, pretending to reach for it.

Emily batted at his hand. "Good posture," she said.

Hugh came down the stairs and invited them to join him in the dining room. Arlen rose quickly to escort Lynnette, and Emily hurried to her father, who tucked her hand into the crook of his arm and walked her to her chair.

Christian followed a few paces behind. Hugh and Arlen were dressed as elegantly as the ladies; he supposed he was the only one who still had work to do.

The meal was served following Hugh's blessing. Christian barely noticed what he ate, absorbed as he was in avoiding any glances toward Lynnette or his brother. Hugh and Emily kept the others in conversation that was easy enough to ignore. Arlen's announcement that he would go into Cottonwood Falls the next day to post some letters and Lynnette would go along was the only thing that made an impression on him.

He tried to convince himself that that didn't interest him either. He wasn't going to miss Lynnette. He would be working and wouldn't catch more than a glimpse of her if she were home. It was ridiculous to feel disappointed that she would be gone, so, of course, he didn't. He discovered he was looking at her and quickly turned away.

When dessert was served, Hugh asked Lynnette about her education, and Christian found himself watching her again. It seemed her father had believed young ladies should have the same education as young men and instead of putting her in a finishing school had sent her to a regular university.

"I'm impressed," Hugh said.

Christian glanced at his brother. *Impressed* did not describe the look on his face.

"I admit I'm surprised," Arlen said. "I had no idea your father's views were so—"

"Liberal?" Lynnette offered.

Christian wondered if Arlen had planned to say crazy.

"Well, yes...liberal," Arlen said. "It seems sort of a...a...waste of, well, resources, don't you think?"

Christian couldn't resist. "How's that, little brother?"

Arlen's cheeks turned pink. Christian didn't dare look at Lynnette. Could he have asked the question out of some deep desire to cause a rift between the two? He wished he could withdraw it.

"Most universities," Arlen began, "must limit their enrollment. A seat to a woman denies one to some man who would actually use an education."

"I'm sure my father felt I would use the education one way or another. At the very least, an education encourages one to think for oneself."

Christian caught a note of challenge in the last statement, but Arlen didn't seem to. He shook his head, chuckling. "Next we'll learn your father believed in suffrage for women." No one else laughed.

"I'm not sure if he did or not," Lynnette offered mildly. "But I most certainly do."

"My dear," Arlen began in a voice lowered to instruct a child. "Suffrage means the right to vote."

"I know what it means, Arlen."

"But that's silly!" Arlen took a deep breath and regained a measure of control. "I mean, women don't need to vote. Men follow the events and decide what's best for everyone. We always keep our women's interests in mind."

"I'm sure you do," Lynnette said, sounding not at all as if she did. "But not all men do."

"This whole issue has been debated time and again," Arlen went on. "It was voted down in '67."

"Of course, along with suffrage for the Negroes, because the people it would benefit weren't allowed to vote."

"You can vote in school board elections," Arlen offered.

"And that's supposed to placate us? Perhaps we should carefully elect school board members who will hire enlightened teachers who will teach the boys the value of women's minds so in fifty years *they'll* allow us full rights as citizens."

Arlen was stunned into silence.

Christian watched him, trying not to smile. He had heard all the arguments against women's suffrage, the primary one being the liquor lobby's fear of prohibition. Most of the rest were just excuses. "If women voted," Christian said, knowing he should keep his mouth shut, "married men would have two votes."

Her eyes locked with his across the table. He knew he should turn away but it was too interesting watching the wheels turn. Her eyes were sharply appraising, perhaps mildly angry.

Spit it out, he silently urged. *Don't swallow what you want to say.* The moment seemed to drag on for far too long. He couldn't guess what the other three at the table thought of their behavior, but they didn't speak. Or perhaps they did, and he simply didn't hear them.

Finally Lynnette spoke. "I don't believe very many men will be so strongly influenced by their wives."

Christian heard Arlen clear his throat. He wanted to congratulate Lynnette on her remark but didn't dare. He flashed her a grin, instead.

"I believe Christian's concern was the other way around," Arlen said gently. "Women would always—"

"I know what he meant," Lynnette said.

Christian shook his head. Arlen didn't give the woman credit for brains. He couldn't watch. "If you'll excuse me, I have a horse to break," he said, rising from the table.

"I don't see how you can think of riding so soon after eating," Arlen said, as if glad for the change of subject.

"I tried to ride him a week ago. Haven't gotten up the nerve since. I just go out every evening to discuss it with him." He turned toward Emily and tugged on a loose curl. "Wait up for me," he whispered. "I won't be late."

Outside, Christian stopped and took a few deep breaths of the cool evening air before heading for the barn. He needed to have a clear head when he worked with the stallion. By the time he had slid open the door and lit a lantern he decided that wasn't possible this evening.

He looked around the barn for some task that would keep him busy until Lynnette went to bed. He headed for the tack room; there were usually harnesses or halters that needed mending, but a careful perusal of all the gear turned up nothing. Perry had evidently found them a way to keep himself busy all winter while he nursed his broken leg. He wanted to curse the man's efficiency.

He found a few tools that he returned to their proper place and even took a broom to the dirt on the floor. Too quickly he was finished. He carried the lantern back to its hook near the door. Perhaps keeping busy wasn't the right idea anyway. Maybe he needed to sit down and think things through. After putting out the lantern, he left the barn, walking the short distance to the cottonwood tree just past the corrals. It was the only tree that grew in the yard and had been a favorite place to play when he and Arlen were young. He had built a small stone bench at the base of the tree, and he sat on it now, deep in the tree's shadow.

He stretched his legs out in front of him and leaned against the tree's rough bark. He couldn't be falling in love with Lynnette. He had known her less than two days. She was beautiful, yes, and he found her attractive. What man wouldn't? He admired her intelligence and spunk. That should make him happy for Arlen. And it did, but...

But what? Christian gazed at the silhouette of the house against the graying sky and listened to the faint rustle of the leaves above him. Was he jealous? Did he wish she was in love with him? That was ridiculous! What kind of a rancher's wife would she make?

The thought, however brief, of Lynnette as his wife sent a warm current through his body. And *that* was the heart of the problem, he decided. His body wasn't interested in what his mind had to say about the situation. Well, that didn't matter. He could certainly control himself. Perhaps it was time he made more of an effort to find a suitable wife from among the neighboring families. He noticed a certain lack of enthusiasm for the project. He hated to think he was lazy.

But then, here he was, sitting under a tree mooning over his brother's girl. Maybe he *was* lazy. He needed a woman, and Lynnette was around. That was all there was to it. It had nothing to do with her personally. When he found his own woman, all these feelings for Lynnette would be gone.

And he could welcome her as a sister. When had his earlier concerns about her possible motives disappeared? In fact, after the dinner conversation tonight, it was clear that she would be good for Arlen. She wasn't easily swayed by his condescending remarks. She could teach him a lot...if he would let her.

And whether he did or not, of course, was none of his business. That was between Arlen and Lynnette. He should put them both out of his mind and work with the stallion.

As he was about to rise, he saw light filter through the curtains in the corner room. Lynnette had gone upstairs. He found himself unwilling to move. An occasional shadow crossed the pale square of light, and he watched transfixed. Finally, the curtains parted, spilling light across the balcony, and Christian discovered he had been holding his breath.

He let it out in a soundless whistle as she stepped through the doors. She had removed the pins from her hair, and it swirled around her shoulders as the breeze lifted it. Her burgundy dress looked black in silhouette, and he realized he had been hoping to see her in the gown she had worn the night before.

Last night, she had put out her light before she stepped onto the balcony, probably thinking he couldn't see her. Tonight, she left the light at her back. She stood at the rail for a few minutes, raising her hand once to toss a thick strand of hair over her shoulder, then turned back into her room.

She pulled the curtains, but left the doors open. Christian watched the wind tease the fabric as her image teased his mind. Did that one glimpse of her undo all his careful logic? Or did it simply prove what he had decided? He hoped it was the latter.

He should go in now and braid Emily's hair. It was a treasured ritual that went back to her first summer on the ranch without a mother to do the task. He knew she would be waiting, though he doubted she was anywhere near ready to retire. Still, he found himself watching for the light to go out. When it finally did he stayed another moment. Did he hope she would step out onto the darkened balcony one more time? He thrust himself to his feet, disgusted, and strode to the house.

Inside he found Emily and their father involved in a game of checkers. ''She's going to beat me again,''

Hugh said. "Can I count on one of my boys to get revenge for me?"

"Christian will play," Emily said, jumping another of Hugh's men.

Hugh shook his head. "The hot bath before dinner took some of the kinks out of this old body, but it'll take sleep to ease the rest." He rose slowly and headed for the stairs. Emily was already setting up the checkers for another game.

Christian sighed, missing the peace of the cottonwood. He brushed it off; Emily would be gone again much too soon. "Hey, Arlen," he called to the opened newspaper across the room. "Come play with your sister while I braid her hair."

The paper barely rustled. "No thanks. I'm checking the papers for any mention of fairs or dances to be held in the county."

Christian scowled down at his sister and discovered Arlen had caught her attention. "Can I come?"

"I'll be working," the voice behind the paper replied.

Emily wrinkled her nose. "Will you take Lynnette?"

"No." The paper started to go limp, then was snapped into shape. "I mean...perhaps later in the summer."

Christian eyed the paper for a moment before he took the seat across from Emily. The girl leaned toward him and whispered, "If Lynnette gets to go, will you help me talk *her* into taking me?"

"I heard that," Arlen said.

Christian winked at his sister. "Who's first?"

"Me."

Christian wondered at his brother's reaction. It seemed odd when he had already mentioned what a campaign asset Lynnette would be. Emily jumped three of his men, and he tried to concentrate on the game. He was only partially successful. It didn't take long for her to beat him.

"Again?" she asked, setting up the board.

Christian shook his head. "Let me braid your hair. I still have work to do." He rose and came around behind her.

"But it's too late to work," Emily protested.

"If it's so late you should be thinking about going to bed."

She turned in the chair so he could reach her hair and pouted. "You work too hard. I won't hardly see you all summer."

"Hey, I spent the afternoon with you, didn't I?" Christian asked, trying not to feel guilty. "How about if I take you to town in a couple days? We can get supplies for Martha and stop at Blainey's on the way home. You and Rose can decide when she will come and stay."

"I'm going into town tomorrow," Arlen said. "I can get any supplies Martha needs."

Emily spun toward the newspaper, and Christian had to move quickly to keep from pulling her hair. "Can I go with you?" she asked.

"I won't have time to stop at Blainey's."

Emily's shoulders sagged.

Christian leaned forward, whispering in her ear. "We'll go even if Arlen gets the supplies."

"Tomorrow?"

"I doubt it. Now hold still." When he finished the braid, he tickled her nose with the end of it. She slapped his hand away. "Tomorrow," he suggested, "you can help Martha in the garden."

Emily groaned in disgust but still hugged and kissed Christian good-night. Back outside, Christian headed once again for the barn. This time he saddled the green-broke mare. What she needed was a lot of time under the saddle, but he couldn't trust her on working excursions like this afternoon's. A trip into town and back would be good for her, he told himself.

But he wasn't going into town to break the horse. The decision had come to him when he entered his home and found himself surrounded by the family he loved. He had too many things on his mind to want to spend the evening with any of them.

Yet it wasn't exactly solitude he sought in town.

Chapter Six

A movement on the bed nudged Christian toward consciousness. His brain resisted. Light burned his eyelids, and he threw his arm up to shield them. The motion and the pain between his eyes woke him completely. With a start that brought him to a sitting position, he looked toward the light and the muffled noises in the room.

"Arlen." He fell back against the bed with extreme relief. For one awful moment he had forgotten that he shared his bed with his brother.

"You came in late," Arlen said softly.

Christian's answer was a low groan as he returned his arm to its former position across his eyes.

"Emily heard you ride out and was worried. Father told her you were probably working with one of the half-broke horses."

That was near enough to the truth.

Arlen kept talking as he moved around the room. "I don't think the horse is the reason you're in the shape you're in this morning, though."

Arlen was quiet for a few minutes, and Christian

hoped he had left. As he started to drift back to sleep, Arlen spoke from beside the bed. "I suppose I should thank you for bathing before you came to bed. I'd hate to go into town smelling like cheap perfume."

Christian couldn't resist a grin. He had bathed last night for his own benefit, not Arlen's. And he wasn't near as hungover as his brother evidently thought. "You're welcome," he said, peeking out from under his arm. The room was nearly dark, lit only by the barest flame in the lamp. "What time is it, anyway?"

"Not yet five. I want to get an early start to Cottonwood Falls. There's a church bake sale and quilt auction in Bazaar at noon. It ought to bring in a lot of people."

"Happy campaigning," Christian said, covering his eyes again. In a minute he heard the door close. Lynnette would be gone more than just all morning; she would be gone all day. He knew that wasn't what he should be thinking about. But assuming he could forget her in someone else's arms was the reason for the headache this morning. A few drinks should have made the willing little tart look inviting. When he had realized if he drank *that* much he wouldn't be able to make it home, he had left.

And it wasn't as if the girl was unattractive—she just wasn't Lynnette.

"No," he murmured, forcing himself to sit up. "That's not it at all." The problem with the tart was that she wasn't the woman he wanted to spend his life with. He had been mistaken when he thought all he needed was one night's pleasure. He needed to find his woman, the woman who was meant for him. *Then* he would forget Lynnette.

He held his head in his hands for a moment. The headache was no more than a mild but persistent reminder of last night's foolishness. The real pain was centered somewhere else.

He threw himself back onto the bed. He needed sleep. Besides, he didn't want to walk into the dining room to find Arlen and Lynnette eating breakfast. None of this was their fault, of course. He just felt too raw at the moment to deal with them.

Morning light filtered through the curtains when Lynnette woke. Her room was cold, and she snuggled deeper into the covers for a few minutes. She was to go to town today with Arlen. They would have a chance to talk without any of the rest of the family around. The country between the ranch and Cottonwood Station was beautiful, and it would be her chance to explore the town of Cottonwood Falls across the river.

She tossed aside the covers and swung her legs off the bed. If she kept this up the entire time it took to get dressed, she might succeed in convincing herself. Throwing on her robe, she moved to close the patio door she had left open the night before. She looked longingly at her notebook on the desk.

A small stirring on her bed made her spin around. Black and white fur slowly dislodged itself from the tangle of blankets and leaped to the floor. Tyrant shook himself before sitting down to glare at Lynnette.

Lynnette laughed. "You again. If you're looking for Arlen, I'm afraid he's one door down."

Tyrant merely glared.

"Would you like to be friends?" Lynnette took cautious steps toward the cat. "You've shared my bed. We ought to introduce ourselves." She giggled at the way that sounded aloud.

The cat cocked his head but remained relaxed. Lynnette bent cautiously and stroked the soft head, then pulled the cat onto her lap as she sat on the floor. "See? We can be friends."

Tyrant allowed the attention for a moment, then tensed, and Lynnette let him go. He walked sedately toward the door and turned to give her a haughty glare. "Well, if you feel it's time to leave." She rose to let him out. "Be sure to visit again soon."

She laughed as the cat took his leave in the most dignified manner. As she closed the door she noticed an envelope lying on her carpet; it had evidently been slid under the door. Picking it up, she found her name scrawled across the front. She tore it open and read the note quickly, then again more slowly. She felt a flood of relief, followed by little prickles of guilt. Arlen had left without her.

With new energy, she dressed in a comfortable day dress. After making the bed she spread a sturdy shawl on it and placed her notebook, tightly closed ink bottle and her pens on the shawl and wrapped them up. She carried the bundle downstairs with her. Immediately after breakfast, she would seek out that inviting bench she had seen the day before.

* * *

Christian wondered if he was the last one up. He couldn't remember when he had slept this late. He wasn't going to have an easy time explaining this to his father—if the old man even gave him an opportunity to explain. It would be more like Hugh to come to his own conclusions and let Christian wonder what he thought. "Well, Pa," he mumbled as he buttoned his shirt, "I went into town to see if a tumble with a trollop would get my future sister-in-law out of my head."

He pulled pants over his legs, and as he tucked in his shirt he continued just above a whisper. "You'll be pleased to know that I didn't follow through. I paid the girl just to show I'm a gentleman, got mildly drunk and came home. So," he concluded, stomping into his boots, "I'm just as bad off as ever." He groaned as he left his room and headed down the stairs.

The dining room was deserted, but that didn't surprise him. Martha turned to fix his breakfast as soon as he entered the kitchen. He got himself a cup of coffee and took a seat at the plank table. He carefully sipped the strong brew, hoping it would dispel the last of the headache.

"The old man been down?" he asked as Martha placed a plate of biscuits and gravy in front of him.

"Hours ago," she said with a grin. "He's in his office, I think."

"Hours?" Christian took a bite while Martha went to fill her own coffee cup.

"Well, one or two. I had about given you up for dead." Martha slid onto the bench across from him.

"Old man that mad, huh?"

She laughed. "Hugh never gives you much trouble."

"Shows what you know," he said between bites. "He gives me this whole...disappointed...routine. It can go on for days." He grinned when he said it; she knew it was an exaggeration, anyway. "I suppose it's too much to hope that Jake did the chores without me."

"He started them, at least."

Christian scraped up the last of the gravy. "Thanks for the breakfast. I better get to work and start my penance." Downing the last of the coffee, he rose from the bench. He stacked his dishes and took them to the sink on his way out the door.

He was halfway to the barn when he noticed her. She sat on his stone bench under the cottonwood tree, hunched over something on her lap. Whatever it was had her undivided attention.

And she had his. He shouldn't go speak to her. He had work to do. He was late already. None of the excuses seemed to make it from his brain to his feet. They had already turned in her direction. What exactly did he think he would say to her? There was still time to turn and head straight for the barn.

In the next moment there wasn't. Lynnette looked up and smiled.

"Good morning," he said. "I thought you were going with Arlen." He reached the cottonwood and crouched on the ground beside her. Her lap contained a writing notebook, the facing page fairly covered with hasty scribbles.

"He left without me." She didn't sound hurt. "Isn't it a beautiful morning?"

"Yes, it is." It came out a whisper. She was looking at the landscape; he couldn't see beyond her lovely face.

"Oh!" She seemed to recall herself suddenly, and he tried to do the same. "I didn't mean to suggest that Arlen simply rode out without a word. He left me a note. It seems his trip has turned into a longer one, and he was afraid it would tire me."

He should wish her happy writing and leave her alone. "What are you working on?" he asked, nodding toward her notebook.

She gave a nervous little laugh and set it beside her on the bench, corked her ink bottle and placed it and the pen on top. "It's just a story I've started."

"Yeah? What's it about?"

She hesitated a long moment. Lord, he liked watching the emotions play across her face. She usually gave away so little. He had caught her at a vulnerable time, he realized. All the more reason to leave. He shifted to sit cross-legged on the ground, relieving a cramping ankle.

"Well," she said finally, "it's set on a ranch."

Arlen, he thought. Well, why not? He waited to see if she would say more.

"Oh, I almost forget. You can help me." Her smile was infectious. He found himself nodding agreeably. "What color do you call that horse you were riding yesterday?"

"Liver chestnut."

She wrinkled her nose. "Liver? You really call it that? Why not just chestnut?"

"That's a different color."

She laughed. "One of the great things about writing is I can change a horse's color just like that." She snapped her ink-stained fingers.

The delight on her face made her more beautiful. "You love it, don't you?"

"I can't imagine not writing. Sometimes it seems like there are characters in my head clamoring for me to give them life. How can I ignore them?" A touch of pain crossed her face for a second and was gone. He was more intrigued than ever.

"You didn't get a chance to answer the other night. Have you had anything published?"

She bit her lip and looked off into the distance. He had hurt her feelings. "I didn't mean to sound like that was all that mattered," he said hastily. "I'm sure it's hard to—"

"That's not it." She turned back, giving him a searching look. God, he felt as though he might melt right into the ground. Finally she came to a decision. "I haven't even told Arlen this, but yes, I've had one novel published."

She looked as though she didn't want to say more. Now he had to know. "You want to swear me to secrecy?"

She laughed, breaking a little of the tension. "That would be nice."

He sat up straighter, placing his hand on his heart, then smiled encouragingly. He had made her smile, at least. "Why haven't you told Arlen?"

"I'm not sure how he'll react." She had lifted her pen from the pile beside her and toyed with it.

"Test it out on me. If I survive, you can tell Arlen."

She laughed again. He wanted to take the pen out of her fingers and twine his own in its place. He waited as patiently as he could for her to decide if she would tell him.

"All right." She took a deep breath. "It's called *Passion's Secret* and it did very well. It's still selling a little, I understand. I can't believe I'm telling you this. *No one* knows. My friends would be scandalized."

He faked a quizzical look. "Passion's what now?" He had made her laugh again. He was absolutely delighted.

"I didn't pick the name. But even without it most people would consider it trash, I guess."

"Do you consider it trash?"

"Not really. It's just a love story. I made it a little more sensational than it needed to be in order to get it published. My father..." Her voice cracked, and he wanted more than ever to take hold of her hand. "My father had a lot of bills, and nothing else would sell."

Christian didn't like the way the conversation had changed her mood. He wanted her laughing again. From where he sat, he could look up into her soft eyes even when she lowered them. He ignored the feeling that this was getting dangerous.

"So, what you're writing now? Is it as scandalous?"

A smile touched her lips. She looked at her lap,

seeming to consider her answer. "It didn't start out that way."

She was flustered and he found it appealing. "I'm sorry, but you're going to have to explain what that means."

She hesitated a moment. "Well, I want my lonely rancher to find the perfect woman and of course when they do...well..."

"Say no more," he said coming to his feet. "I'll wait till I can buy it. Is there a pen name I should be looking for?"

She shook her head even as she answered. "Silver Nightingale, but don't look for it."

She craned her pretty neck to look up at him. "I should tell Arlen, shouldn't I?"

"You should tell Arlen, and I should get back to work." He turned to go.

"Christian?"

The sound of his name from her lips made his heart lurch. She had never called him by name. It shouldn't matter. It *didn't* matter. He had his reaction in tight control when he turned around. "Yes?"

"Thanks for helping with the horse. Would you mind if I have other questions, about horses and ranching, I mean?"

"My pleasure," he said. He hoped it sounded sincere. The more he tried to convince himself there was nothing to his infatuation beyond loneliness, the more strongly he reacted. He hurried toward the barn and the normality of chores.

After a few minutes he sent Jake off to exercise the horses and finished cleaning the stalls alone. He wasn't fit company for the boy, and he knew it. Lynnette was driving him crazy. He had no willpower where she was concerned. He told himself to stay away from her, then sat at her feet like a disciple and listened to her secrets. His own poor judgment astounded him.

As he walked away from her, Lynnette closed her eyes. What had she been thinking? She couldn't tell her fiancé, but she could tell his brother? The idea, shameful as it was, of keeping it a secret forever had come to her more than once. That was ruined now. Christian knew.

When she opened her eyes a moment later she was relieved to find he was out of sight. How could she not have told him? No one else had ever shown as much interest in her writing, not even Amanda. She was starved for an opportunity to talk about it.

Well, she would have Arlen to talk to about it. Somehow she would make him see how much this "nonsense" meant to her. He truly wanted the best for her; he would understand. She just hadn't given him a chance. And she would explain about the book. She found herself imagining asking his forgiveness and was irritated that that should be the way of things.

She picked up her notebook. She wouldn't think about Arlen now. She reread the last two pages and, with Christian's dimpled smile fresh in her mind, returned to her story.

She had no idea how much time had passed before she heard Emily call, "Here you are." The girl sprinted toward her.

"Hi, Emily. You're looking fresh this morning."

Emily flounced the ruffles on her pale yellow gown. "How long have you been out here?"

Lynnette riffled the pages of her notebook, noting how many more were filled than before. "Quite a while, I guess."

"It's almost time for lunch."

Lynnette put the stopper in the ink bottle. "I should go in and freshen up."

As Lynnette gathered up the pens, Emily picked up the notebook to carry it for her. "Is this a story?" At Lynnette's nod, she asked, "Can I read it?"

"When it's done, I'd love for you to read it."

They walked toward the house together, Lynnette mentally assessing the content of the book from a young girl's point of view. There wasn't anything objectionable in it, yet. And there wouldn't be, she resolved. She wanted Arlen's approval. And he needed the approval of the voters.

In the house, Emily followed her upstairs and into her room. She set the notebook on the desk and looked around. "Jeez, Arlen doesn't like pictures much, does he?"

"The room seemed a little bare to me, as well. I thought perhaps he hadn't wanted to force his tastes on me." Emily shrugged and walked toward the framed photograph. "Do you know who those people are?" Lynnette asked her.

"Mother's family. It was taken shortly after she married Father. Arlen always liked it because he looks so much like most of them." The girl turned and smiled. "So do I, I guess."

Lynnette came closer and studied the photograph.

An older couple were seated in the center, the woman holding a small boy who had moved and blurred his face. They were flanked by four younger adults. Emily was right, they did look like Arlen, except for one man who was the image of Christian. She couldn't help herself. "And this man?" she asked, pointing.

"Father." Emily laughed. "Surrounded by his in-laws. I better let you get ready for lunch."

Lynnette forced her eyes away from the photograph and bade her goodbye. Twenty minutes later she descended the stairs, her face washed, her hair freshly pinned up, and her skirt brushed.

Christian stood on the center balcony, looking off across the valley. Lynnette stopped just short of the bottom step and studied him. What was he thinking? Was he contemplating his domain, reliving the past, longing for the woman who would complete his life? Oh God! This was *Christian,* her future brother-in-law, *not* the hero of her book. And she would prove she knew the difference. She stepped onto the balcony with him. "Does one ever get over how beautiful this is?"

He turned toward her. She didn't seem to have startled him; perhaps he had heard her on the stairs. A full minute passed before he answered softly, "No."

At least it seemed like a minute. Her heart had beaten the appropriate number of times, but perhaps that wasn't a good test. She wanted to tell herself it was the view or the distance to the ground that made her heart race, but she was afraid it was Christian. She forced herself to swallow. "I'll see if Martha needs any help."

She turned quickly and left him. How could this have happened? She had been so sure her interest had been for the sake of her character. But why had she chosen Christian for her hero? That had been a mistake, she decided. She should burn the story and rewrite it with Arlen as the hero.

She paused just outside the kitchen door. In spite of her boast to Christian, changing her story wasn't so easily done. The characters had taken on lives of their own, and it was difficult to abandon them. But she would, she resolved.

She pasted a smile on her face and pushed through the door.

Christian waited for the sound of the kitchen door. It seemed to take forever. When he finally heard it, he still didn't turn around.

She had no idea. She was polite and friendly, and he was falling in love with her. He cursed himself, but it did no good. He couldn't undo what had happened. He braced his hands against the railing and hung his head. Ten years from now, when Arlen and Lynnette brought their children to visit, would he still be in love with her? Would he marry some woman he didn't love so he could have a family too?

Could he go to Arlen and beg him to break the engagement? He hated himself for even thinking it. *I'm sorry, Arlen. I never meant to betray you.*

He heard the kitchen door again and heard Emily's skipping step on the stairs. Cheerful voices reached him, but they only made him more miserable. Listening to her laugh, seeing her smile, knowing he could never have her, tore at his heart.

He would certainly avoid situations like this morning. The temptation to declare his love might become too great. He could ruin her life and Arlen's, as well as his own.

It would be difficult with her here all summer. Then Arlen would marry her and take her away. The tiny sense of relief he felt lasted barely long enough for him to identify it. Would time and distance make any difference? Would his heart heal?

He heard his father's voice mixing with the others and knew he had to go in. He felt a closer kinship to Hugh now, though he could never tell him. Hugh had loved Felicia, that much he had understood even as a boy. But she had left him. And he had gone on to live a life, and raise his sons.

Had time dulled the pain? Was it worse for him because he had believed she loved him too? Or did the anger at her betrayal make it easier to forget the love he lost? Not exactly things he could ask his father.

He straightened, running his fingers through his wind-tossed hair. He couldn't stall any longer. He had to join the family and pretend.

Emily was coming to get him when he turned. "Nothing out there can be that interesting," she said, catching his arm and dragging him toward the table. "We're starving."

He helped Emily into her usual seat and took his place beside her. Lynnette was already seated. He tried not to look at her, but she was the only person seated on the other side of the table. He thanked God she wasn't directly across from him.

Hugh said the blessing and light conversation accompanied the platters around the table. "Lynnette's writing a book," Emily announced as the last platter made the rounds. "She promised to let me read it."

Christian looked at Lynnette. He couldn't help it. She had glanced at him as well. There was uncertainty in her eyes as if she expected him to object. Or was she afraid he would give away her secret?

"It's a long way from finished," she told Emily. He pulled his eyes from her face.

"Is there anything we can do to make the writing easier?" Hugh asked. "I'm sure Arlen's things are still in the desk upstairs. We could find you something else."

"No, no. Don't go to any trouble. I'll just take the notebook and wander around."

Christian didn't look up to see if she shook her head, if the tiny wisps of hair that escaped her careful styling danced around her ears. He swallowed a bite of something that might as well have been sand.

"I think this is wonderful," Hugh said. "A writer here under our roof. Can you tell us about it, or will that break some deal you've made with the muse?"

She laughed. God, why did she have to laugh? Of course, it was time he looked up or his behavior would appear rude. He ventured into the conversation. "She's setting it on a ranch." Emily and Hugh turned toward him and he added. "She told me this morning."

Was it his imagination, or had his comment been a

little out of place? He didn't even know how to talk with his family anymore. He let the others carry on without him. He ate as much as he could force down and excused himself, uncertain by then just what he interrupted.

Lynnette tried not to watch him go. He was uncomfortable. Or unhappy. Whatever it was, it had nothing to do with her, she told herself firmly. And with him gone it should be easier to concentrate on Emily's questions. It was the oddest thing, being surrounded by people who weren't put off by the fact that she wanted to be a writer. They were encouraging her, in fact.

"Let's raid the library," Emily suggested. "We can take turns reading to each other."

"Perhaps Lynnette wants to continue her writing this afternoon," Hugh said gently.

Instead of looking disappointed, Emily looked contrite.

"I'd love to read," Lynnette said quickly. "After all, that's how I learned to write, by reading everything I could get my hands on. I have books in my trunk we might choose from."

Emily pushed her chair away from the table. "I'm embroidering roses on a nightgown and Mother says I simply must finish it this summer. I'll go get it." She stood and kissed her father's cheek before scurrying to the stairs.

"That's very kind of you," Hugh said.

Lynnette smiled. "I'm happy to do it. I wrote all

morning, and I think I need a break. Besides, I enjoy Emily's company."

"If you can get a word in."

Lynnette tried not to laugh aloud—it wouldn't do if Emily heard—but she nodded her agreement. "If you'll excuse me, I want to talk to Martha. I have no sewing project, so perhaps I can borrow some socks to darn."

She rose from the table at Hugh's nod and went to the kitchen. The family was around the plank table. Perry reached for his crutch as Jake came to his feet. She motioned them back down.

"What can I get for you?" Martha asked, slight irritation evident in her voice.

"I'm sorry to interrupt," Lynnette said. "Emily and I are going to take turns reading and sewing this afternoon, and I wondered if you might have some mending I can do."

Martha seemed stunned by the request. She stared at Lynnette as if she expected to hear the rest of the joke.

"We'll send Jake in with it," Perry said.

"After he's finished eating," Lynnette said. "I'll take the first turn with the book." She apologized again and hurried out of the kitchen. She had made another mistake with Martha. It seemed every time she tried to do something for her, it went wrong. Of course a careful seamstress wouldn't want to trust her family's seams to just anyone. Lynnette went up the stairs vowing to take the tiniest, most careful stitches of her life.

Emily waited outside her door, holding a pretty woven sewing basket. "What kind of books do you have?" she asked as she followed Lynnette into the room.

"All kinds," she said. She opened the trunk and took them out one by one, handing them to Emily.

Emily stopped her with a squeal. "You have Jane Austen!"

"I have several." She found the rest and set them before the girl.

Emily went through them hastily. "Oh, this one, this one! It's my favorite. Don't you just love the way she writes!" She clutched the book to her breast.

They both laughed. "I love the way she uses the characters' points of view to make you feel like you're in the story."

Emily eyed her a moment and shrugged. "I like how there's no stupid war and politics stuff to skim through to get to what's really interesting."

"Let's read it," Lynnette said. "I can straighten the mess up later."

Emily ran ahead of her, still clutching the book. Lynnette picked up the forgotten sewing basket and followed her down the stairs. In the living room, Emily moved a huge stuffed chair closer to another and curled up in one. "Can I read first?"

"My sewing hasn't arrived." At Emily's raised brows she added, "Jake is to bring some mending for me to do. Why don't I read until he comes?"

Emily relinquished the book with good grace and took up her sewing basket.

Lynnette made herself comfortable in the other chair and turned to the first page. She read, remembering how much she had loved these words the first time she had read them. Emily's only interruptions were an occasional sigh. She had read two of the short chapters when footsteps made her look up. Jake carried a laundry basket to her.

"Thank you, Jake." She turned over the open book and rested it on her knee.

"It looks like a lot," he said, "but most things are little tears or buttons gone and the like." He set it down beside the chair and turned to Emily.

The girl pretended to ignore him, but the needle wasn't making any progress in the tiny pink rose. "You can go now, Jake."

Jake grinned at her. "Miss Lynnette," he said. "Don't let Emily put any of her crooked little stitches on my clothes."

"Don't worry, Jake." Emily looked up and flashed the poor boy a devastating smile. Jake's grin faltered a little, and he turned and hurried from the room.

"Now it's my turn to read," Emily said, wadding the gown back into her basket. She grabbed up the book, scooted deeper into the chair and quickly found where Lynnette had left off.

A couple of hours into the afternoon, Martha brought them lemonade, and after the drink, Emily declared herself ready to continue reading. Lynnette only read once more and then for only half an hour before Emily tired of sewing.

The afternoon passed more quickly than Lynnette would have expected. Emily was a third of the way through a book that Lynnette had barely heard when Arlen came home.

Chapter Seven

Lynnette watched the buggy come up the road then disappear as it got closer to the house. She had been gazing out the window as she flexed her fingers, stiff from hours of sewing.

"Arlen's back," she said when Emily paused for breath.

Emily uncurled her legs and stretched them out in front of her, looking more like a little girl than the young woman she was becoming. "Maybe there's a letter from Mother," she said after a demure yawn.

"Ah, letters," Lynnette said with exaggerated anticipation. "I haven't written to my friend Amanda, and I promised to write every day."

Emily leaned forward in the chair. "Put the date you left on the first page and a new date on each page afterward, and she'll think you did. I do it to Mom all the time."

"Good idea," Lynnette whispered as they heard the back door close.

Emily went on in a hushed tone, "Of course, sometimes it's hard to think of that much to say, so I write kind of big and let on that I miss her more than I really do."

Arlen came into the room smelling of wind and sunshine and dust. He had left his hat on the way in and run his fingers through his curly dark hair. Strange that she never quite remembered how handsome he was. Perhaps he looked more handsome every time she saw him.

"My two favorite girls, and I've caught them whispering," he said, coming to kneel beside Lynnette's chair. "Did you have a good day?" He laid one hand on top of hers, and she wondered if he tried to hide the ink stains.

"We've been reading and sewing," Emily said. "I got two whole rosebuds done."

"Two?" Arlen seemed unimpressed.

"She did most of the reading," Lynnette added quickly. "She's quite good."

"I'm glad you enjoyed yourself." Arlen gazed adoringly into her eyes. She wanted to feel some deep response to it but only felt mildly uncomfortable. She tried gazing back.

"Mail." Emily's voice penetrated Lynnette's brain easily, but since it was spoken to Arlen and he didn't look away, she didn't either.

"Hey, lovebirds, give me the mail, and I'll leave you two alone."

Lynnette couldn't hide her amusement. Arlen scowled at his sister, but he took a small stack of letters from an inside pocket. He sorted them quickly and handed one to Emily then placed the rest on the floor beside him. He returned his attention to Lynnette.

Lynnette used the excuse of Emily's leaving to avoid facing Arlen for a moment. She took the book from Emily, promising to find something to mark the page, and watched the girl drop the letter in her basket and head for the stairs.

"Now I can give you my present," Arlen whispered.

"You don't need to buy me presents," she said.

"Yes, I do. Besides, this one's an apology." He pulled a paper-wrapped parcel from another pocket and handed it to her.

"Apology for what? Arlen, I truly didn't mind staying here today." Perhaps she shouldn't have been so honest. It sounded as though she hadn't missed him. She gave him her sweetest smile as she took the present.

"I shouldn't have discouraged you from writing," he said, drawing her attention back to his face. "All day I thought about what I said. If it amuses you and gives you something to do when I'm gone, than I want you to write all you wish."

Lynnette pulled the string loose and unrolled the paper. White cloth gloves dropped to her lap, three pairs of them.

"They'll save your fingers a little," he said. "Can you forgive me for objecting?"

Lynnette couldn't mistake the hopeful note in his voice. It comforted her to know he regretted what he had said, and she knew he meant well with the gift. "Of course, I forgive you," she said, leaning forward to kiss his cheek. "It's sweet of you to think of gloves."

Christian took a backward step out of the living room. He had seen Arlen drive in and, since it was nearly time for dinner, had decided to come inside. Now he wished he hadn't.

They were kissing. He shouldn't have been surprised. And it wasn't likely to be the last time; he would have to get used to it. It seemed like an impossible task.

Quietly, he walked down the back hall to the kitchen. Inside, Martha turned from the stove to see who had entered. "What do you need?" she asked with a smile.

"Food." He crossed the room, pretending more interest in what she was cooking than he actually felt.

"Am I to hurry dinner?" She scowled at him, and he had to laugh.

"No. I don't care about them. I just want my food. Can you have Jake bring it to the barn?"

"Something is bothering you tonight."

It wasn't a question; she knew him too well, probably better than anyone. "No, it's just part of my continuing penance for this morning."

"I don't believe you."

He tried to look stern. "Martha, fix my dinner and send it out to the barn."

"Right, boss." She returned to her work. "Whatever you say, boss. Right away, boss."

Christian let her mumble awhile, then walked up behind her, placing his hands on her shoulders. "You make me feel guilty."

"That's the idea. It's the houseguest, isn't it?"

Christian gritted his teeth and forced himself to relax. "I'd tell you if I could," he whispered. He kissed her temple and left her.

Martha told the family that Christian had asked that his dinner be brought to him. She didn't say why.

Emily was cross about it all through dinner. "What's so important that he can't eat with us?" she asked. Her father's reminder that he had also been in a hurry at noon didn't placate her.

Arlen was happy to talk to his father about the people he had met during his outing, and Hugh listened intently, adding what he knew about certain influential men.

Lynnette had Arlen beside her and tried not to notice the empty chair. She was sure she would have been successful if Emily hadn't continued to call it to everyone's attention.

By the time the meal was finished, Arlen was visibly perturbed at his pouting sister. "Why don't you go out to the barn and ask him why he missed dinner?" he suggested.

His tone was just sarcastic enough to indicate his doubt that she would do it.

"Excuse me, then," Emily said, rising from her chair. She fairly flounced across the room toward the kitchen door, the shortest way out of the house toward the barn.

"I wouldn't want to be Christian about now," Arlen said, his eyes twinkling. "And I feel somewhat responsible for having suggested it."

Hugh just laughed. "Christian handles her flights of

temper as well as anyone. Shall we retire to the living room?"

They all rose, and Arlen tucked Lynnette's hand into the crook of his arm. He walked her slowly, trailing behind Hugh. As they passed the stairs, he gave her a quick kiss on the cheek that Hugh didn't witness and turned her loose.

"A game of chess?" Hugh asked the room in general.

Arlen answered first. "I picked up today's copy of the *Courant* while I was in Cottonwood Falls. If you don't mind, I'll go through it tonight. It's a weekly," he explained to Lynnette. "But it's the only paper in the county and most events are announced in it."

"Then Lynnette will play," Hugh said, setting out the board. "It's going to be deathly boring otherwise, with just me to talk to."

"I doubt that," she said, coming forward, "but I'll play just the same."

Arlen read his paper with only an occasional rustle. Hugh played a quiet game, making few comments beyond the game itself, and Lynnette was left to wonder what Christian and Emily were talking about. She tried to remember Christian's advice of two nights before, but thinking of him sitting nearby made her less able to concentrate on the game. Hugh beat her handily.

"You want revenge, I imagine," he said, setting up for another game.

"No, I know when I'm doomed. I think I'd rather use your washroom for a real bath, if that wouldn't interrupt anyone else's plans."

"Be my guest," he said, rising as she did. "I'll send Martha in to help with the water."

"That won't be necessary," she said quickly. "I'm sure I can manage."

If Arlen noticed her departure, he showed no sign. In her room, she gathered up clean undergarments and a bar of scented soap. She added a hairbrush and wrapped them all in a towel. She considered going back through the dining room and kitchen so she wouldn't have to walk past the men but realized she would likely meet Martha if she did. She chose the living room. Hugh had a letter in his lap and one in his hand and told her to take as long as she liked. Arlen's newspaper rustled slightly.

She found the washroom door open and Martha inside adding wood to a small stove. "I told Hugh not to bother you," she said, wondering if the woman would believe her.

"I always start a fire this time of day," Martha said, pumping water into a large kettle. "Christian will want a bath when he comes in."

"How soon will that be?" She wanted to be out long before he wanted the room.

Martha set the kettle on the stove and shrugged. "There's a hook on the door, so you don't need to worry."

"I didn't want him to have to wait," Lynnette mumbled. Talking about Christian and baths at the same time made her feel a little giddy. "I can take it from here."

Martha considered Lynnette a moment, then shrugged. She picked up an odd-shaped rubber stopper and placed it in the tub. "Pull that out when you're finished," she said and left, closing the door behind her.

Lynnette turned to hook the door and realized she was still clutching her bundle. She fumbled one-handed with the hook, making sure it was securely in place. The last thing she needed was Christian accidentally interrupting her bath. The thought made her nearly drop her clothes.

She put her things on a bench and unbuttoned her dress, stepping closer to the tub as she did so. It was quite large and rigged to drain out of the house. She hadn't expected such luxury on a ranch. She hadn't expected Arlen to have so large a house, either. *Or a fascinating brother.*

She tried to shrug off the thought as inconsequential. The whole family had been a surprise. She quickly hung up her dress and sat on the bench to remove her shoes and stockings.

By the time she had pumped water into the tub and added a few kettles of hot water, she decided she preferred a smaller tub and less work though it was nice not to have to empty it when she was finished.

When she slid underwater to wet her hair she understood the appeal of the huge tub. With all the long-legged men in the family it was probably appreciated. She sat up, squeezing the excess water from her hair. She was picturing Christian again. She tried to picture Arlen taking a bath in the huge tub, but he seemed to keep his clothes on. She tried to imagine him taking them off, but that only made her feel guilty. The hazy image of Christian came back unbidden, full of provocative mystery.

She washed as quickly as possible, running through the alphabet, remembering the Roman numerals, reciting the names of the states in order of entry into the union, then she tried to alphabetize them. Anything to keep control of her thoughts.

In a few minutes, she was clean and dressed. She wanted to put the towel around her shoulders to keep her dress dry but she couldn't walk through the living room with her undergarments in plain sight. She ran the brush through her wet hair one more time and wrapped everything but the soap and brush in the towel. She felt immodest for leaving her hair down, but it was too heavy to pin up until it dried.

She took one last look at the washroom, determining that she was leaving it in good condition, turned down the lamp and lifted the hook. She squared her shoulders, prepared to walk as quickly as possible past the men and up to her room.

She swung the door inward, stepped into the dimly lit hall and collided with Christian. He had been merely walking past the door when she stepped out and hit him broadside. He turned to catch her and knocked the bundle out of her arms. The brush and the soap hit the floor first, followed by all her unmentionables, which seemed to flutter down like leaves on a lazy breeze.

She watched them in a detached sort of way. She stood inches away from Christian, his hands warming her arms. They were both completely still but for the steady rise and fall of their chests. His breathing appeared to be as labored as hers.

She studiously kept her head lowered; to raise it would be to come face-to-face, quite literally, with a man whom she had just imagined naked.

"Are you all right?" he asked just above a whisper.

She nodded, not taking her eyes off the mess on the floor.

He let go of her arms slowly, as if testing her balance, and stepped back. She thought he would go on his way and allow her to gather her things and hide them once again in the towel. Instead he crouched as if to help her.

She knelt quickly, bumping her knee against his, and nearly lost her balance. He reached out and steadied her again. "I can take care of this." She had meant to whisper, but it came out a hiss. "Please," she added, looking into his face for the first time.

What she saw made her catch her breath. He watched her with open admiration. Not the way Arlen did, but more sizzling and hungry. The look frightened her even as it excited her.

But in a second, it was gone. He looked down and started to pick up a lacy petticoat. She practically snatched it out of his hands. "I can manage," she said firmly. "Thank you."

He raised his hands in surrender and grinned at her. It went a long way toward dispelling the tension. "Just trying to be a gentleman," he said softly.

She noticed then that the grin didn't quite reach his eyes. *He feels it too,* she thought. *Dear Lord, he feels the same attraction!* An instant later he was on his feet moving toward the living room.

"What kept you?" Emily's voice reached her as she gathered her clothes. "I thought you were coming right in."

"Oh, I ran into a little something I had to take care of," was Christian's reply.

She heard more voices, including Arlen's, but didn't know what was said. By the time she was ready to join the others she was convinced she had imagined everything. Everything except the solid body and the gentleman's offer to help. The hall was practically dark, after all. What could she have seen?

Now she had to face the gauntlet of the long room and three men with her hair down around her shoulders. She had been braced for it once, and look what had happened.

She entered the room and her eyes were drawn to Christian first. He was building a fire, with Emily watching over his shoulder. She turned quickly to find the other men. They both looked up from their reading, and she smiled a nervous greeting. She would have walked past them, but Arlen came to his feet.

"Come sit by the fire until your hair dries," he said. "The nights still get cool, and you shouldn't go to bed with wet hair." When he was close enough to touch her, he inhaled deeply. "You smell wonderful," he said, not quite softly enough to keep the others from hearing.

She tried to smile at him as he led her toward the fire. Christian had finished, and he and Emily moved away. Lynnette sat on the hearth where Arlen indicated, and, when he sat down beside her, she put her bundle down on her other side. "Your hair is lovely," Arlen said. "I pictured it a little longer, though." He touched the end of a lock where it fell between her shoulder blades. "It looks as if it's been cut."

Lynnette tried not to notice where Christian had gone. She was a terrible person to even think about him now.

"Really long hair is too difficult to pin up," she explained, wishing he would quit talking about it. Of course, they were all used to seeing Emily's dark mane...and watching Christian braid it.

She couldn't help looking toward the pair. They had chosen a chair across the room, and Christian sat on its edge while Emily knelt on the floor. He didn't take his eyes off the thick rope in his hands. For the first time in Lynnette's life, she envied someone's waist-length hair.

"It never occurred to me that women trimmed their hair," Arlen said, drawing her attention again. "Emily seems to manage some clever styles, and her hair is down to her waist."

He was trying to suggest that she quit trimming her hair. Odd that it would irritate her when she had been thinking the same thing. Of course a husband would want a say in his wife's appearance, but it still made her want to grit her teeth. "Not without help, usually," she said.

"I suppose," Arlen said and turned to Hugh, changing the subject. He mentioned an article he had read in the paper and soon he and Hugh were deep in conversation.

With the attention off her, Lynnette pulled the brush from where she had tucked it in her bundle and began brushing her hair. Anything, she thought, to hasten its drying and thus her chance to escape. Once she thought she saw Christian pause and look at her, but it was seen from the corner of her eye and when she turned he was as busy as ever.

"Oh, I forgot to tell everybody," Emily said suddenly. "Christian and I are going to town tomorrow."

"That's nice, Emily," Arlen said in a tone that said the opposite. "Aren't you old enough to know better than to interrupt?"

She gave him a pouty frown, then ignored him. "We'll stop at Blainey's and invite Rose. She can come any time, can't she, Father?"

"Of course, dear," Hugh said fondly. He didn't seem as eager to return to his conversation with Arlen as the younger man did.

"Emily," Lynnette started, effectively cutting off Arlen who had just begun to speak. "Sorry."

He motioned her to go ahead. "If I get a letter written to my friend, can you post it for me tomorrow?"

"Sure. I'll have one for Mother anyway."

"Thank you, Emily. I'll go write it now." She gathered up her things and hurried for the stairs.

A short time later, her things put away and her dress exchanged for a nightgown, she sat down at the desk with writing paper before her. What would she tell Amanda?

Christian was being tortured. With the sweet scent of Lynnette still clear in his memory, he was forced to listen to her voice, watch her brush her thick wavy hair and pretend not to care. It was a wonder Emily didn't notice how clumsy he was.

He was glad when he could kiss his sister goodnight and head back into the cool evening air. At the barn he headed straight for the stallion's stall.

"It's your lucky night, boy," he said softly. He slipped the halter over the sleek black head and led him from the barn. He tied him to the snubbing post and took a few minutes to rub the long neck. "Want another chance to knock my brains out?" His tone was soft and soothing. "I'll get the saddle."

Lynnette finally put down the pen, stood and paced across the room. Should she tell Amanda everything? *Arlen's a charming young man, but I'm fascinated by his brother. Did I say fascinated? I may be in love with him.*

She shook her head. She and Amanda used to share everything, but that was before she started her double life as Silver Nightingale. This was even more shocking than her book.

Or it would be if it were true. Which it wasn't. It was all her imagination! Her heart pumped blood through her body; it did not govern her emotions. Her mind did that. She would forget her interest in Christian now that she had decided not to finish the story.

She remembered Amanda's questions about her love for Arlen and knew she could have answered yes to all of them, if they had been speaking of Christian.

"Fanciful," she said aloud as she had to her friend and almost believed it.

She headed back for the desk, determined to write to Amanda about the house and what she had seen of the ranch. Instead she found herself stepping out onto the balcony. She left the door standing open behind her.

A frantic movement in the pen below caught her attention. In a moment her eyes adjusted to the dark, and she made out the shape of a horse and rider. As she tried to make sense of what she was seeing the rider sailed off the horse to land hard on the ground. She gasped, covering her mouth to hold back a scream, then realized she probably shouldn't have. She was on the verge of running for help when she saw the figure come to his feet.

It was Christian. It had to be. The gray shirt she had seen him in earlier looked white in the moonlight. He brushed himself off and walked slowly to the horse. He rubbed the horse's neck, caught up the reins and swung onto its back again.

Lynnette watched in horror, her hands pressed against her mouth. The horse turned in a tight circle, then jumped as if its legs were springs. How Christian could stand the pounding was beyond her. The horse twisted to one side, and Christian flew off again. He rolled and came to his feet.

She didn't want to watch anymore. She wanted to run inside and write her letter to Amanda and pretend she didn't know Christian was out here. But she couldn't move. Someone had to watch, she told herself. What if he didn't get up next time? Who would get him help?

He held the horse's halter and stroked its neck for

a moment. She even imagined he whispered something in the horse's ear. She felt a shiver go down her neck as if he were beside her. She stood frozen in fear as he swung into the saddle. After another terrifying ride, the horse threw him once again. She held her breath until he came to his feet.

This time, instead of following the horse, Christian walked to the fence facing the house and leaned there. She thought for a moment that he had seen her but realized he watched something below her. In a moment a woman came into sight.

"Where's Jake?" The woman's raised voice barely carried up to her. "You know someone should be with you."

Even through the moonlight, Lynnette thought she could see him grin. "I would have invited him to watch, but I hate to show off."

"Don't try to tease me out of scolding you. Has it ever worked before?"

"Well, yeah, most of the time."

"You, don't get back on that horse until Jake gets here. Understood?"

"Yes, ma'am."

Martha hurried away from the house, and Christian walked slowly back to the horse. She thought he might be limping, and she choked back a sob. He caught up the reins, led the horse to the center post and tied him there. Then rubbed the horse's neck, talking softly.

The horse sidestepped, and Christian looked up. She knew he could see her silhouetted against the back-lit curtains. What was he thinking, knowing she had been watching, knowing she had listened to his conversation with Martha?

She should go in now. Jake would be there to run for help if he got hurt. She forced herself to turn toward the door. When the wind hit her face, she realized it was wet with tears.

Chapter Eight

Somehow Lynnette was able to write the letter to
Amanda. All the while she heard Jake's muffled cries
of encouragement or dismay. She never had the nerve
to see which. When the letter was finished she fell into
a fitful sleep.

She was up early, and dressed in a simple cream
gown. She had plenty of time. Unless Christian could
work miracles, Emily wouldn't be ready to leave for
hours.

She reread the letter to her friend. It told of getting
lost and riding down the steep slope behind Christian,
of Arlen's enthusiastic conversations with his father
on politics. She mentioned watching Christian break
the horse in the moonlight. Everything in the letter was
completely true. It was only dishonest in what it left
out.

With the letter folded and sealed and Amanda's address carefully written on the outside, she stepped out
on the landing. The lamps that hung in sconces on the
walls were not lit and the only light came up the stairs
from the windows below. The effect was almost like

a dark box above a bright theater. She crossed in front of the stairs and turned toward Emily's room as the door next to her opened. She now shared the landing with Christian.

Neither spoke for a moment. Would he ask why she had watched from the balcony? What would she say? *I hurt for you every time you fell? My soul feels as bruised as your body probably does?*

She surprised herself by speaking first. "Are you all right?"

His smile was kind and dimpled, not the teasing grin she was used to. "I'll make it. Thanks for asking." She saw his eyes twinkle suddenly and wondered if he teased his family so much to avoid the serious issues. "I'm afraid if we had run into each other just now, I might not have stayed on my feet."

"You're hurt."

"No. Just the usual stiff joints, a few bruises."

"You could be killed." She took a step closer without meaning to.

"Not likely. Broken bones are a possibility, but a horse can throw you anytime. In the winter you can slip on ice and break your leg...or your neck."

It was none of her business. But then, she had never been able to resist an argument. "That doesn't make sense. Accidents can happen anytime, sure, but you're doing this on purpose."

He seemed surprised but not especially put out. "I'm breaking the horse. That's how it's done."

"I hate it!" That surprised them both. Lynnette was glad at least that she hadn't said it very loudly.

He went still. "Then don't watch." There was no

resentment in his tone; he said it with complete kindness. She could imagine stepping into his arms and accepting his comfort. That should have been enough to make her move away. Instead she stood and stared at him, listening to her own pulse race.

Then he did the most amazing thing. He stepped forward and wrapped one arm around her shoulders, bringing her gently against his side. "Don't worry," he whispered. "It's all right."

A tingle went down her neck and all the way down her spine. She felt herself tremble.

He gave her shoulder the slightest squeeze. "Trust me. I don't let Arlen do it. I've never let Arlen do it."

His words startled her back to reality. He thought she was worried about Arlen! Her trembling stopped, and he let her go.

She took a step away from him. "Thank you," she murmured for lack of anything better to say. How was she to end this encounter? The letter was still clutched in her hand. She raised it, using it to point toward Emily's door. "I—" She had to stop and clear her throat. "I was on my way to give Emily my letter to mail."

"Let her sleep another hour. I have chores to do before we can leave. I'll take the letter."

"All right." She didn't know why she hesitated to hand it to him until she actually did it. It was a small letter. They already stood too close in the narrow landing. But she was careful and their fingers didn't brush.

He held it in one hand and tapped it gently on his other palm. "I'll just put it with my things." He motioned over his shoulder toward his door. "I could mess it up during chores."

"Yes. Fine." She was glad he turned away. He opened the door to his room, and she headed down the stairs. If her legs had felt steadier, she might have run. He had practically held her in his arms, and *he* had been thinking of Arlen.

She reached the bottom of the stairs and looked out on the tip of what must recently have been a colorful sunrise. A new beginning, she told herself. A new story to write. She would start it today.

Christian didn't go into his room. He placed the letter on a chair just inside and eased the door shut. Arlen, thank God, was still asleep. Christian leaned his back against the door, waiting for Lynnette to reach the bottom before he followed.

What if Arlen had happened into the hall while he stood with his arm around Lynnette? Of course, Arlen was so trusting, he would understand at once when he told him what had happened. Christian cursed himself. Arlen would never guess the truth.

He didn't want to eat breakfast with Lynnette. Once she was settled in the dining room, he would make his apologies as he went by. His trip to town was an excuse, and he could grab something on his way through the kitchen. He pushed away from the door. The plan was good except for the fact that he was starving.

Hugh's door opened before he made it to the stairs. "Good morning, son," said his father, coming forward. "I see you survived your ride last night."

"Looks that way."

Hugh started down the steps, and Christian fell into step beside him. "Can I do anything for you while I'm in town?"

"Get a list from Martha," he suggested. "Why, here's Lynnette to eat with us."

They had reached the bottom of the stairs, and Hugh went to greet Lynnette where she stood by the center balcony. Christian hung back, wanting a chance to leave, unwilling to take it now that it was offered.

"I'm pleased to see you're an early riser," Hugh was saying. "Maybe we can find something besides the ranch to discuss at the breakfast table."

She laughed, a quiet feminine sound that made Christian smile. "And here I was hoping that's just what you would discuss," she said.

"Ah yes, the book. I'm sure we can tell you more than you want to know. Does Martha know you're down?"

She shook her head, and Hugh headed for the kitchen, leaving Christian and Lynnette to face each other. He took the last few steps to the floor. She looked almost as uncomfortable as he felt. With an open palm, he directed her toward the table. Hugh returned in time to hold her chair. Christian had been afraid to offer; he had come too close to her already this morning.

"There we are," Hugh said, moving to his own place. "Emily isn't likely to join us, Christian. You might as well sit here beside me."

It was reasonable. This was where he sat when Emily was in Topeka. But Lynnette wasn't sitting across from him then. He pulled out the chair on his father's left and sat down.

Hugh said the blessing, and Martha brought in a platter of scrambled eggs, returning a moment later with coffee and toast. Christian tried to concentrate on the food and not the beautiful woman in front of him.

His plan to see a prospective horse buyer while he was in town was the only information he volunteered. He let Hugh answer the rest of her questions. Soon Hugh turned the conversation toward her life in Topeka and her friends, including Felicia. She mentioned how much she had loved her father's big quiet house filled with books.

"She fits right in here, doesn't she?" Hugh said then.

Christian nodded. And if she didn't, he would change the place until she did. How could Hugh have let Felicia go? Wouldn't a man move heaven and earth to be with the woman he loved…if there wasn't a beloved brother in the way? At that moment, Arlen's footsteps could be heard on the stairs.

"Excuse me. I better tend to the chores," he said, tossing his napkin on the table and scooting back his chair.

"When should we wake your sister?" Hugh asked.

"I'll get her up when I come in to change." He gave Lynnette a polite nod and headed for the kitchen. He thanked Martha on his way through and hurried to the barn. He was eager to be on his way to town and away from Lynnette Sterling.

Lynnette enjoyed her breakfast. She hesitated at first to mention Felicia but discovered Hugh was pleased to hear about her. She found him perceptive and understanding and would have enjoyed the conversation immensely if she hadn't been always aware of the man across the table.

She wanted to know what *he* was thinking. She wanted to know more about his dealings with the horse buyer, what he thought of parting with the horses he had raised and trained. But she no longer had the excuse of a novel to ask those questions. She tried to put Arlen in the role of her rancher, but it didn't ring true.

She was relieved that Christian had to leave before Arlen joined them. She found the older brother too distracting and could give Arlen the attention he deserved only if Christian wasn't around.

Arlen let Martha know he wanted some coffee and took his place at the table. "You look lovely this morning," he murmured to Lynnette.

She smiled. "There are still some eggs, though we seem to have eaten all the toast."

"No thanks," he said, moving his cup and saucer onto the plate in front of him. "The only thing worse than eggs in the morning is cold eggs in the morning."

Martha brought the coffee and left the pot.

"Lynnette's been telling us about her life in Topeka," Hugh said.

"I'm sorry I missed it," Arlen said. "But perhaps you wouldn't mind repeating yourself. We can take the whole day to get better acquainted."

"I thought perhaps we could go riding," Lynnette suggested.

PLAY...

"ROLL A DOUBLE!"

PEEL OFF LABEL AND PLACE INSIDE

GET 4 BOOKS

AND A

FABULOUS MYSTERY BONUS GIFT

ABSOLUTELY FREE!

SEE INSIDE...

NO RISK, NO OBLIGATION TO BUY...NOW OR EVER!

GUARANTEED

PLAY "ROLL A DOUBLE" AND YOU GET FREE GIFTS! HERE'S HOW TO PLAY:

1. Peel off label from front cover. Place it in space provided at right. With a coin, carefully scratch off the silver dice. Then check the claim chart to see what we have for you – FOUR FREE BOOKS and a mystery gift – ALL YOURS! ALL FREE!

2. Send back this card and you'll receive brand-new Harlequin Historical™ novels. These books have a cover price of $4.99 each, but they are yours to keep absolutely free.

3. There's no catch. You're under no obligation to buy anything. We charge nothing – ZERO – for your first shipment. And you don't have to make any minimum number of purchases – not even one!

4. The fact is, thousands of readers enjoy receiving books by mail from the Harlequin Reader Service®. They like the convenience of home delivery...they like getting the best new novels BEFORE they're available in stores...and they love our discount prices!

5. We hope that after receiving your free books you'll want to remain a subscriber. But the choice is yours – to continue or cancel any time at all! So why not take us up on our invitation, with no risk of any kind. You'll be glad you did!

"There's no reason to," Arlen said. "We can talk better here."

It was midmorning before Emily was ready to leave. Of course Christian hadn't expected anything else. He handed her up into the waiting buggy. He didn't have to check his shirt pocket to remember the letter was there. The crisp paper seemed to carry its owner's heat directly to his skin.

"I'm surprised Lynnette didn't beg to go since Arlen left her behind yesterday," Emily said.

"I imagine she wants to spend the day with Arlen." This wasn't what Christian wanted to talk about.

"So they can make goo-goo eyes at each other. Why did he leave her behind, anyway?"

"He wanted to make a side trip to Bazaar and was afraid it would tire her."

"Pooh." Emily wrinkled her nose. "He wasn't that late. We'll be even later, I bet."

Christian grinned at his sister. "We will if we stop to see Rose. But then Arlen got an earlier start."

Emily shrugged, refusing to take offense. "I suspect he was afraid she'd talk about women voting and upset his followers."

Christian tried to hide his surprise. His little sister's occasional bursts of intuition were usually close to the truth. "So you think Arlen intends to keep her away from the public?"

"My guess is he'll spend today teaching her what to say."

Christian gave a surprised laugh. "I don't think that's going to go over."

Emily shrugged. "Never worked with me." Christian could see she was already bored with the subject. He wasn't surprised when she said, "Tell me everything about everybody in town."

"That's a tall order," Christian said, smiling down at her.

"It's a long ride."

Christian had related all the best gossip by the time the buggy crossed the bridge. The town of Cottonwood Falls lay before them, with the beautiful new courthouse dominating the view at the end of the street.

He fed his horse first, then his little sister at the finest restaurant the town had to offer, and left her to shop and visit while he met with the prospective buyer. An hour and a half later he joined Emily at the store.

Emily hadn't piled as many goods on the counter as he expected. Perhaps their country store didn't offer the assortment she was used to. She appeared to have had a good time, however, and was reluctant to end her conversation with Mrs. Kaiser and two young female shoppers.

At the back of the store where Mr. Kaiser had his watch repair shop and post office, Christian traded Lynnette's letter for one addressed to her. With this new letter in his pocket, he wandered the aisles searching for things on Martha's list. He found several but resigned himself to having to interrupt Mrs. Kaiser to find the rest. On his way past a collection of books, a red cover practically jumped out at him. *Passion's Secret.* Lynnette's book! "Don't look for it," she had said. Well, he hadn't been looking for it. He glanced at the circle of women.

Only one seemed at all interested in what he was doing. Miss Waters, a preacher's daughter, looked away quickly, her cheeks turning pink. She would probably watch him until he left the store. She tended to do that even though he had been careful not to encourage her.

Nothing in his hands gave him a place to hide the book. He considered slipping it into his shirt, but that would look like he was stealing it. He left it where it was and moved on. Finally, he took the list to Mrs. Kaiser to find the last few items, effectively breaking up the gathering. Miss Waters and her friend moved toward the door and Emily followed, expressing her wish to see them again during the summer.

Christian hoped she would follow them outside, but she came back to show him what she had picked out, including a gift for Lynnette that made him smile. The packages were wrapped and paid for, and Emily didn't leave his side. He followed Emily out to the buggy, where she lifted the leather flap on the boot and he deposited the packages inside. As he fastened the cover in place, part of him tried to forget about the book, the rest tried to figure out how to get it.

He handed Emily into the buggy. "Oh, shoot! I got Martha's things and forgot my own. I won't be a minute."

He hurried back into the store, thinking quickly. He palmed the book on his way to the hardware and in a few minutes was back at the buggy, stashing his purchases in the boot.

"I needed a sack of penny nails," he told his sister. "Sorry to keep you waiting." She seemed unconcerned, and he relaxed as they headed for the Blainey Ranch.

Morton Blainey's ranch was nearly as large as Hugh's but the house he had built tended more toward comfort and lacked the drama of the Prescott home. Rose saw them coming and ran to meet the buggy. Rose was a tall slender girl, quiet and reserved, an unlikely companion to Emily. She had blond hair and a pale complexion.

Odd, but Christian had once thought Arlen was interested in her. He watched her gather Emily into her arms and laughed at himself. She was Emily's best friend and therefore a child forever.

The girls walked arm and arm into the house as Morton came to greet him. "Come on inside and have a cool drink. One of my men will look after the horse."

Christian followed the older man inside. The girls had claimed the parlor, and Morton led the way to his office. "Ruby knows you're here," he said. "She'll bring the girls some lemonade. How about a real drink?"

Christian accepted the small glass of bourbon. They talked cattle and horses for an hour with the sound of girlish laughter in the background. "I better let you get back to work," Christian said finally. "By now, the girls should have decided when Rose can come visit."

"It might be a week or more before Rose'll go,"

Morton warned. "Her mare's due to foal about then, and she doesn't want to miss it. Emily'd be welcome here, though."

Christian shook his head. "Pa and I see her so seldom, we wouldn't want to part with her."

"I understand. Well, let's go break up the giggle fest and see what they've decided."

Emily gave up trying to talk Rose out of waiting for the horse when the men came, admitting she might feel the same. Morton promised to bring Rose to visit Emily as soon as the colt was born.

"She won't want to leave her colt, either," Emily said, pouting, on the way home. "She probably won't come all summer!"

Christian wanted to comfort her but couldn't promise that Rose would come. He took a deep breath and told her what he knew she wanted to hear. "If she doesn't come in two weeks, we'll let you stay with her."

It worked. Emily threw her arms around his neck. "You're the best brother in the world."

"I may tell Arlen you said that," he threatened, but her smirk told him she knew he was teasing.

Lynnette had spent the entire day with Arlen. When she retired to her room for a rest before dinner, she felt she knew him quite a bit better. She had the feeling that he hadn't learned much about her, however. She couldn't explain why she felt that way; he hadn't interrupted her or refused to let her talk. He simply assumed a great deal without question.

She shrugged at her face in the mirror. Perhaps she

imagined it. At any rate, it had been a pleasant day, especially the picnic lunch Martha had packed. They had walked to a spot along the trail where she had walked the first day. Lynnette would have liked to eat by the little stream, but Arlen was sure it was too far.

She scrubbed her face again. She should be ashamed of herself, finding fault with such little things. Arlen had been attentive and kind. "It was a lovely day," she said aloud.

She decided to heed Arlen's suggestion and rest before dinner. She wasn't especially tired, but welcomed a few minutes alone. She wondered when Emily and Christian were expected. It was Emily she was missing, of course.

She lifted a book out of her trunk, not caring which one it was, and took it to bed with her. After reading three pages without noticing what they said, she set it aside and closed her eyes. Almost instantly she drifted into a half sleep, where her imagination was freed yet she knew she was dreaming.

She and Arlen were having a picnic by the stream. Christian appeared beside them, holding an identical basket. "Wouldn't you rather eat with me?" he asked.

She got up quickly and ran to his side.

"But Lynnette," Arlen cried. "You promised to marry me. I love you. I love you."

He seemed to get farther away from her, but his plea grew louder. "I love you. I love you."

Lynnette jerked herself awake. A cat's steady mewing sounded from the balcony. She laughed and rose to let him in. "Are you the one saying 'I love you' in my sleep?"

The cat mewed again and strutted past her to spring up onto the bed. He curled up in the center and glared at her.

"All right. You're Arlen's cat. You have a right to be upset, but I can explain. It wasn't Christian. It was the hero of my book. They look alike, I know, but I can tell them apart."

The cat squinted and looked away. Lynnette watched it for a moment. "I won't write that story anyway," she whispered.

Since she was up and her bed was occupied, she decided to dress for dinner. When she was ready to go down, she left the balcony door ajar and the hall door standing open. As an afterthought she tucked the book she had chosen before her nap under her arm. She would take it out on one of the downstairs balconies and at least pretend to read.

She was gazing off into the distance when a buggy rose over a hill and sank out of sight again. "Christian," her mind whispered. "And Emily," she added quickly. She wanted to stand and watch for them to reappear but knew they would be thirsty from the trip. She turned resolutely away and headed for the kitchen, leaving her book on a step as she went past the stairs.

Martha was in the kitchen, busy with dinner preparations. She looked up from her work, and didn't seem as unfriendly as she had before. "They're almost home," Lynnette said. "I saw the buggy come over a hill."

"Emily will want her lemonade," Martha said. She glanced at the mess around her as if uncertain where to start.

"Let me make the lemonade," Lynnette offered.

Martha hesitated only a moment. "The packets are in the pantry. We have to have lots on hand when Emily comes."

Lynnette found the flavored sugar packets and the vials of concentrated lemon juice and brought one of each back to the sink. The glass pitcher was on a shelf above the sink, and she lifted it down as Martha spoke again. "Well water will be colder than what's in the cistern. But that means a trip out to the well."

"I think I can do that," Lynnette said, carrying the heavy glass pitcher out the back door. The wind had come up since she and Arlen had had their picnic, and it brought a chill that contrasted with the warm sunshine. She set the pitcher down carefully at the well and worked the handle.

Unfortunately she didn't think about the wind blowing the stream away from the spout. By the time she had managed to fill the pitcher, she had fairly soaked her skirt. At least it was a cotton dress, she thought gratefully as she headed back to the kitchen door, not velvet or satin that would be ruined by water.

Martha glanced up and stared. "Oh, I'm sorry!" She started toward Lynnette. "I'll finish this. You go up and change."

Lynnette laughed and waved her away. "It's nothing, really. You go ahead with dinner." She shook out her skirts, willing them to dry.

Martha seemed perplexed but returned to her work. Lynnette heard the buggy go past the kitchen door as she mixed the lemonade. A moment later she heard

Emily burst through the door. She left the lemonade and went to the back hall to meet her.

She assumed Emily would be alone. Christian, she was sure, would want to take care of the horse before he came in. She hadn't thought about their purchases. Christian was a few steps behind Emily, his arms laden with paper-wrapped parcels.

"Come see what I bought," Emily said as she took Lynnette's arm and walked with her to the living room. "I had the best time, but Rose isn't coming, maybe ever."

Christian deposited everything on one of the big chairs. "Rose will probably be here in a couple of weeks." He grinned at the face his sister made. He explained to Lynnette, "She's waiting for her mare to foal. What happened to your skirts?"

Lynnette had nearly forgotten them, caught as she was in Emily's excitement. She shook them a little, laughing. "I had a battle with the pump over a pitcher of water for lemonade. I'm pleased to tell you, I won. Let me get it."

She left them quickly and put the pitcher and three glasses on a tray. She half hoped Christian would leave before she returned—and half hoped he would stay.

Back in the living room, she found them sorting through the parcels. A few had been partially opened to see what was inside. Emily left the project and came for her lemonade. Lynnette poured a glass for her, then one for Christian. She carried it to him where he knelt on the floor.

He took it, smiling his thanks. "I think this is all

of Martha's things," he said, studying the pile in front of him.

Lynnette found it impossible to take her eyes off him. His hair was wind-tossed, practically calling to her fingers to straighten out the long blond strands. From where she stood above him his shoulders seemed impossibly broad. She could see his muscles flex under the thin cotton shirt when he raised the glass and drained it.

He handed the empty glass to her and their eyes met. It took a conscious effort for her to reach out and take it, careful to keep their fingers from touching, afraid she would drop the glass if they did. She hurried to the tray to set it down.

"This is for you," he said, reaching into his shirt pocket. She reluctantly returned to him and took the paper he offered without looking at it. It was warm. She held it between both palms to absorb the heat before it was lost.

Christian turned his attention to Martha's parcels, and Lynnette stepped to the table where she had set the lemonade. She tucked the corner of the letter under the tray and poured herself a glass. She wasn't really interested in the lemonade, but at least it kept her from gazing at Christian. She didn't relax until he had gathered Martha's things and headed for the kitchen.

Emily was sitting on the floor where she had been opening all of her purchases, scattering the string and paper around her. "Come see what I got," she said. Emily had found a white lacy chemise and a ruffled petticoat in a pale peach. "This is just a shade lighter than a dress I have," she said, holding up the petticoat.

She added in a loud whisper, "I know they're not supposed to show, but they do if you work at it."

Her attention shifted to some folded delft-blue fabric with appropriate sewing notions piled on top. "Rose and I always make something together when she comes, and it was supposed to be my turn to get the dress."

"Do you really think she isn't coming?" Lynnette asked, crouching beside the girl.

"I suppose she is. Eventually. I just wanted her to come today." Emily's pout didn't last very long. "Look. I found this for you."

Emily rummaged under some wadded wrapping and pulled out a small silver pin and handed it to her. She laughed in delight. It was in the shape of a feather.

"If you wear it like this—" she turned it in Lynnette's hand "—it looks like an old-fashioned quill pen."

"I love it," Lynnette said. She pinned it to the collar of her blouse.

Emily reached out and touched it. "Perfect. Everyone will either know you're a writer or think you're an Indian."

They were still giggling over that when Arlen came in. He gave his sister and the mess around her a fond smile. "Did you have a pleasant trip? It looks like it was fruitful, at least."

"Yeah," Emily said, gathering her purchases together. "How long till dinner?"

"Close to an hour, I believe." He assisted Lynnette to her feet. "What happened to your skirt?"

"Oh," she began, wishing he hadn't noticed, "the

wind blew water on me when I filled the pitcher for the lemonade.'' She turned to put her glass on the tray.

"Why were *you* making the lemonade?"

Lynnette blinked at him. "Martha was fixing dinner."

Emily saved her from whatever Arlen might have said next. "Help me get my loot upstairs," she said. "I want to change out of this dusty dress."

Lynnette helped her gather her things, leaving behind the paper and string. She wondered if Arlen would clean it up or go get Martha to do it. She knew she was being unfair, but she couldn't help it. Little things Arlen said irritated her, and she couldn't talk herself out of it.

Upstairs, she helped Emily deposit her things in her room, then went to her own. She supposed she would have to change her skirt now that Arlen had noticed it. She slipped it off and hung it over the back of the chair. The petticoats seemed barely damp, but she took off the outside one and spread it out on the bed. She picked a skirt that went with the blouse and slipped it on.

Checking herself in the mirror in preparation for going down, she touched the silver pin and smiled. It was nice of Emily to think of her.

She considered loitering in the room until Emily went down, but what would she do? Suddenly she remembered the letter. It was probably from Amanda. She went quickly down the stairs to retrieve it. The living room was empty, Arlen no doubt having returned to the study.

In a few minutes she was back in her room with the

letter. She sat on the edge of the bed and broke the seal.

Amanda came right to the point. Julian Taggart had been to see her, demanding to know where Lynnette had gone. Amanda described Taggart's behavior as suspicious. "He paced and questioned and muttered," she wrote. "I found his visit most upsetting and have informed my staff that I will not receive him again unless Bill is with me."

Amanda went on to assure her that she didn't tell Taggart where she had gone but was afraid he would find out from some other source. She closed the letter with a warning. "Please be careful of him if he comes there. I don't believe he is at all rational."

Lynnette slowly folded the letter and placed it on the stand beside the bed. Her first reaction was frustration. Why couldn't the man forget her as quickly as she had forgotten him? He frightened her. Irrational people's behavior was unpredictable. He might very well follow her to the ranch and cause her trouble with Arlen. As if she didn't have enough already.

Chapter Nine

Lynnette sat on the bed for long minutes listening to the wind rattle the glass door and thinking about Taggart. What could he do if he came? Demand that she go with him? She could simply refuse. Tell Arlen lies about her? Surely Arlen would believe her instead. Was he capable of violence?

A thought crept into her mind. *Christian can handle him.* She had to laugh at herself. When she heard Emily come out of her room, she was happy to leave her thoughts behind and follow the girl downstairs.

Christian missed dinner again. Emily wasn't quite as unhappy as she had been the night before. Evidently spending the whole day with him made it easier for her to forgive him. She spent much of the meal relating everything the ladies in town had told her and everything Rose had said.

Lynnette could sense Arlen's impatience with his sister's monopoly of the conversation. She didn't care. She was too preoccupied with Amanda's letter to want to talk herself. And she didn't want to listen to Arlen.

In a break in Emily's monologue, she asked if the family planned to attend church the following day.

"The nearest is a little community church about six miles from here," Arlen said. "Everyone in the neighborhood goes. Of course we never know if we can get Emily around in time."

Emily favored her brother with a smirk. "You'd rather go to church in town where there are more voters."

Hugh cleared his throat and both of his offspring looked contrite. "Normally," he said, directing his words at Lynnette, "we take a lunch and eat at church after the services. Of course, if you have some other preference, we'll do what we can to accommodate it."

"No. A country service sounds charming." She smiled at Hugh. An escape from the table had just presented itself. "I think I'll go and arrange to help Martha with tomorrow's lunch."

She was half out of her chair when outbursts from Arlen and Emily stopped her.

"That isn't necessary."

"You don't need to—"

Lynnette sat back down. "What's wrong?" she asked. The table was silent.

She looked at Arlen for an answer. His eyes flicked to his father and away. Finally he spoke. "It's just that you're a guest. It isn't proper for you to be working in the kitchen."

Lynnette didn't respond. She turned to Emily. "Is that what you were thinking as well?"

Emily twirled her fork but didn't answer.

Lynnette decided Arlen needed to see a little more

of her defiance. "Tomorrow," she began softly, "is Sunday. How can you enjoy a day of rest knowing a fellow Christian is working in order to make that possible? Excuse me."

She rose and turned from the table. She heard Arlen hiss, "You're just afraid she'll make you look bad."

"Then what's *your* problem?" Emily retorted.

Hugh's "Children!" followed her into the kitchen.

Martha and her family were around the table, and once again the men started to rise as Lynnette entered. She waved them down and seated herself at an empty place. Martha looked too stunned to remember to chew.

"I'm sorry to interrupt," she said. "I just wondered what your plans were for the lunch tomorrow."

After a moment Martha said with exaggerated patience, "I planned to fry a chicken. Did you want to change the menu?"

"No," Lynnette said, hoping her smile would make the woman relax. She knew Martha didn't like her, but she wasn't backing down now. "It must be difficult to cook and attend worship so I'm asking to help."

She saw Martha's eyes narrow and added hastily, "I'm not suggesting that you can't handle it, but it must be hectic, and there are more to feed than usual. Besides, when we had servants, Father always gave them Sundays off so I'm used to it." She didn't add that the servants had been gone for years and she was used to doing all the cooking.

"Oh, I'm happy to accept your offer," Martha said

in a tone that sounded anything but happy. "I'll start frying the chicken at sunup. You can join me any time."

"Thanks," she said, wondering if her own smile looked forced. "Tonight's roast was very good."

"Don't you want dessert?" Jake asked. "It's chocolate cake."

She had been about to turn him down but reconsidered. "May I take it to my room?"

Jake laughed, rising from the table. "You found her weakness, Mom." He winked at Lynnette and led her to the counter where the cake sat. "Trays are over there," he said, pointing. "Want a cup of coffee?"

Lynnette crossed the room and poured herself a cup. She was returning to claim her cake when the outside door opened with a gust of air that swirled her skirts around her ankles. She found herself facing an equally startled Christian. His hat, which he removed quickly, had been pulled down tight against the wind.

"You here for cake, too?" Martha asked, her voice far warmer than Lynnette had ever heard it.

"Rumor says it's chocolate," he answered, not taking his eyes off Lynnette. "Were you elected to fetch dessert tonight?"

"No, I..." Why did just the sight of him affect her? "Actually, I'm just here after my own."

Christian laughed, moving away and releasing her from his gaze. "A storm's blowing in," he said over his shoulder.

Lynnette quickly returned to Jake and put a slice of cake on her tray. She was about to leave the kitchen when Emily came in. Jake met her with a tray con-

taining three more slices, and Lynnette left them to
tease each other without her.

"Emily will be along in a moment," she told Hugh
and Arlen. "If you don't mind, I'll take my dessert to
my room."

Arlen was on his feet before she made it past the
table. "Are you feeling all right?"

"Yes, I'm fine." She hoped her smile was reassuring. "Christian picked up a letter from a friend when
he was in town. I thought I would reread it and perhaps answer it tonight."

"We understand perfectly," Hugh said.

She couldn't tell if Arlen understood at all, let alone
perfectly, but he stepped aside. It was funny, she reflected as she went up the stairs. Earlier, she had been
eager to leave her room, but now she found the company of the family no more comforting than her own
thoughts.

Christian got up early the next morning. The rain
might change the day's plans. It didn't take much to
turn the roads to quagmire. In which case, the household rules were the same. Martha fixed lunch early,
and had the rest of the day off. The rain would make
the chores take longer, though that didn't matter if
Hugh declared the roads impassable and they didn't
need to hurry off to church.

Normally, he looked forward to Sunday mornings.
Instead of the usual breakfast with his father and a
discussion of ranch business, he ate with Martha and
Perry and Jake.

Today, however, he dreaded the community gathering—and watching Arlen introduce Lynnette to all the neighbors as his future wife. Every time the sound of rain against his windows had lightened, he had prayed for a downpour, and he thought a little guiltily that he might have gotten it. If he sank in mud over his boot tops and his chores took him all day, he would deserve it—and he wouldn't half mind.

As he pushed open the kitchen door he heard Martha's voice. "Do you want your breakfast in the dining room, Miss Sterling?"

"Whatever's easiest," came the reply.

Christian hesitated in the doorway. Lynnette, dressed in a simple gown that somehow made her perfect face look more beautiful, eyed the table curiously. He turned his gaze there and saw the fourth place Martha had set.

"The easiest," he began, recalling the conversation he had overheard, "would be for you to join us here."

"I would enjoy that," she said. "If Martha doesn't mind." She turned toward the older woman and waited for her nod. "I wondered whom the extra place was for."

He turned away from her before her eyes became too hypnotic and gathered the silver needed to set another place. Last night he had skipped dinner with his family to avoid her, and now she showed up here for breakfast. "It's set for me every Sunday," he said finally. "I suppose that seems a little strange to you." He laid out the silver on the table to avoid looking at her.

"It seems strange to Arlen that I should want to help with lunch." He looked at her then. She must have read his surprise because she added, "Yes, Arlen's china doll actually asked to help cook."

Christian turned away to hide his smile. Arlen must have called her that, and from her tone she hadn't been flattered. He grabbed a cup from the shelf and started for the stove. "Will Arlen's china doll have coffee?"

"Aren't you afraid the paint will crack?"

He turned to find she had followed him, an empty cup in hand. "Well," he said softly as he poured. "Perhaps Arlen is."

"Would that be so tragic?"

He became aware of Martha working nearby and led Lynnette back toward the table. He should tell her he didn't want to be involved in any disagreements between her and Arlen, but even that statement seemed an involvement. It would be better to change the subject.

"Evidently you've heard about our Sunday routine," he said, offering her a corner place at the table. He stepped over the bench and sat down beside her.

"Only briefly. What time do you usually leave for church?"

"Nine. But it may have rained too much to go."

She looked surprised for a second, then light seemed to dawn. "I hadn't even thought of the muddy roads."

"You could have slept late after all," Martha said from behind them. Somehow she didn't sound sympathetic.

Lynnette cast Martha a nervous smile over her shoulder. If she had intended any other response, it died on her lips. By turning she had put her face mere inches from his. Her soft hazel eyes looked troubled, vulnerable. Her pink lips parted slightly as the smile faded. He tightened his grip on the coffee cup to keep from reaching out to touch her.

The squeak of the back door made it possible for him to break away. Perry and Jake entered, dripping and gasping, and Christian rose to greet them. If they were surprised to find Lynnette at their table they covered it well. Soon they were all seated and Martha brought the food. Perry returned thanks, asking a special blessing for their guest, and Jake started the food around the table.

Christian tried to encourage a normal conversation, but both women were uncomfortable. Perry cast his wife furtive glances as if he were afraid she would say something she shouldn't. Jake was the only one relaxed enough to enjoy the food.

Why had Lynnette agreed to stay if the family made her so nervous? Christian wondered. The thought that he was the one making her uncomfortable crossed his mind and was easily dismissed. He was the one affected by her presence.

Martha's behavior reminded him a little of her manner around Felicia. No doubt she saw Lynnette's presence as an invasion.

Which was how he saw it himself. She had invaded his family, his home...his heart. And she sat only inches away from him. If he wasn't careful his leg would brush against her skirt, or his elbow would touch her arm. He was sure he could feel her body's heat. One irrelevant thought kept coming back to him: How could Arlen have actually called her a china doll?

Lynnette thought breakfast would never end. She was constantly aware of Christian beside her, and it was more disconcerting even then having him across from her. He, on the other hand, seemed at ease. More at ease, perhaps, than he was with his own family. It was strange, as he had said. Did he fit in better here?

After the tense breakfast, the morning of cooking seemed to rush past. Martha assigned her a task and seemed surprised that she asked for another when it was done. An hour into the preparations, Jake told them the roads were too muddy to make the trip to church. Plans were quickly changed to leave the meal warming on the stove, but the pace of preparation didn't let up. Finally, everything was ready and the women parted.

In her room, Lynnette pulled aside the curtains and watched the rain streak down the glass. She hoped Christian wasn't out in the rain. She had only the vaguest idea of what his morning chores might be and hoped they were all in the warm, dry barn. She shook off the thought and turned away.

She changed into the burgundy-colored dress she had worn on an earlier evening and rearranged her hair. She wasn't sure what the family did on Sundays when they didn't go to church, but she imagined them sitting around the fire, reading and playing checkers as they did most evenings.

She smiled as she patted the last strand into place. In an odd sort of way she had enjoyed her morning with Martha. She had felt useful for the first time in days.

In the course of the morning, she had asked Martha

about wash day and learned that it was always Monday, weather permitting, of course. She had considered trying to take care of her own laundry herself, but that would have been difficult without bothering Martha for supplies. Besides, doing the laundry together would give her and Martha a chance to visit.

She was on her way to the door when the oddest thought struck her. She almost wished she was here to work for the household instead of marry into it. Of course that was ridiculous; Martha's life only seemed simpler from a distance.

She reached for the doorknob and stopped. *Martha isn't on the verge of marrying someone she doesn't love.* Was that what bothered her this morning? Doubts about Arlen? But what did she know of love anyway? Just romantic notions she had picked up from books and Amanda, and had mimicked in her own writing.

She turned and walked slowly toward the glass door. Rain still dripped from the gray sky but not so heavily now. It seemed as if she had had doubts about her decision since she came here. Why should they crowd in on her and make her feel especially melancholy today?

Was it because she had spent the day before with Arlen and several little things he said had disturbed or irritated her? But she was far from perfect herself. She should accept Arlen the way he was. Wasn't that really all anyone could ask?

She turned away from the glass. Perhaps it was the weather. A warm family gathering downstairs would lift her spirits.

* * *

"How long have you worked for the Prescotts?"
Lynnette had just dumped an armload of white undergarments into the tub of hot soapy water. Martha
added more wood to the little fire where more water
heated.

They had set up for wash day on a rock-paved area
just outside the kitchen door. Jake had helped, then
hurried off. The sounds of hammering drifted from the
far side of the barn. Yesterday's wind had torn some
shingles loose, creating a few leaks in the barn's roof,
and Christian had asked Arlen to help with repairs.
The sound, echoing through the huge structure and off
the rocky hill behind it, seemed somehow reassuring
to Lynnette. She decided that was because they
weren't working where she could see them, high above
the ground.

Martha took so long to answer Lynnette's question
she began to wish she hadn't asked. She took the long
wooden paddle and stirred the clothes. Finally the
older woman spoke. "I came just before Christian was
born, to look after his mother."

"Felicia," Lynnette said, almost absently. Nothing
in the current batch of clothes needed real scrubbing.
They could come out as soon as the rinse water was
ready.

"Felicia isn't Christian's mother," Martha said.

The paddle froze in midcircle. Lynnette tried to
sound only vaguely interested. "I didn't know that."

"No," Martha said, stirring her hand around in the
rinse tub. Jake had carried water from the well until it
was half-full, and Martha had been adding kettlefuls
of boiling water.

Lynnette watched the older woman. Was that all the information she would get? She turned the paddle thoughtfully. At least she understood why Christian looked so different from his brother and sister. Was he the little boy with the blurred face in the picture in her room? How old was that child, five or six? Did Christian remember his mother? Had she died or had she, like Felicia, left Hugh? And her little son?

That was an uncomfortable thought. She wished Martha would volunteer more information. Her imagination was liable to be far worse than the truth.

Several minutes later, Martha carried one of the kettles from the fire to the rinse tub. As she raised it above the rim, Lynnette asked, ''What happened to her?''

''Anna?'' Martha glanced up before turning her attention back to the steaming water pouring from the spout. ''She died when Christian was three. She was never very strong.'' The kettle was empty, and Martha let it hang at her side for a moment. ''I better put this on to heat for the next batch.'' She headed for the pump to refill the kettle.

Three, Lynnette thought. There must have been at least a couple years between Anna's death and Felicia's arrival if the picture was taken shortly after Felicia and Hugh's marriage. And who would have looked after the little boy but Martha?

Martha joined her again in a few minutes and took the wooden paddle from her. She used it to lift garments out of the water then pushed them between the rollers on the wringer while Lynnette turned the crank.

When she had dropped three garments into the rinse

tub, Lynnette's curiosity got the better of her. "What was she like?"

Martha smiled. "She was a sweet little thing. She wanted everyone else to be happy and felt responsible if they weren't. Christian's like her that way."

Lynnette was trying to phrase another question when Martha continued, "That was before this house was built." She tipped her head in the direction of the big stone structure. "That was built for Felicia. Hugh and Anna lived in the frame house where Perry and I live now. I moved in to care for Anna and watch the baby after he was born. It was almost like he was my own."

Lynnette looked up to see Martha smiling into the wash water. *It still is,* she thought. Martha seemed to recall herself. "I'll get the next batch." She headed for the kitchen.

Lynnette slid the paddle around the tub one more time, came up with a white stocking, and ran it through the wringer. Perhaps she shouldn't ask any more questions. Yet, if she was going to be part of this family, wasn't it acceptable for her to be curious about it? She tried to dismiss the idea that it was mainly Christian she was curious about.

In a few minutes, Martha returned with an armload of clothes. Her wash-day method called for starting with the cleanest, lightest-colored clothes and working toward the dark, dirt-caked work pants. The water lasted longer that way. A few badly-stained items had been put to soak in buckets to get a head start on the dirt.

"What was Arlen's childhood like?" Lynnette

asked as she stirred the new batch of clothes. She could almost believe that was really the question she wanted to ask.

"Pretty normal, I guess. Whatever else I might say about her, Felicia was a loving mother."

"Whatever else you might say?" As soon as it left her lips, Lynnette realized that she had overstepped. Family history was one thing; gossip with the help was another.

But Martha only laughed. "No, we didn't get along, if that's what you're asking. I think she was jealous of Christian's relationship with me. She found fault with nearly everything I did. Hugh wouldn't fire me, though. He knew Christian needed me. I think she was relieved when I married Perry and we had Jake, but by then Christian was nearly grown."

Martha moved to help Lynnette run the rinsed garments through the ringer again. "I didn't drive her away, if that's what you're thinking," Martha said softly. "I wouldn't have hurt the boys—or Hugh—like that. She wasn't cut out for the loneliness here or for the work. She's happier in the city."

"Does she ever visit?"

Martha shook her head. "Hugh's been to see her, and of course Arlen comes and goes."

And she tells Emily to give Christian an extra hug for her.

When the last garment had been through the ringer and dropped into a basket, Martha sent Lynnette off to the clothesline with a bag of wooden pins. As she hung the clothes on the line, she thought about the little boy who had lost his mother when he was three, then braided his little sister's hair after her mother was gone.

More questions burned in her mind, about Christian, but she knew she couldn't ask.

"How is it, brother, that you can always find work to do?" Arlen sat braced against the scaffolding, hammering a shingle back in place.

Christian glanced at him from his higher perch. "And exciting work, too," he said.

"Yeah. This roof doesn't look so steep from the ground."

"This isn't steep." Christian grinned at his brother. He had intentionally given Arlen the safest place to work, if any place on this huge roof could be considered safe. "You ought to work on the house's gables some time."

"I'll look forward to it." Arlen eased over and found another loose shingle. "Can I ask you something?"

"Go ahead."

"Lynnette is a lady, of course, so she isn't going to…well…enjoy my touch, so to speak. But what if she actually refuses me after we're married?"

Christian's hammer missed the head of the nail and bent it double. He felt lucky he hadn't smashed his thumb. He straightened the nail enough to still be usable as he tried to frame an answer.

Arlen took his silence as a need for clarification. "I mean she lets me kiss her. She doesn't push me away. And I don't expect her to actually be inviting or anything."

Inviting? God, Christian thought she was inviting! He remembered sitting at her feet while she talked, longing to touch her. He thought of standing in the dark hallway and pulling her against him. She hadn't resisted his touch, had been soft and pliable in his arms. He tried to brush the thoughts away. His thumb could get it yet.

"As you said, she's a lady." He tried to make his voice sound normal. "What are you asking?"

"How much force should I use?"

"None!" Christian almost dropped his hammer.

Arlen moved closer to him. "I didn't mean that, exactly. I mean how forceful should I be? I'll want to do it, and, of course, she won't. I assumed she would have been taught to submit, but I'm not so sure anymore. She's argued with me on more than one occasion."

Christian had never in his life wanted to strike his brother—until now. If they hadn't been perched on the barn roof, he thought he might have. He made an effort to be calm. "Arlen, the fact that she argues with you simply proves she has a brain. It has nothing to do with sex. And do you really want a woman who merely submits?" He realized he hadn't been entirely successful at staying calm.

"Of course it's not what I *want*, but it's all I can expect from a lady. And a lady is what I need for my career."

Christian turned away, trying to go back to work. "I have absolutely no experience with unwilling women," he said tightly. Did he really hope his brother would let it drop? Somehow, for Lynnette's sake, he needed to straighten out Arlen's thinking. But this was the last thing he wanted to be talking about.

"I was just worried, that's all." Arlen sounded hurt. Christian felt his jaw clench. "It can be very difficult for men in politics to take a mistress."

That did it. "You aren't even married, and you're talking about a mistress? I thought you were in love with her."

"I am," Arlen said. "But love doesn't have anything to do with sex, either."

Arlen sounded as though he were explaining something to a simpleton. Christian had heard him use that tone on Lynnette and wondered where in the hell he had learned it. He reminded himself to stay calm. His brother was obviously misguided.

Christian took a deep breath. "When I first brought her here," he said evenly, "she seemed embarrassed when I kissed Emily. I don't think she's used to any displays of affection. I suggest you make sure you're alone." Oh yes! I don't want to ever see it! "Then...seduce her."

"What!" Arlen was incredulous.

"I think your best bet is to teach her to want you." He turned away so Arlen couldn't see his face. He wanted to scream at him not to ever touch her. Instead he went back to work on the roof, grateful that Arlen kept any further thoughts to himself.

Chapter Ten

Arlen's behavior had changed. Lynnette noticed it on Monday afternoon. He took her for a walk past Martha's house and garden. Once they were beyond the house's dooryard, the walking became difficult. They picked their way around rocks and puddles until they were assured of privacy.

Arlen found a rock on which to sit, removed his coat to serve as a cushion and helped Lynnette to be seated. The rain had left the air clear and fresh-smelling; the sun made it virtually sparkle. She gazed off across the grassy slopes and tried to fit the man beside her into a novel. She couldn't have a politician for a hero; no one would believe *that*. Where did he fit in her imaginary ranch? As a banker? A lawyer? He was supposed to be the hero.

"Your skin reminds me of the petals of a wild rose," he said softly.

Lynnette hoped her face didn't register her surprise. Arlen had always been free with the compliments, but there was something different about his tone, something...well...seductive. Besides, her skin was far from wild-rose pink, it was actually starting to tan.

She might argue with everything else, but she didn't normally argue with compliments. She turned toward him and hoped her smile looked appropriately grateful. *His* cheeks had a definite rose hue about them. She bit down on her lower lip to keep from giggling.

"Such cruel treatment of tender lips," he said, taking her chin in his hand. "You should leave them to me to take care of." He moved slowly toward her and gave her lips the barest brush with his own.

His eyes were closed as he slowly drew away. She was struck again with how handsome he was, his face almost artist perfect. A doctor, she decided. His eyes opened slowly, and she shook herself. She had to get back to the here and now.

"Did I scare you with the kiss?" he almost whispered. "I don't want to scare you."

"No," she answered truthfully. "You didn't scare me."

"Good." His voice was a sultry whisper. "I don't want you to be scared of me. I want you to like me to touch you." He ran a finger along her jaw to her ear. "Your lips taste like honey."

Taste? She bit her lip again. How could he have tasted anything? She might not have much experience with kissing, but she had read about it. Lovers could do considerably more tasting than that, which, she realized, was exactly his intent.

His hand slipped to the back of her neck and held her firmly. His lips made gentle contact with hers and stayed there. After a long second, his lips parted, allowing his tongue to tease the slit between her lips. Curious, she parted hers as well.

His reaction startled her. He shifted slightly, and her upper body was pressed closer to his. How was that possible? His other hand was at the small of her back. Of course. She hadn't noticed it there before.

And his lips! They certainly weren't just *touching* hers anymore. They were molded to them. They were engulfing them. They were somehow commanding hers to return the pressure, for survival, she thought. His tongue made a brief foray into her mouth, then traced the inside of her lips.

She felt his body shudder and wondered if his seat on the rock was less than secure. Surely he would break the kiss and catch himself before he tumbled off. It was his problem, though, she thought. She was busy enjoying the kiss. She would be able to write about kissing much better now.

Abruptly Arlen broke away. He was breathless, but didn't appear to be in danger of losing his balance. What did one say after a kiss? Thank you? That was very nice? She decided silence was better. She looked down at her hands, which had remained folded on her lap.

''I better take you back.''

She thought she detected a tremor in his voice. Perhaps he had had to work harder at kissing than she had. After all, all she had had to do was sit still. At any rate he seemed exhausted, and she decided returning was a good idea.

A similar incident occurred that evening, another on Tuesday morning and twice more on Tuesday afternoon. Each time, Arlen was a little bolder with his tongue and with his hands. Occasionally his touch, close to her breast, for example, made her feel uncomfortable. She tried not to let it show, but he must have sensed it for his hand always moved away.

Being married to Arlen wasn't going to be bad, she decided. Particularly if he refrained from talking. His outlandish compliments always made her want to giggle. One time her eyes started to water at the effort of holding it inside. She could only imagine how hurt he would be if he knew what emotion had made her misty-eyed.

At least, she reasoned, he no longer objected to anything she said or did. Of course, he hadn't started any political discussions in her presence. Still, it was nice to have his encouragement when she went off to write—about the handsome young doctor on the frontier.

By Wednesday morning, she had to admit the story wasn't going well. Her characters didn't seem real, even to her. And she was starting to dream about the rancher she had buried in the bottom of her trunk. He crawled out at night and demanded to be given life.

Thinking of the rancher, of course, made her think of Christian. She had barely seen him since Sunday. He skipped most meals or ate elsewhere. He made an appearance in the evening only to braid Emily's hair. He and Emily had ridden out to check on the cattle Monday afternoon. He had spent Tuesday showing horses to a prospective buyer, the one he had met in town on Saturday. That day Arlen had taken her and

Emily on a picnic at noon so the other three men could talk business over lunch.

She missed Christian, her rancher hero. She sat on the balcony off her bedroom with the notebook on her lap. The weather had turned from warm to hot, and she knew there would be more of a breeze on one of the balconies downstairs on the other side of the house. But she couldn't bring herself to move. Downstairs, Arlen was bound to seek her out, and she needed a respite from his attention.

Besides, she was more likely to catch a glimpse of Christian from here. She had vowed to set aside the fantasy along with the rancher novel. She had worked hard for two days to concentrate on Arlen. "My future husband," she said under her breath, as if forming the words would help impress them on her mind.

And it was working, she told herself. This morning was simply a minor setback, cold feet, perhaps. She slammed the notebook shut, gathered her writing supplies and moved resolutely to a downstairs balcony.

Two hours and half a page later three riders came into view below. They were all well dressed, and none rode with the easy grace she was used to seeing when she watched anyone on the ranch ride. Lynnette watched them pass the front of the house and turn up the drive beside the barn. She placed the stopper in the ink bottle and went in search of a family member.

She found Arlen in the study. At her brief description of the visitors, he came to his feet, elated. "What are they doing way out here?" He brushed past her and hurried to the back door. Lynnette considered following, but the back hall was narrow. Besides, Arlen would probably wish to introduce her in a more formal setting.

In the living room, she took a seat in one of the leather chairs and reached for a book on a nearby table. It was one of Emily's. She leafed through it absently. It occurred to her that she was posing, making herself ready for Arlen to display to his friends. How had she fallen into this? She was trying to do what she knew he would want. That wasn't necessarily wrong, but it didn't feel right either.

She hastily closed the book and returned it to the table as she rose. She was hurrying toward the balcony when she heard the back door close and voices in the hall. She took the notebook onto her lap and waited. In a moment, the voices faded behind the study door. So much for knowing what Arlen wanted.

She stared off across the valley. Was everything she did pretense now? She pretended to write about Arlen when she wanted to write about Christian. She pretended to enjoy Arlen's kisses when she really only studied them. She pretended to be what Arlen wanted, when she knew she never could be. And she still hadn't told him about *Passion's Secret*. After all the time they spent alone, how could she claim she hadn't had a chance?

She should share all of these things with Arlen— well maybe not the part about his kisses—but the rest. She should be completely honest with him. If she couldn't do that, it was reason enough to know she couldn't marry him.

The old panic came back in a rush. Where would

she go? What would she do? And, to her shame, she didn't want to leave and never see Christian again.

Christian. Dear Lord, he was the center of it all. If she had never met him she might have fallen in love with Arlen—or not, but she would know it was because of Arlen, who he was rather than who he wasn't.

But she *had* met Christian. And that changed everything. Whatever the personal cost might be, she would have to break up with Arlen and leave. If either of the men knew how she felt, it would destroy their relationship. She couldn't let that happen.

"Lynnette! Where are you?" Arlen's call broke into her contemplation. She rose and stepped into the living room. "There you are. I need to go to Topeka. I'm going to pack a few things and leave with my friends. Will you tell the family?"

"Of course."

He kissed her on the cheek and hurried up the stairs. She found herself alone with three very curious young men. She motioned them toward chairs and took one herself. "What's the emergency?" she asked.

"A meeting he has to attend," the nearest one explained. "We couldn't count on a telegram being delivered out in the country so we took the late train out yesterday."

"And rented horses this morning," offered another. "I don't relish the thought of riding back to town."

Lynnette tried to hide a smile. "Can I get you gentlemen something to drink?"

They all shook their heads. "The maid brought us lemonade already," the nearest said.

They glanced at one another, and one cleared his

throat. She had the impression they wanted to ask her something, but none had the nerve. Arlen hadn't mentioned who she was. Of course not, he hadn't had the time. It seemed awkward now for her to introduce herself. Arlen would no doubt explain later that she was his intended bride—though it was no longer true. She tried her best to smile at them.

Arlen returned a moment later, ready to travel. He must have told Martha to have someone saddle a horse because the four riders went past the house a few short minutes after they had left the living room.

And just that quickly, Arlen was gone. She found herself taking a deep breath as if a tight corset had just been loosened. She hadn't even thought to ask when he would return.

Christian saddled the horse and saw his brother off. Arlen said he would be back on Friday. Three days, Christian thought, when the torture would ease up a little. He walked slowly back to the barn.

Had it been only two days since he had advised Arlen to seduce Lynnette? It seemed like an eternity. Every time the two of them walked away together, he *knew* what they were doing. Every time they reappeared, he studied her for signs of just how far it had gone.

There had been no rent seams or grass clinging to her hair. Of course, she would be very careful about things like that. Still she always seemed unruffled, in demeanor as well as clothes.

But Arlen. God! Arlen came back looking like Tyrant when he had made off with something tasty from

Martha's kitchen. He was puffed up and flushed and entirely too pleased.

He wished he'd told Arlen something else. He had long since decided that the altitude of the barn roof had kept him from thinking clearly. Why hadn't he used the opportunity to tell Arlen not to marry her? He knew why, and it wasn't because he was thinking of Arlen's happiness. If Arlen ended the engagement she would leave, and he would never see her again.

He still should have come up with something that wouldn't be such hell to watch. Or something that would have made her so mad at him *she* would have broken it off. He even imagined her running to him for protection.

He slumped against the wall in the tack room, grateful that he was alone in the barn. He could never have done it. He loved his brother, and it wasn't in his nature to trick people anyway. He wanted to see Arlen happy. And Lynnette happy, too.

No, he had done the right thing. If Arlen could coax her to passion it could go a long way toward future happiness for both of them. He was just grateful that for a few days, he wouldn't have to watch.

He didn't have time to moon around. He grabbed three halters off the nails on the wall and headed for the corral. He had told Jake to turn the three-year-olds into the corral while he saddled Arlen's horse. It was time he got back to work.

He found Hugh waiting for him. His horse was tethered to the fence, and he stood impatiently beside it. Christian handed the halters to Jake and walked to meet his father.

"Can I have a word with you, son? Is there something wrong between you and your brother?"

His father's blunt question took him by surprise. "Wrong? What makes you ask?"

"You're missing far more meals than your work justifies. I don't think it's Emily. You and I get along well enough at breakfast so I don't think it's me. That leaves Arlen. Are you avoiding him?"

Damn! If he denied it would Hugh think of Lynnette next? He needed to prevent that conclusion. "It was nothing important," he said. He was studying the toes of his boots and tried to force his gaze upward. "We patched it up just now, before he left."

"He left? I must have missed him."

Good. Let's change the subject. "Three friends from Topeka came out to get him. There's some meeting or other they think he needs to attend. Say, how did everything look out there?"

"Fair. It was a pretty general rain but we could use some more." He threw an arm around Christian's shoulder and started back toward the corral. "So everything's patched up, then? We can expect you at lunch?"

"Sure. Uh, I'm sorry about before. I just didn't want any tension between us bothering the ladies." God, it was hard to lie to his father.

"I understand. It's wonderful to have them here, isn't it? Their pretty dresses and their laughter, they just brighten up the place, don't they?"

He nodded. "They've changed everything," he said.

* * *

Christian showed up for lunch. Lynnette was watching Emily rearrange the flowers on the table when he came around the base of the stairs. Her first reaction was elation—her second was shame. Aside from a brief nod in his direction she refused to look at him.

She heard Emily greeting him with some saucy remark and him making a teasing response. She wasn't listening. Her third reaction, now that she had a moment to think, was fear. She didn't even have Arlen here to distract her.

And things were different from the last time she had eaten with him. She knew herself to be in love with him. At the thought an unexpected joy rose in her breast before she had a chance to tamp it down. There was nothing, *nothing,* to feel joy about. It was an impossible love.

She glanced in his direction. His attention was solely on his sister. Did he give any thought to her at all? She shook herself. Of course not! And she should be glad! Things were bad enough as they were.

Hugh joined them, and they all took their places. Christian told Emily where Arlen had gone and when to expect him back. Friday, Lynnette thought. She would have until then to treasure every moment she could with Christian. Of course that would be somewhat awkward since she hadn't yet entered the barn and that seemed to be where he spent most of his time.

What was she thinking? she scolded herself. She wasn't going to start flirting with Christian. It would be best to avoid him as much as possible, then let Arlen down easy and go.

Go where? She had no idea.

Christian watched Lynnette while trying to appear not to. She was preoccupied. Once in a while she would recall herself and eat for a few minutes, even smile at Emily, but soon she would drift away again.

She missed Arlen already. The boy must have done a fine job. He would have to tell him he was proud of him. If he could fight off the urge to punch him in the mouth.

He pulled his eyes away. Emily was trying to talk their father into letting her go to Rose's tomorrow. She had tried several arguments, but Hugh wasn't giving in.

"You've barely been here a full week, and you're ready to leave?" Hugh kept saying.

"You should have used all your fine debating skills on Rose," Christian suggested.

"Well, I did!" she declared. "But she has to wait for her dumb old horse to foal. I even told her if she came now she'd be here when Elayne foals, and that would be just as good."

"Only a city girl would see it that way," he said. His eyes went directly to Lynnette, who was listening for once. His luck. "No offense intended," he said.

She laughed, and he could have sworn his heart skipped a beat. "I'm afraid I was about to agree with Emily," she said with a wide-eyed innocence that was just a tad overdone.

"See," Emily said. His peripheral vision suggested she had made a face at him, but he didn't take his eyes off Lynnette. He couldn't. She laughed at Emily now, her eyes dancing, so different from the pensive look of a few minutes before.

Emily gave up the subject and went on to other things. She and Lynnette arranged to read and sew during the afternoon. Hugh asked Lynnette about her writing, and she answered briefly and noncommittally. Emily expounded on a story she had been forced to write in composition class.

Soon the meal was finished, and he was on his way back to work. He was glad he had come in for lunch. The brief exchange of innocent smiles with Lynnette would stand out as the bright spot in his day. Though he knew he should dread it, he was already looking forward to dinner.

"Do you mind if we skip a few chapters? I've been reading ahead."

Lynnette smiled at Emily. "That's fine. I've read the book several times already. I'll be able to follow along."

"Good. I didn't want to have to reread." Emily settled into the chair and soon became engrossed in the book.

Lynnette had been unable to borrow any sewing from Martha so she stitched a tiny pink rosebud on Emily's nightgown. She was determined to concentrate solely on the stitches and the story. As a result neither of them noticed when a buggy pulled into the yard. The first they knew they had visitors was the burst of noise as the back door was flung open.

"Rose!" Emily shouted, tossing aside the book.

Rose flew into the room and threw herself into Emily's arms. Christian and an older man she guessed to be Rose's father followed behind, both of them laden with bags.

Emily introduced Rose to Lynnette and the girls headed for the kitchen in search of lemonade. Lynnette didn't think of following; her attention was centered on Christian. He had dropped the bags on the floor and instructed his companion to do the same, promising to take care of them later.

"Let me introduce our houseguest," he said, advancing on Lynnette. "Lynnette, this is Rose's father, Morton Blainey. Morton, meet Lynnette Sterling, Arlen's future wife."

Lynnette wished the words hadn't come so easily for him. Was she hoping he felt some of the pain she did? How selfish! She smiled warmly at Rose's father and extended her hand. He shook it, and Christian indicated they should sit down.

"Emily will play hostess and bring the lemonade. Would you care for something stronger, Morton?" Christian had already opened a cabinet and removed a glass decanter.

"A shot of something wouldn't hurt," Morton said.

Christian filled a small glass. "Lynnette?"

She had been watching every move he made, every flex of his shoulder, arm, fingers. Hearing her name on his lips made her jump. Was he asking why she stared at him?

The next instant she realized he was holding up the decanter, offering her a drink. "No, thank you," she said hastily.

He poured a second glass half-full and put the decanter away. Handing the full glass to Blainey, he settled into another of the leather-covered chairs.

"Not a very generous drink you poured yourself," Morton said, savoring the smell of his own.

Christian shook his head. "I'm working with some young horses out there, and I don't want to give them any advantage. I'm barely smarter than they are as it is."

His smile was devastating. She hadn't seen him in the role of host before. He was friendly, charming and relaxed, even though he had left his work to usher them into the house.

Hugh came in from the study. "I thought I heard someone arrive," he said, walking quickly toward the guest. Blainey rose to shake his hand, then both men were seated again, Hugh in the chair beside Lynnette that Emily had vacated. He removed the book that was wedged between him and the armrest and cast Lynnette a rueful smile.

"We weren't expecting to see you so soon," he said, turning his attention to Blainey. "Did your daughter change her mind about waiting for the foal?"

Blainey's expression turned serious. "No. We lost it yesterday." He nodded at everyone's sympathetic reaction before he went on. "She's understandably upset. Her mother and I thought coming here would be the best thing to lift her spirits."

"I'm sorry about the foal, Morton," Hugh said. "But I'm grateful for your daughter's arrival. Emily's been pestering me to let her go to Rose."

"I don't pester," announced Emily. She carried a

pitcher of lemonade, and Rose followed with a tray of several glasses.

"That's right, Muffin," Christian said. "I wouldn't call it pestering. I'd call it…nagging."

Emily sneered at him. Turning to Rose, she removed a glass from the tray and filled it. "I don't believe Christian gets any lemonade." Her tone was soft as if she were giving the other girl instructions.

Christian laughed. "I'll regret it the entire afternoon." He set the liquor aside unfinished and rose to his feet. "Good to see you again," he said to Blainey, giving his hand a shake. He nodded to the rest. "Rose," he said, gracing her with a sincere smile, "we're glad to have you here."

Lynnette watched him until he disappeared. She felt a pang of jealousy at the way he looked at Emily's young friend. She turned toward Rose, but it was too late to read the girl's reaction. She should have looked sooner but had been unable to take her eyes off Christian.

While the girls served the lemonade, Lynnette studied Rose. She was a lovely girl, more beautiful than Emily in a simple, less sophisticated way, taller and more slender. She looked to be a few years older than Emily, sixteen perhaps. Her blond hair was shiny with windblown tendrils curling around her face.

Of course Christian would find her attractive. She was, besides being beautiful, a country girl who understood why one foal was not the same as the next. She swallowed a sip of lemonade to wash down the bitterness. He had seen her as a city girl from the beginning and dismissed her.

No. She was being stupid. He had seen her as Arlen's fiancée and had too much integrity to see anything else. She was the one at fault. She looked back at Rose, now in whispered conversation with Emily.

The men stood and Lynnette realized they had carried on a conversation beside her, and she hadn't heard a word. She could only hope neither one had tried to include her. Rose ran to kiss her father goodbye, and Hugh saw Blainey to the door.

The girls returned their glasses to the tray and ran to the pile of bags. Rose chose one for Emily to carry and picked up one herself, then they ran chattering up the stairs.

Lynnette sat in the sudden quiet. What could she do now to distract herself from thoughts of Christian? She eyed the gown draped on top of Emily's sewing basket. Sewing allowed far too much room to think, but evidently a room full of people did as well. Nothing would stop her from thinking of Christian.

With a sigh she stood and gathered all the dirty glasses, including Christian's. The temptation to touch her tongue to the rim of his glass appalled her. She quickly set it on the tray with the others and carried them and the pitcher to the kitchen.

The kitchen was empty. Martha had cleaned up from lunch, and it was too early to start dinner. Lynnette found a kettle of warm water on the stove and used it to wash the glasses. Images of Christian swirled in her mind the entire time. She laughed ruefully at herself as she put the last glass in its place on the shelf. If she was going to spend the afternoon preoccupied with Christian, she might as well put it to constructive use.

The anticipation built as she left the kitchen and hurried to her room. She was about to release her rancher hero from his prison in the bottom of her trunk.

Chapter Eleven

The girlish chatter in the house seemed to have doubled. Christian washed for dinner and headed for the dining room. He rounded the stairway and stopped, watching the scene. All three ladies were clustered near the table, talking and laughing. He could pick out only an occasional word of their discussion and decided it had to do with fashions. How any of *them* followed the discussion was a mystery. There were two voices audible at one moment, and whispering or giggling the next.

They had all chosen bright-colored dresses, Lynnette's cheerful blue gown being the most subdued. Still his eyes fell on her instantly. Her back was to him, and he took the opportunity to admire her narrow waist and feminine hips.

There had evidently been some conspiring, for each lady's hair was styled quite elaborately, including Lynnette's. It was caught up high in the back and cascaded down in soft ringlets. He was dying to know if she left curls around her face the way Emily liked to. Or if she would think that was too untidy.

If they knew he was there she would turn around, but he was reluctant to end this chance to stand and watch them unobserved. The younger girls had evidently taken her into their confidence. She was doing her share of talking and laughing.

A touch at his shoulder made him glance aside. Hugh had joined him. "Lovely, aren't they?" he murmured softly.

He nodded, his eyes on Lynnette as she turned around. He caught his breath. Her face was framed with thin wisps of curls that softened the delicate features. She looked more doll-like than ever, or would have but for the saucy grin on her face.

"How long have you been standing there?" Emily demanded, bringing one fist to her hip.

"We were just enjoying some of nature's beauties," Hugh said, stepping forward.

"Imagine our surprise," said Christian, trying to keep his eyes on Emily—and off Lynnette, "to come in and find a flock of magpies in our dining room."

This was greeted with a small outburst of indignation and barely stifled giggles. Christian stood back and watched his father hold a chair for each of the ladies. He noticed Rose was seated at his usual place beside Emily. It didn't take a genius to know where that left him. He waited until Hugh took his place before he rounded the table to sit beside Lynnette.

After the blessing, food was brought to the table. The ladies exchanged conspiratorial glances as the food was passed.

"What were you ladies discussing?" Hugh asked.

It sounded for all the world like a casual question, not an effort to get to the bottom of all that giggling.

Christian leaned forward, repeating the question with his own emphasis. "Yes. What *were* you ladies discussing?"

"We were discussing...fashion," Emily said. The other ladies tried unsuccessfully to hide their grins. "*Men's* fashion," she added.

"That's right," offered Lynnette. "We were discussing what each of us thought looked good on men."

"Well!" Christian stated with exaggerated shock. "I'm not sure that's proper at all. How did my costume rate?" He tugged at the front of his shirt and waved away imaginary dust.

"Better than you might think," Emily murmured.

He couldn't hide his surprise. "Better than I—?"

Lynnette cut him off. "But I don't think we should discuss our findings."

All three shook their heads, pursing their lips.

Rose spoke for the first time. "As my mother always says, men are funny about things they don't understand."

Hugh and Christian exchanged looks of wounded pride. "We're outnumbered," Christian said.

"And unarmed," stated Emily firmly.

The conversation turned to Emily's plans while Rose was there. Christian happily left it to his father to listen and comment. He tuned it out and concentrated on the woman beside him. Her mood was strikingly different than that at lunch. He had decided then that she missed Arlen, was disappointed that he had left. If that had been the case, she'd gotten over it!

He was certain that she barely followed what Emily said. He knew he shouldn't give in to his curiosity, but he leaned toward her. "Have you been listening to that all afternoon?" he asked softly.

She stifled a laugh, biting her lip. He noticed the barest glance at Emily before she turned to him. "The walls upstairs muffled it sufficiently."

"Good," he murmured. Sufficiently for what? For writing, he supposed. Was that what had her filled with anticipation? He knew he didn't imagine it. He could sense the excitement in the tension in her body, in the light in her eyes. If he didn't know better, he would think she was expecting to meet a lover.

He excused himself early and left to start the evening chores. His evenings were a little freer with Rose here because the girls braided each other's hair. And, with Arlen gone, he could dig the book out of its hiding place and get some insight into the thinking of Lynnette "Silver Nightingale" Sterling.

Christian stared at the streak of moonlight angling across his ceiling. He couldn't get the smile off his face. *Passion's Secret* had few secrets and less passion. Basically, it was a sweet love story. No one who actually read it could declare it scandalous.

The author could be accused of some lack of humility, perhaps. Every detail of the dark-haired heroine could have described Lynnette herself. But maybe he wanted to picture Lynnette as the heroine and had filled in the details himself.

His ego had taken a blow where the hero was concerned. He was dark and sophisticated, a wealthy man with no designated source of income. His formal attire got enough attention for this evening's girl talk to take on a different light. It wasn't the *cut* of the clothes she described so much as the *fit*. She had spent considerable time and interest looking at men.

But not touching. He was sure of that. She had no idea what consuming desire felt like, even if she knew the phrase and liked to use it.

Or at least she hadn't known when she wrote the book. Arlen might have changed that. He groaned aloud. It had been impossible to put Arlen out of his mind while he read. He would have enjoyed it a lot more if he could have. And now, he would have liked to lie here and imagine himself teaching her all the things she didn't know. But again Arlen intruded.

It was late. He had read the thin volume straight through and most of the night was gone. He closed his eyes and tried to put Lynnette out of his mind.

Someone called her name. She heard it on the edge of sleep and struggled awake. Father! He needed her again, as he did so often at night. She sat up and threw the covers off her legs before the room solidified around here.

She couldn't have heard her father. He was dead, gone now for several weeks. What had she heard?

"Tyrant?" she whispered. There was no answering mew.

Perhaps someone had called to her from the hallway. She got up and crossed to the door, opening it a crack. No one was there. The house was quiet.

She returned to the bed and snuggled under the covers. She must have dreamed it. She couldn't remember dreaming about her father, but it was possible.

She had come to some upsetting decisions yesterday. She was surely feeling the strain of those decisions. The last time she had felt this lost was after her father had died. Surely that was what had caused the dream.

Yesterday she had buried herself in her story, had even written after dinner and into the night. It had worked to keep her mind off her situation, but the distress had evidently caught up with her in her sleep.

She closed her eyes, recalling the last scene she had written, letting her imagination take her into the next. She fell asleep with a smile on her lips.

"I'm sorry your mare lost her foal," Emily offered. Rose hadn't been her usual self, and Emily was at a loss as to how to cheer her up. They had taken a light breakfast, then gone back to Emily's room where Rose had flung herself across the bed and expressed no interest in doing anything Emily suggested.

Rose sighed. "Thanks, Emily. Elayne will do better, don't worry."

"I wasn't thinking about that," Emily said, sitting on the corner of the bed and watching her friend's face. "Do you want to go riding this afternoon?"

Rose shook her head. "I don't know." Her eyes narrowed. "Do you like her?"

"Who?" Emily asked.

"*Her.* Lynnette."

Emily smiled. "Sure. She's nice. Don't you think so?"

Rose looked more mournful than ever. "Yeah, I guess I like her too."

Emily couldn't hold back a laugh, her friend looked so funny. "Are you afraid she'll become my new best friend?"

"No," Rose said, sitting up. "Though that would make it even harder to bear."

"Rose, you're not making any sense."

"She's going to marry Arlen." Rose flopped backward and threw an arm across her eyes. "How could he do it?"

Emily shrugged. "He's old. He's supposed to get married. What difference does—?" She gasped, leaning toward her friend. "Are you in love with Arlen?"

Rose nodded, flinging her arms outward to gaze at the ceiling. "Since forever!"

Emily stared. "Arlen? Why? I mean...Arlen?"

A dreamy look came over the soft features. "He's so handsome, and cultured, and polite."

"Well, yeah, but..."

"I didn't even know about *her* until I got here. He's never even given me a chance."

Emily leaped to her feet and paced across the room. "We ought to make him give you that chance, Rose."

Rose sat up to watch her. "What do you mean?"

"Well—" Emily tapped her lip with a finger "—I like her fine, but not the way I like you. If I could choose, I'd rather have you as my sister. Besides, I don't think Christian likes her."

"What...?"

"You saw the way he hurried off after dinner when he had to sit beside her." She talked faster, warming to the subject. "He's hardly ever around, and I think it's because of her."

Rose waved her to silence. "No, I mean what do you mean about Arlen giving me a chance?"

Emily came to sit on the bed. "I don't know. But we have to do something before it's too late."

The girls stared at each other. Emily finally spoke. "Do you think you could...uh...get his attention?"

Rose eyed her quizzically.

"You know," said Emily, raising a saucy eyebrow and dropping her voice, "get his attention."

"Flirt with him?" Rose seemed horrified at first, then a slow smile spread across her face. Emily could see the doubts fade then reassert themselves. "I don't think I know how. I mean, I know how to flirt, but this would have to be...good."

Emily nodded, her mind racing. How could she help her friend? Then she remembered. "Rose," she whispered, leaning toward her friend. "When I was in town with Christian, I saw a book in the store. It was called *Passion* something-or-other."

"That would have been great," Rose whispered, then covered her mouth.

"The great part," Emily went on, "is that Christian bought it. He went back after I was in the buggy so I wouldn't know, but I saw him through the window. I know it was the same book because it had a bright red cover."

The girls stared at each other. Rose shook her head. "Christian won't let us read it."

"Of course not," hissed Emily. "That's why we have to search his room." Emily grabbed her friend's hand.

"Right now?"

"Shhh!"

"What if *she* hears us?"

Emily stopped just outside the door. "Let's see if she's up here." With Rose waiting behind her, Emily walked resolutely to Lynnette's door and knocked loudly. She turned back and grinned at her friend. When there was no answer, she opened the door and stuck her head inside. "Lynnette?"

She closed the door again and waved Rose forward. "She isn't here."

Rose joined her outside Christian's door. "What would you have done if she'd been here?"

Emily shrugged, walking calmly into Christian's room. "Asked to borrow a ribbon or something. Close the door in case someone comes up."

"What if Christian comes up?"

"Hmm," she murmured, scanning the room for possible hiding places. "I'll tell him..." She started through the dresser.

Rose went to the desk and tentatively opened a drawer. "You have no idea what you'll tell him, do you?" she whispered.

"I'll think of something if he comes, which isn't likely. Let's see. Where would...?" Her eyes lit on the small stand beside the bed. A red-covered book lay casually on top. Emily ran to snatch it up. "Here it is!"

Rose looked up from her search. "He left it out? Won't he miss it if we take it?"

Emily froze. "Maybe." Her indecision lasted only a moment. "We'll just have to return it before tonight." She grabbed Rose's hand and ran out of the room. Safely back in her own room, she leaned against the door and gasped for breath.

Rose tumbled onto the bed. "I can't believe we did that."

"I can't believe it was so easy." With one last sigh, she scurried toward the bed. "Move over." Giggling, the girls settled in to read.

Lynnette slowly climbed the stairs to her room. She had been unnerved by another lunch with Christian. The girls had gotten trays and gone back to their room, and with just Christian and Hugh at the table, she had used the opportunity to ask them several questions about the ranch. She should be excited about working those details into what she had already written.

Instead she was restless. She had spent the morning on the bench in the yard, writing. She kept remembering how Christian had come and talked to her when she had written there before. After trying so hard to concentrate on her imaginary hero, lunch with the real thing filled her with longings she couldn't identify. Or didn't want to identify.

She mustn't dwell on the fact that she was in love with Christian. Surely that would make it more difficult to pretend she wasn't when he was around. If she spent any more time alone, her hopeless love was bound to be all she thought about.

The sound of voices and laughter from Emily's room caught her attention. The promise of a carefree afternoon beckoned. Her hand was poised to knock when Emily's voice stopped her.

"'Robert's eyes lingered on her face, drinking in the fragile beauty of her features. After a breathless moment, he drew her into his arms and held her against him with restrained passion.'"

"He held her with restrained passion," Rose moaned.

"Unrestrained passions sounds more fun to me," Emily quipped.

As the girls giggled, Lynnette backed away from the door. Where had they found it? Did they knew it was hers? No. No one could have told them but Christian, and she was sure he wouldn't have given away her secret.

Rose must have brought it, she decided as she made her way to her own room. Half the fun was knowing the adults would not approve. Arlen especially, she realized.

She pulled aside the curtains and opened the door to the balcony. She had planned to tell Arlen that, while she was fond of him, she didn't love him. She had hoped if she could emphasize that she was not the right woman for him, she could end the engagement without hurting him.

Now she realized all she had to do was tell him about the book. It would prove that she was not the woman he thought she was. Perhaps that was why she hadn't been able to tell him sooner. Since she had first met him in the attorney's office, she had truly *wanted* to be the right woman, but she couldn't change who she was.

And Christian. She stepped out on the balcony and leaned against the rail, hoping to see him working below. Without Christian she might have tried to do it. She might have married Arlen and settled into a life of pretending.

As if on cue, Christian and Jake rode out of the tall barn doors, turned and disappeared beyond the barn. Lynnette wished they had ridden in the opposite direction, where she could watch Christian for a while as he slowly left her behind.

"Parting should be quick," she whispered. But she didn't believe it. She wanted as much time with him as she could possibly grab.

Christian was absent from dinner. Lynnette wasn't surprised. She had spent the afternoon on the balcony and would have seen him return. The girls were too wrapped up in themselves to comment on his absence, if they even noticed, and Hugh evidently knew about whatever job had called him and Jake away.

Hugh kept Emily from doing all the talking by drawing Rose out with questions about her family and her own activities. Lynnette was glad that responsibility hadn't fallen to her. Pretending to eat was all she could manage.

Tomorrow Arlen would return, and she would have the difficult task of breaking their engagement. And then she would leave. Christian would be lost to her forever.

Over the quiet dinner conversation, Lynnette heard the back door close. Christian had returned! She schooled her features not to reveal her elation. As upsetting as his presence was, his absence was worse.

She pretended to listen to what Rose was saying. She didn't dare look in his direction, but she charted his progress through the living room and to the base of the stairs by the sound of his footsteps. In a moment he would be beside her, and if she dared a glance, she knew just the sight of him would make her heart race.

"You're home early, son," Hugh said, rising and extending his hand.

The greeting offered an excuse to look. She turned and nearly gasped. "Arlen!"

"I didn't mean to startle you," he said. He shook his father's hand and took the seat beside her, kissing her cheek in the process. "Didn't you hear me come in?"

"I...ah...no, I guess not."

"I caught the late train," Arlen explained. "My friends have set up appointments for me next week with some of the most influential men in Kansas. I wanted some time at home to prepare myself. If you don't mind, Father, I'll need the study all morning tomorrow."

"It's all yours," Hugh said.

Lynnette thought the girls had exchanged a conspiratorial look while Arlen was talking. She watched them curiously, and in a few minutes they excused themselves and scampered up the stairs. A signal, she supposed, dismissing it.

When Hugh proposed they retire to the living room, Lynnette laid a hand on Arlen's sleeve. "I'll be there in a moment, Hugh," she said. Hugh graciously left them alone. "Could I speak with you a moment?" she asked Arlen softly.

"Can it wait until tomorrow? I'm really beat." He was already rising from the table. "It's wonderful to see you again." He cupped her cheek with the palm of his hand and gazed at her for a long moment. "Good night," he whispered, bending to kiss her lips.

Lynnette remained in her chair as he crossed the room. She should run after him and insist he take time for her, but he did look exhausted.

With one foot on the bottom step he turned. "I like your hair much better this way," he said. He gave her a warm smile that she tried to return and went up the stairs.

In Emily's room the girls, dressed in their nightgowns, sat cross-legged on the bed, their heads close together.

"You heard what he said," Emily whispered. "He's going to be in the study all morning."

"But how does that help *me*?"

"You go in, say you're looking for a book, then stay and...you know."

Rose took a deep breath, her eyes wide. "Won't he think it's odd that we're not together?"

Emily hesitated. "Tell him you need the book for

us to read together. If you're successful, he's not going
to remember your excuse, anyway."

Rose still looked uncertain. "What if Lynnette
comes in? Or your father?"

"Grab a book and run, I guess. But Papa won't
bother him while he's working, and I'll take care of
Lynnette."

Rose looked at Emily for a long time before a smile
started to spread across her face. "This is my one
chance, isn't it? Now I'm too excited to sleep."

"The book!" they said almost in unison.

Emily scrambled to the head of the bed and removed the book from under a pillow.

"I thought you were going to return that to Christian's room."

Emily shrugged. "I'll do it tomorrow. Arlen's in
there now, anyway." At Rose's skeptical look she
elaborated, "I'll put it on the floor, almost under the
night table, and he'll think he missed it tonight because it had fallen off the table. Don't worry. Besides,
it's only Christian. It's not like I took something that
belonged to *Arlen*. Then I'd be in trouble."

Rose glared at her. "You should be in trouble."

"Oh, don't get grown-up on me now," Emily said,
leafing through the pages. "You've enjoyed the book
as much as I have, whether it helps you with your
mission or not." She gave her friend a wink and settled in to read.

Christian and Hugh were just finishing breakfast
when Arlen joined them in the dining room. "You're
up early," Christian said by way of greeting.

"I wanted to get an early start on things this morning."

"I have a few things I'd like to retrieve from the study," Hugh said, rising. "Enjoy your breakfast."

Arlen poured himself a cup of coffee and offered the pot to Christian. He took it and refilled his cup. He was finished, ready to start his chores, but he lingered. Arlen was gone most of the time, and he found himself avoiding him the rest. He didn't want it to be that way with his brother.

Arlen asked in a quiet voice, intended not to carry, "Did you stay out all night?"

Christian shook his head. "I got in late and saw your horse. I didn't want to wake you, so I slept on the cot in the tack room."

Arlen eyed him skeptically. Christian took a sip of coffee, hoping to hide the fact that that wasn't the whole truth. "So what're you up to today?"

"Studying," Arlen said. "I've got some important meetings next week, and I don't want to mess up on a single fact."

"Better you than me, little brother." Christian toasted him with his coffee cup.

Light footsteps on the stairs drew their attention. Christian glanced up once, then watched his brother's profile as Lynnette came into view. Arlen studied her with narrowed eyes, a possessive smile on his face. Both men stood when she reached the bottom of the stairs. Arlen helped her into the chair beside him, kissing her cheek, before he returned to his own seat.

Christian found himself unwilling to remain. He didn't want to sit across from them and watch. He hated the way Arlen looked at her, and was afraid his brother would have a similar reaction if he happened to notice how *he* looked at her. After giving Lynnette the warmest good-morning he could muster, he stacked his dishes and took them to the kitchen.

Lynnette wished Christian weren't leaving. Here was a perfect chance to talk to Arlen, and she didn't want it. She wanted to put it off for one more day. She wanted one more day with Christian.

She watched Arlen pour her some coffee and tried to shake off her foolishness. "I'm glad you came home early," she lied. "I've been wanting to talk to you."

"I want to be with you, too," he said softly. "You're my life. I'm sorry I can't spend the whole day with you. But I really need to get to work."

"I only need a few minutes," she said.

"Ah," he murmured, taking her face in his hands. "You ask so little. This afternoon I should have more time. But now I really need to get to work." He gave her one of his slow lingering kisses. "Enjoy your breakfast," he said cheerily as he left her alone.

Lynnette listened for the sound of the study door closing. "I ask so little," she muttered under her breath.

Chapter Twelve

Lynnette was finishing her breakfast when Emily found her. The girl was dressed in the pants and shirt she wore when she went riding. "There you are," she said, sliding into a chair across from Lynnette. "Do you have any plans for today?"

Lynnette felt a surge of anticipation. Would she be invited to go riding with the girls? "Nothing definite," she said.

"I thought I'd show you around the barn," Emily suggested. "You haven't had a chance to explore it, have you?"

Lynnette shook her head, hiding her disappointment.

"I can find you some pants so your gown doesn't get dirty."

Lynnette considered a moment. Would wearing pants increase her chances of getting to ride? But then, what did she care whether she rode or not? Christian would be in the barn. Did she want him to see her in pants like Emily wore? It was daring and exciting and would absolutely horrify Arlen. "That would be great," she said, tossing aside her napkin.

Upstairs, Emily walked into Christian's room as if it were her own. Lynnette followed hesitantly. While Emily rummaged through a drawer, Lynnette looked around. The room was cluttered, but two men were sharing it temporarily.

"Which one of Christian's shirts do you want?"

Lynnette turned to see Emily holding up three of her brother's shirts. She recognized one as a shirt she had mended. The thought of wearing any of them next to her skin made her tingle. "Perhaps Arlen has something...."

"Nope. We'd have to ask his permission. Do you think he'd give it?"

The girl had a point. Lynnette reached for the mended shirt, feeling at least a familiarity with it. She laid it over her arm and resisted the urge to caress it.

Next Emily came up with a worn pair of denim pants. Emily promised to put the dresser back in order, and Lynnette went to her room to change.

She stripped down to her drawers and chemise and tried on the shirt. It went well past her hips. She rolled the sleeves up three times and reached for the pants. They were far from a good fit. They were indecently snug across her hips, and the waist was too loose. She cinched it in as best she could with the wide ribbon tie from her straw hat.

She looked down at herself and decided she looked ridiculous. But it was too late to turn back. She just prayed that Arlen wouldn't see her. It wouldn't exactly put him in the mood she wanted him in for their discussion. Or maybe it would. Perhaps a little indignation would shield his ego.

Head high, she left the room and found Emily sitting on the top step waiting for her.

"Where's Rose?" Lynnette asked.

"She wants to stay in bed this morning," Emily said, starting down the stairs.

Lynnette caught up with her. "Is she ill?"

"Monthly," Emily whispered.

Lynnette accepted that, though it seemed odd that Emily would desert her friend. Perhaps Rose truly desired to be alone. She followed Emily through the kitchen and out the side door. As they crossed the yard, Lynnette found her anticipation building. This could be her last day here, and she was spending it, as much as possible, with Christian.

They stopped outside the double doors. In the shadows of the darker interior, they could make out the moving shapes of men and horses. Lynnette was intrigued. What exactly did they do?

She started forward, but Emily caught her arm. "They're cleaning out the stalls. Let's see the top first."

Emily headed toward the ramp that led to the third level, and Lynnette reluctantly followed.

Christian tightened his grip on the lead ropes and stared after Lynnette. If he wasn't mistaken, those were his clothes she was wearing. He would never see either of those garments in quite the same light again.

"Are they wanting us to saddle horses for them?" Jacob asked, coming to stand beside him.

"Emily wouldn't have hesitated to ask. My guess is they have something else in mind." He tugged on the ropes and started the three patient horses moving again.

Jacob, following with three more horses, called, "Why else would they dress like that?"

"Beats me." Darn little Emily. Trust her to raid his room. And he had left Lynnette's book sitting on his night table. When he had gone in last evening for a clean shirt, he hadn't even thought about it.

They tied the horses to the rails around the stock tank. Christian cranked the windmill's tail into position and hooked up the shaft while Jacob put the pipe that would divert the water to the tank into its position on the spout.

They walked back into the barn to begin cleaning out the stalls. Christian tried to concentrate on his work, but his mind kept drifting to the denim-clad beauty somewhere above him.

Jacob's voice was a welcome distraction. "The spreader wagon's going to be full," he said, tossing a pitchfork-load of old hay into the wagon.

"Maybe your pa…" Feminine voices caught his attention. On the ladder in the center of the barn, Emily was skillfully making her way to the bottom. He left his pitchfork and walked to meet her and discovered Lynnette descending more slowly above him. It was a most intriguing view. One he shouldn't be enjoying.

He looked away quickly, meaning to say something to Emily, only to find that she was already moving across the barn. His eyes were drawn upward again. The tight pants showed him just exactly how slender her legs were, how rounded her little bottom was. He felt his groin tighten and took a hasty step backward.

Four feet from the bottom, her toe slipped off the rung. She hadn't shifted her weight to that foot yet; she might have easily caught herself. These things didn't cross Christian's mind until his hands had already wrapped around her narrow waist.

If she had let go, he could have swung her to the ground...or into his arms. He wasn't sure which. But she didn't let go. She caught her balance, and continued down the last few steps. His hands didn't leave her waist until her foot touched the floor. He stepped back and let her turn around.

"Thanks". She was breathless. The climb down, he supposed.

What was his excuse? He was breathing harder than she was. A smile and a nod was all he could manage in response. She hadn't taken her eyes from his, and the desire to step toward her was almost overwhelming.

"Lynnette," Emily called.

She turned away, and he watched her feminine hips as she joined his sister near where Jacob worked.

"They're almost done," Emily said. "The saddle horses live in these stalls. Every day they're taken out and watered and exercised and their stalls are cleaned."

"And fresh hay is dropped into the stalls from the holes in the ceiling," Jacob provided. "Did Emily show you?"

At Lynnette's nod, Emily added. "We don't want

to be down here when they do that. The dust'll choke you.''

''We'll leave that to Jacob, then,'' Christian suggested, coming forward. ''You ladies can help me exercise the horses.''

Lynnette seemed delighted with the prospect. Seeing her step toward him was almost enough to make him forget what else he needed to say. Almost. He tore his eyes away from her, ignoring his sister's scowl. ''When you're done, Jacob, see if your pa can unload the wagon on the oats.''

''Sure thing.''

He started out of the barn, Lynnette at his side. He didn't know if Emily followed or stayed to harass Jacob. He found himself hoping for the later.

''How can Perry unload the wagon? He can't even walk without the crutch,'' Lynnette asked.

Christian was momentarily startled by the question. He sensed concern for Perry mixed with her curiosity. It was foolish to find such a little thing heartwarming. ''It's a spreader wagon. Other than pulling a lever to tighten the chain, all Perry has to do is ride. It'll chop the…ah…fertilizer and drop it on the field as it goes.''

They had emerged from the barn. He turned to look at her in full sunlight. She was turned toward him, too. He didn't know when they had stopped walking.

''I never thought about what a rancher did with all the barn waste,'' she said.

''We spread it on the cropland.'' He barely kept his mind on what he was saying. ''Most of this land isn't fit to grow crops, but we have a few little fields in the valley.''

Field crops were the farthest things from his mind. The sun gave her skin an almost golden glow. He could have sworn there were golden flecks in her green-brown eyes, as well. He almost stepped toward her to see but caught himself and turned away.

"As Emily said, we have to exercise these horses every day if they aren't ridden." He walked to the tank where the horses were tied. He disconnected the windmill shaft while he talked, glancing up only to be sure she had followed. "The draft horses will take the wagon out, but these other four need to be walked around a bit."

"What about them?" She had walked past the well and was looking down at the lower corral.

"Since they're not kept in the barn they can get their own exercise. They need to be fed, though." He wasn't sure when he had moved to stand beside her. She watched the horses, and he watched her.

"They're beautiful," she said.

"Hmm," he murmured, realizing how dangerous this was. "Do you want to exercise one of the saddle horses?"

She swung around to face him, her face alight with anticipation. "Can I? You'll have to show me what to do."

"Nothing to it." He was ridiculously pleased with himself for thinking of something that made her so happy. He had to work to turn away from her. The lunge line was just inside the barn and he hurried to fetch it, meeting her back near the horses. He picked out the gray gelding and led it farther into the open barnyard.

"This is Trooper." As Lynnette joined him, he switched the lead rope for the thirty-foot lunge line. With one hand on the cheek strap, he dropped the coiled rope on the ground. He rubbed the horse's nose as he watched her face. She was torn between fascination and fright. He drew Trooper one step closer to her. "Get to know him a little."

She reached out a tentative hand and touched the horse's nose. Trooper tossed his head and moved forward, nuzzling her cheek. She jumped back, a startled laugh escaping her lips.

"Hey," he said, pulling the horse away from her. "No kissing on the first date."

She laughed, her eyes twinkling.

"Here," he said, handing her the lunge line. He let go of the halter and stood beside her. "Give him a little more rope." Their hands brushed as he helped her. With one hand covering hers, he moved to stand almost behind her.

Trooper started walking, and Lynnette tensed. "What do I do?"

"Just turn," he said softly, conscious that his lips were only inches from her ear. He guided her in a slow circle, his body nearly pressed against hers. "Trooper knows what to do."

As Trooper picked up speed, he felt her relax. He wanted to move closer, press her backside against his thighs. He tried to distract himself by talking. "Normally I'd do this in the pen, but if you drop the rope, all Trooper's going to do is head for his stall. With any of the other horses I need a whip to get 'em started and keep 'em moving."

"He's beautiful," she said. Her voice trembled a little, but he didn't think she was still afraid.

"I look for any signs of illness or injury as he runs."

"There aren't any, are there?"

"No." He couldn't resist the slightest brush of his cheek against her head. He pretended it was meant to soothe her fears. This was insanity. It wasn't going to make his life as her brother-in-law any easier. He should move away; she didn't need his help with the horse, anyway. They turned in two more slow circles, and still he couldn't bring himself to let her go.

"I'll do one," Emily called.

Christian started at the sound. Lynnette stumbled, and he caught her against him until she regained her balance. "All right, now?" he whispered. "Can you do this alone?"

She nodded hesitantly.

"When you get tired, just pull in the rope." He eased his hand from her, finally stepping away entirely. He left the circle behind the horse and walked to Emily. He told himself he was glad Emily had interrupted, but that didn't explain the loss he felt, the emptiness that made him ache inside.

He got Emily started with the other gelding in the pen, then led the draft horses into the barn and hitched them to the wagon. Stepping outside, he intended to stop Lynnette, but one look at her face made him want to stand back and watch.

She was enthralled. With the horse's beauty? His graceful motion? He wasn't sure. Her lips were parted, her eyes dreamy. He felt a pang of jealousy. What would it be like to put that kind of expression on her face?

He cursed himself. He ought to take a dunk in the stock tank. He had no business thinking about sex when he looked at Lynnette.

He stepped forward, let Trooper run past then joined Lynnette in the center of the circle. "Let's haul him in," he said, helping her gather the lead rope. Trooper trotted toward them and nuzzled Lynnette's shoulder. She wobbled, practically falling into Christian's arms. He grabbed the halter and pulled Trooper away, keeping one arm around Lynnette. "You all right?"

She laughed, "I'm just a little dizzy, I guess." She pushed away from him far too soon, one small hand against his chest. He wanted to take the hand and hold it there, press it against his heart. He did no such thing.

"Trooper's trying to sweep you off your feet," he quipped.

"He did a fine job of it." She rubbed the horse's nose with her fingertips, apparently still hesitant around the animal. "What next?" she asked.

"Now we rub him down and put him away." He led the gelding toward the barn, and she fell into step beside him.

"Is Elayne, the horse Emily mentioned, kept up here?"

"She's in the lower corral with the young stock." He knew he shouldn't encourage her to spend time with him. Hell, he shouldn't even look at her when he answered. She was looking at him with an eager curiosity he found irresistible. "I'll show her to you when we're done."

She smiled. For a second he felt as if he had gotten a glimpse of heaven. More like hell, he decided.

Jacob came to meet them, and they stood aside as Perry drove the spreader wagon out of the barn. "Want me to exercise the mare?" Jacob asked.

Christian glanced toward the pen where Emily was working with the liver chestnut gelding. "Check and see if Emily wants you to relieve her first," he said. "If you work with the mare, don't let her bite you."

Jacob nodded and headed for the pen. As Christian and Lynnette moved on toward the barn, she asked, "The mare bites?"

He shrugged. "Women."

She scowled at him, but her eyes were dancing. "She's the light brown one, right?"

"Dun," he corrected.

"Dun. And the black horse with her at the tank is the one you were riding the other night."

"*Trying* to ride. I'll try again this afternoon."

"Thanks for the warning."

Her smile had vanished, and he wished he hadn't mentioned it. No, he decided, it was just as well. He needed something to put a little distance between them.

At Trooper's stall, Lynnette wasn't content to watch him rub down the horse. She had to do it as well. There was no way to show her without standing next to her, guiding her hand, inhaling the scent of her hair. Trooper got the most thorough rubdown he had experienced in his life.

At one point he heard Emily muttering to herself as she led the other gelding to his stall. She didn't ask for his help so he ignored her. Instead, he gave himself up to this stolen opportunity, reveling in every chance touch or glance. He even allowed himself to imagine, just for the moment, that she was feeling the same attraction he felt, that it was desire that brought her breath in little puffs between parted lips, that it was love that gave her eyes their shine.

When he heard Emily leave the other gelding, he knew it was time to quit. "Now you're an expert," he said softly, taking the brush from her hand.

She turned her face up and smiled at him. He thought her eyes were misty, but she turned away too quickly to be sure.

"I should go in," she said.

"Wait." It was out of his mouth before he even thought. "I wanted you to see Elayne. Besides, your tour of the barn isn't over until you've seen the lowest level."

She seemed reluctant, her judgment being better than his, he thought. Still she relented. He led her to a ladder in the corner of the barn and started down. He enjoyed the view once again as she climbed down after him. He more than half hoped she would slip and let him catch her.

He showed her through the isolation stalls that occupied about half of the lowest level. At the outside wall he opened a window by raising the hinged panel and fastening it to the hook overhead. From here they could watch the horses in the corral.

"The other half of this level is open shelter," he explained as she came to lean on the sill beside him. "The black there. That's Elayne."

"She's beautiful. Are you going to break all these horses? There's more than a dozen."

"Nineteen. But I won't break them all. Some buyers prefer to break their own. Besides, there are three new colts and their mamas. I can leave them alone for a while. There are only three horses old enough to start real training. I'll probably start breaking them this summer."

"When you've broken the stallion."

It was on the tip of his tongue to say, "Or he's broken me." Considering her opinion of his methods, she wouldn't think it was funny. "I may let him have his way," he said instead. "I keep thinking he'd make a great mount, but he may be more stubborn than I am."

"What will happen to him if you give up?"

A little colt had noticed their presence and came closer to investigate. He watched Lynnette's profile as she reached a hand toward the baby.

"We'll keep him for stud." This was not considered a proper discussion for mixed company, but she didn't seem horrified.

"Maybe he knows that's the option," she said, turning her grin from the colt to him. One eyebrow danced upward. "And that's why he's so stubborn."

He had no ready quip for that. He watched her turn back to the colt that had taken one more hesitant step forward.

They heard Emily's long call from near the house. "I better go," Lynnette said.

Christian unhooked the panel and lowered it back into place. "We can get out here," he said. He led her out a door and up a path between the corral and the windmill.

He stopped and watched Lynnette and Emily walk toward each other. Lynnette turned once to look at him over her shoulder. He raised his hand in a brief wave. He felt a loss as acute as if she had just ridden out of his life.

"I wondered where you were," Emily said.

"Christian was showing me the horses in the lower corral," Lynnette answered, though she knew that was probably obvious.

"I wanted to let you know I was going in. I checked, and Rose is through…uh…napping."

"I'm sure she'll be glad for your company again. Thanks for showing me through the barn."

Emily nodded. "I'll see you at lunch." She turned and trotted toward the house.

Lynnette watched her go. She didn't want to follow. It was still a couple of hours before lunchtime. But she had no real excuse to stay outside. She had seen all of the barn and had imposed on Christian more than she had any right to. Still it was too nice a day, and she was filled with too much tension to want to return to her room.

She turned around slowly and found Christian standing where she had left him a moment before. She was far enough away that his face was hard to read, but she imagined it reflected some deep sorrow—directed toward Emily, she supposed.

He turned quickly and moved to the stallion that

still waited at the tank. The horse nuzzled against him, and he rubbed the sleek black neck affectionately.

She didn't know when she started moving, but she found herself standing near enough to touch the stallion. "He doesn't seem wild," she said.

Christian barely glanced at her. There was a distance between them now that hadn't been there before. "He's gentled down a lot during the past week," he said.

His eyes were on the lead rope as he untied it. The horse nudged his shoulder hard enough to make him stumble forward. He caught the halter in one hand and worked on the rope with the other. The horse tossed his head, trying to shake off the hand.

Lynnette stepped back, alarmed at the horse's behavior. "Perhaps I'm making him nervous," she said. "I think I'll take a quick walk before lunch. I won't go far."

She started toward the path that skirted the far side of the barn. She could hear Christian speaking softly to the horse, "Sure, now you're my best friend."

It reminded her of his voice close to her ear as he instructed her and calmed her fears. He had stood so close she had been afraid her knees would buckle. They had, in fact, at one point, and she had fallen into his arms.

Her knees trembled now as she walk faster, needing to burn off the energy that coiled inside her. Dear Lord! While they had rubbed down the horse, she had pretended that his tone was meant for her, his soft words were endearments whispered in her ears. She had never wanted anyone to touch her the way she wanted Christian to. She wanted his gentle hands to slide over every part of her.

When the buildings were no longer in sight behind her, she crumbled to the ground, burying her face in her hands as she tried to catch her breath. She had felt his breath fan against her cheek. Each brush of his arm against her shoulder or his thigh against her leg had fed the fire inside her.

And they hadn't all been accidental touches. She had actively worked at leaning into him, moving subtly against him. And he hadn't moved away from her touch. In fact, she thought she had seen an answering fire in his eyes when he looked at her. She had convinced herself that he felt it, too.

Now she was ashamed. She had promised herself she wouldn't let Christian know about her feelings. She wouldn't complicate his life when there was no hope for them. But deep in her selfish heart, she wanted to know that he loved her, too.

She wrapped her arms around her legs and rested her chin on her knees. Had she imagined the warmth in his gaze? Had his attentiveness been mere politeness? Away from him, that was easy to believe. Did her love completely blind her to everything except what she wanted to see?

She got to her feet and dusted off the denim pants. She should go back. She would need to get cleaned up before Arlen saw her. A bath would probably be a good idea so he didn't detect the scent of sunshine and horses on her skin. She closed her eyes and inhaled deeply, letting a smile curve her lips. She smelled like Christian. He had a scent all his own, and she had been close enough to detect it. The memory of it was enough to make her dizzy.

She opened her eyes, resolving to get control of herself. She would go back and get ready for lunch. Somehow she would act as if nothing unusual had happened. And she absolutely had to talk to Arlen this afternoon.

Lynnette tried to still her screaming nerves as she came down the stairs for lunch. She was clean and fresh; Arlen could have no complaints. She had even washed her hair, afraid that it might have absorbed too much outdoor scent. In the interest of saving time, and cooling her blood, she hadn't heated the water. As she dressed, the memories of Christian seemed to warm her more than sufficiently.

It was, of course, Christian she worried about seeing. What did he think of her behavior this morning? Had she flirted with him? She couldn't even remember what looks she might have given him. She remembered every detail on his part, but not her own.

All but Arlen had assembled when she entered the dining room. Upon seeing her, Hugh directed everyone to their chairs. "Arlen asked for a tray in the study," he said.

In moments the meal was begun. She found herself next to Christian again. He had brought in all the outdoor scents, filling her with remembered feelings. She tried to shove them aside, to save them until she was alone.

She had no interest in conversation, though she tried to respond when spoken to. Emily was talkative as usual, describing how hard she had worked this morning. Rose seemed preoccupied, but Lynnette assumed she still wasn't feeling well.

Christian, when she dared to glance in his direction, seemed lost in thought. She wished she could read his mind. She thanked God he couldn't read hers. He ate quickly and excused himself, as always taking his dishes with him to the kitchen.

Once he was gone, she had no desire to stay. "I believe I'll check on Arlen," she said. Hugh excused her, and she rose to leave. As she came around the table, she caught a glimpse of the girls' faces. Emily scowled, and Rose looked disappointed.

They knew! They knew about her attraction to Christian. She hadn't been able to hide it. Emily must hate her for betraying one brother with the other. And Rose. Poor Rose was probably in love with Christian herself. At least those two people would be glad to see her go.

At the door to the study, she steeled herself and knocked. There was a long pause before Arlen finally answered.

He swung the door open. "Lynnette." He seemed surprised to see her.

His reaction threw her. "I came...ah...to see if you needed anything." She nodded toward the tray on the edge of the desk.

"No, no, I'm fine."

She took a step into the room, though he didn't invite her. She had to collect herself. "Arlen, I need to talk to you."

"Oh, dear. I'm sorry. I did promise we would spend

the afternoon together. But I got so little done this morning. There were...distractions. I need to study these things undisturbed.''

"I understand." She didn't want to spoil everything for him next week. Her refusal to marry him would surely be more than a distraction. She would have to wait until his studying was done and hope it didn't ruin his concentration at the actual meetings. "I'll leave you alone then," she said.

"Thank you, darling." She had started out the door when he stopped her. "I almost forgot. I picked these up for you yesterday." He lifted a small stack of letters off the desk and brought them to her.

She nodded her thanks and left the room. When the door was closed behind her, she looked down at the letters, not wanting to believe what she thought she had glimpsed. The upper left-hand corner of the top letter said "Julian Taggart."

Chapter Thirteen

Dearest Lynnette,

It seems you've run away from me. Imagine my disappointment to call and find the house deserted. And I thought we understood each other. But no matter. I've finally found you. Did you really think I wouldn't? Come back to me, little one. Don't make me come and get you. You should never have tried to keep *secrets* from me.

With undying love,
Julian Taggart

P.S. I long to fold you in my arms and swear my eternal love.

Lynnette's hands trembled as she refolded the letter. The last was a quote from *Passion's Secret*. He knew, and he had found her. He was going to cause some sort of trouble. It didn't matter. She would be leaving soon, though she didn't know where, certainly not back to Topeka. Not now.

There were two more letters. One from Amanda and

another from Taggart, posted four days after the first. She couldn't bring herself to open his second letter. She broke the seal on Amanda's instead.

Amanda, bless her, had written a cheerful letter full of trivialities. She had attended this tea and that cotillion. And at the end of the letter, the best news possible. She was expecting a child.

Lynnette read the letter through again, using it to block out the other. She was delighted for her friend. Romantic, frivolous Amanda with a little child! That was something she dearly wanted to see.

But would she? Would she ever dare visit her friend? Had Taggart found her through Amanda?

She tossed the letter on the bed beside the others and moved to the balcony. She opened the door and stepped through the curtains, hoping the warm, fresh air would revive her. Instead, her eyes were drawn immediately to the pen below. Christian sat atop the bucking stallion. But only for a moment. He fell and hit the ground with what seemed like terrible force.

She covered her mouth to stop the gasp. Jake watched from the fence, and Christian was already coming to his feet. She turned away. This was the last thing she wanted to watch now.

Inside the room, with the curtains billowing at her back, she eyed the letters. She would have to read Taggart's second letter eventually. She walked to the bed and lifted it. She held it for a moment before breaking the seal, and read.

Dearest Lynnette,
I find myself becoming angry when I think of

how you deceived me. I have to fight to control my temper. I asked you nicely to come back. I waited for days but heard nothing! Do you think I will stand this treatment? You know how much I love you. You declared your passion for me in a book the whole world can read, then ran away from me. I will not let you get away.

My everlasting love, the real Robert.

P.S. Robert laid his lover on the bed and ran a finger over the bloodless lips and gazed into her staring eyes. 'Now we will always be together.'

Lynnette dropped the letter, clasping her hands to her mouth to stifle a sob. *Blood-red* was what she had written. *Starry eyes*. Not bloodless and staring! Taggart's Robert had killed his lover!

Panic washed over her, and she scrambled to retrieve the letter from the floor, crumpling it in her hands. She snatched up the other, tearing Amanda's in her effort to release it. Shaking, she ran to the fireplace and tossed them on the cold hearth. Searching frantically, she found a jar of matches on the narrow mantel. She knelt and opened the jar, spilling the matches on the floor.

She grabbed one and struck it hard against the stone hearth. It snapped in two, skinning her fingertips. Her hands were so cold she barely felt it. The next match flared, and she held it to a corner of a letter. It caught, and she tossed the match in the center of the wadded pile. A second tiny blaze started there. Still panicking, she struck a second match and lit another corner. Then a third. Finally she stared at the burning paper, a fourth burning match in her hand and no place left to light with it. She dropped the match into the flame just as it burned her finger.

She stuck the fingers in her mouth, tasting sulfur and blood. She watched until every particle of the letters was consumed. The pile of black ashes was too much for her to stand. With the hearth broom, she scattered them over the hearth, whisking them into the far corners.

Her hands shook as she gathered up the scattered matches and placed the jar back on the mantel. She walked slowly to the bed. Amanda's letter still lay there, a two-inch tear on a crease. She lifted the letter gently and folded it. Clutching it to her heart, she fell across the bed, fighting tears.

She had to leave. She couldn't tell anyone where she was going, not Amanda and not Christian.

The stallion stood as sweet as you please for about two minutes, just enough time for Christian to imagine he was making progress, but not enough to put him off guard. He was determined to stay on this time. Perhaps that was why the stallion tried a new tactic. He stayed so close to the fence that Christian wondered if they would both go through it. Neither one did, but Christian hit it so hard he was stunned for a moment.

Jake was by his side before his vision cleared. "You all right, boss?"

Christian swore. The stallion stood watching from the far side of the pen. "Yeah, I'm all right. Help me up."

"Are you sure nothing's broken?" Jake asked as he helped him to his feet.

Christian flexed his arms and rolled his shoulders, then took a deep breath, feeling his ribs. "No, I'm fine."

"You lost all the skin off your shoulder, boss," Jake said, lifting a piece of torn shirt. "You better let Ma clean you up."

"Damn," he muttered, trying to twist enough to see the damage. He could feel his neck and shoulder stiffening up. Now that he was aware of the injury, it stung like the devil. "Let's get the saddle off him and rub him down."

In the barn, Jake removed the saddle while Christian stood at the horse's head, ensuring his cooperation. The stallion was almost affectionate now that he had won. Again. Once Christian was sure that the horse wouldn't give Jake any trouble, he headed for the kitchen to find Martha.

He suffered through her doctoring and lecture, which together amounted to mothering, kissed her on the cheek and went upstairs for a clean shirt. On the landing he heard voices from Emily's room, but could sense Lynnette's presence in her own. He stood for a moment looking toward her door, longing to go to her. But there was nothing he could possibly say.

In his room, he eased a clean shirt over the bandage Martha had tied around him, tucked it in and was buttoning it as he opened the door.

Lynnette's door came open at nearly the same moment. He froze when he saw her. Even in the dim light, he could see she was upset. Pain, sorrow, fear seemed to compete on her beautiful features.

His fingers were too clumsy to manage the buttons, and he left them undone and went to her, was drawn to her. "Lynnette," he whispered. "Are you all right?"

"Yes, I..." She looked down, back into her room, anywhere but at him. "I was going for a walk."

Before he could stop himself, he took her chin and turned her face toward him. Her skin seemed wonderfully warm against his fingers. "You're upset," he said.

She licked her lips. Light from the windows in her room found the shine of moisture left by her tongue. He felt himself growing hard, and cursed silently. She was unhappy, and he was thinking of sex. Again. It was not his place, but still he whispered, "Please tell me what's wrong."

"It's nothing really." She struggled for breath. "Letters. I mean, I got some letters, and there was bad news."

He wasn't sure he believed her. "I'm sorry," he said softly. "Is there anything I can do?"

"No. I was going to take a walk. I'll be fine."

He realized his hand was still under her chin, his thumb less than an inch away from rubbing her lips. But the anguish in her eyes made it impossible to pull away. "You have a family now. You don't have to bear this alone."

Her eyes misted over. Whatever it was, he had managed to make it worse. He bent and brushed his lips against her forehead in what he hoped—pretended—

was a brotherly kiss. ''I'm sorry,'' he said and backed away.

With one furtive glance at his face, she brushed past him and practically ran down the stairs.

At dinner Emily decided this was the most miserable group of people that ever lived. She knew why Rose picked sadly at her food. She had spent the morning being rejected by the man she loved and the afternoon reliving it—over and over again. Arlen was straight across from her now so she never once looked up from her plate.

But Arlen wasn't eating either. Or talking. Did he spare poor Rose a single thought? It seemed as though he glanced at her once in a while, but he glanced at Lynnette sometimes, too. Of course, Arlen could be preoccupied with his precious politics.

Christian, at the end of the table, acted for all the world as she did when she knew she had done something wrong and would soon be in terrible trouble. She couldn't imagine Christian doing anything wrong, though. He was a grown man and could do as he pleased, couldn't he?

Lynnette seemed the most miserable. She alone had offered an explanation of sorts. Arlen had brought her letters from town, and one of them contained some bad news. She hadn't shared what that bad news was, so maybe she was lying. Maybe she had found out about Rose flirting with Arlen, and she had decided to be heartbroken over the whole thing. Had Arlen been dumb enough to tell her? Maybe a woman would know something like that.

Her father was either completely blind, or a marvelous actor. He ate enthusiastically and asked questions of everyone, receiving short, curt answers most of the time. *She* was forced to do more than her share of the talking. Normally that didn't bother her, but she was too angry at everyone else.

Fortunately, no one cared to linger. Arlen was the first to excuse himself. Lynnette seemed about to ask him something but changed her mind. Maybe she had decided not to speak to him and had nearly forgotten.

Christian left next, heading outside through the kitchen. Lynnette said she was tired from her walk and went off to bed. Rose asked to be excused and nearly ran up the stairs. Her father said something about it being a fine night for reading on the balcony and went up to his room.

She was the youngest one here and the *only* one who was acting at all grown-up!

Christian had just gotten to the barn after breakfast when Lynnette appeared in the doorway. He watched her as she let her eyes adjust to the relative darkness. She was dressed in his pants and shirt again, and memories flooded his senses. He moved toward her, uncertain what he planned to do or say until he stood beside her. "Do you want to exercise the horses again?" he asked.

"I want to ride one, if I may." Had he imagined a quiver in her voice?

He had moved too close to her; one step, and he could have taken her into his arms. He needed distance, emotional and physical. He backed off a step. "You should ask Arlen."

She moved toward him. "Arlen doesn't think I need to learn to ride. But Arlen and I—"

He raised a hand and stopped her. "You have to leave me out of any problems you're having with my brother. I don't want to listen to your complaints about him." *I'm too likely to want to comfort you.*

"I understand," she said. "But I'm going to leave soon, and I've never ridden."

He didn't want to risk it. He couldn't spend any more time with her or his heart would be broken beyond repair.

"Please," she whispered.

Her face was turned up to his, looking vulnerable in the soft light. "Wait here. I'll saddle the horses."

He led Trooper from his stall and was cinching Emily's saddle into place when Jake joined him. "Are you taking the ladies for a ride?" Jake asked.

"One of them," Christian answered.

Jake looked curious but didn't ask any more questions. He set about beginning the chores.

Christian saddled the mare, then led the gelding toward Lynnette. "You remember Trooper." At her nod, he dropped the reins and moved to stand just forward of the saddle.

He didn't have to coax Lynnette to join him. She stepped up to the horse, but stopped. The scent of soap in her hair filled his lungs. She turned uncertain eyes toward him, and he remembered where he was. "Grab the saddle horn," he instructed. "Put your left knee in my hands. When you're in the air, throw your right leg over the saddle. Got that?"

She nodded, looking even more uncertain.

"Easy as pie," he assured her. He bent a little. With the slightest lift of her leg, he took her calf and tossed her into the saddle. She gasped, then looked extremely pleased. "I told you," he said.

He adjusted the stirrups while she sat clinging to the saddle horn. "Just sit tight for a minute," he said, giving Trooper's neck a pat. As long as the reins were on the ground, he would stay put. Probably.

The mare had to do her usual dance step with a few sideways jumps before she decided to behave. He rode her around in front of Lynnette. Gathering up Trooper's reins, he urged the mare forward until the horses were side by side and he was facing Lynnette. With one hand, he brought the reins to either side of Trooper's head, slid his hand to the proper length of rein and held them for her. She looked at them. "You have to let go of the saddle horn."

She did, with the right hand at least, and took the reins. He closed his hand over hers. Her fingers seemed so tiny. He held her hand first to one side then the other, showing her how the reins turned the horse's head. "Right, left. Back toward you is stop."

She pulled the reins toward her, and Trooper stepped back. She immediately eased up. "What's go?" she asked.

"Well, go could be a problem since you're not wearing spurs. I'll ride on out of the barn, and you kick him just as hard as you can."

He reined the mare back away from Trooper and

turned her. Outside the barn he stopped and turned again. Whether Lynnette's heels had made any impression or not, Trooper had gotten the idea. He came trotting out of the barn.

Christian put the mare into a walk, and Trooper slowed his pace to fall into step beside them. Lynnette relaxed quickly. They rode around the barn and along the path toward the meadow.

"This is wonderful," she said.

He turned to her, and she smiled. He found himself smiling back. "I'm glad you enjoy it."

"I suppose you're so used to this—" she made a quick gesture that encompassed their surroundings "—that it seems common."

He shook his head. "Never common exactly. I'm used to it, I guess. But once in a while I'm struck with how beautiful it is, how much I love the ranch, the horses, the life here."

"I think I can understand that," she said.

She wasn't just saying it. She truly believed she understood. He turned away quickly, kicking the mare ahead so they could go single file along a narrow place in the path. The first woman who understood, who might learn to love the ranch the way he did, was out of reach.

She had said she was leaving soon. Had she meant she was going to Topeka with Arlen next week? Something about the way she had said it made it sound as if she wasn't coming back. At the time he had been more interested in the plea in her eyes and his own inability to resist temptation. Now he had to know.

When the path widened he dropped back to ride beside her again. "When are you leaving?"

"Possibly this afternoon."

He turned away. It wasn't any of his business. He wanted to ask if she was coming back, but didn't know how to keep from showing how much he would miss her.

The path forked, and he took them down the slope toward the little stream. There he stopped the mare and loosened the reins, letting her have a drink. Lynnette followed his example.

"I'll never forget this place," she said softly.

She didn't sound like someone who was going away for a week. It sounded like forever. Suddenly losing her completely seemed more unbearable than losing her to Arlen. He knew he should mind his own business, but he had to know what she was planning. He tried to think of how to ask without giving himself away.

When the horses had drunk enough, they splashed across the stream and started up the narrow path that wandered up the hill then topped out in a high meadow. They rode side by side in silence until they came to the rocky summit of the hill.

He swung off the mare and tied her reins to a branch of a gnarled pine tree. He moved to Lynnette's side to help her down. She was attempting to dismount by herself but hadn't kicked her left foot out of the stirrup. He caught her before she fell.

When she turned to face him he could see tears in her eyes. His first thought was that the ride had been too long for her. He caught her shoulders, afraid she might be about to fall.

She seemed to take strength from his touch and fought off the tears. "I'm sorry," she said. "I'm all right now."

He let her go, and she turned toward the rocks. She found a place to sit and he joined her, keeping a safe distance between them. "I thought you were going to spend the whole summer," he said finally. "I thought you would plan the wedding—"

"I'm calling off the wedding."

He absorbed that in silence. It explained yesterday, he supposed. She and Arlen had barely spoken to each other at the table. There had been tears in her eyes when he had met her on the stairs. A letter with bad news had no doubt been a quick lie to explain her sorrow. Arlen must have done something to disappoint her. He wasn't sure he wanted to know.

Still, if it was something like Arlen's efforts to seduce her, perhaps he could take the blame and right things between them. It was difficult, but he finally asked, "Why?"

She smiled sadly. "I thought I was supposed to leave you out of our problems."

"That was before I knew it was this serious. You've both really decided it's over?"

"I have. Arlen doesn't know."

He didn't know when he moved closer to her, but he found himself inches away from putting his arm around her shoulder. He stopped himself. "What did he do?"

She sighed. "It's not anything he did. I'm just not right for him."

"He seems to think you are."

"He thinks I'm someone I'm not. He created an idea of a perfect wife, and he's trying to shove me into it. It's not a good fit." She glanced at him, measuring his understanding. He held his tongue. It seemed a betrayal of his brother to agree with her, but he did.

In a moment she gazed off across the prairie and continued. "It's not all Arlen's fault. When I first met him I thought I could become whatever he wanted. I was wrong. And I'm not in love with him." She turned to him and whispered, "I'm in love with you."

All the air had been knocked out of his lungs. She was in love with him. Had his own love for her made it happen? Had he stolen his brother's woman simply by wanting her?

He hadn't found his voice yet when she stood, pacing nervously in front of him. "I'm sorry. I swore I wasn't going to tell you, and then I blurted it out. It wasn't at all fair, of me. I don't want you to feel any obligation, and you're not to blame for what's happened between Arlen and me. It wouldn't have worked anyway. I'm just not his china doll. I *want* to ride horses. I don't *care* if I have ink on my fingers. I—"

How long she would have babbled away, he didn't know. He listened to all he could stand before he stepped in front of her, taking her by the shoulders. "I'm glad you told me."

Tears sprang to her eyes, and he folded his arms

around her. ''Shhh,'' he whispered. ''It'll be all right.''

She shook her head, and he felt her damp cheek brush dangerously close to his lips. ''Shhh,'' he whispered again. It was the most natural thing in the world to kiss that cheek, to kiss away the tears. Suddenly her face was in his hands, and his lips had moved downward, tracing a trail to her mouth.

He took her mouth then, and she let him. He felt her strain upward to meet him, felt her tremble in his arms. Her lips parted with the barest pressure from his tongue, and he tasted her sweetness until he was trembling too.

He raised his head and sucked cooling air into his lungs. When she made a move to leave his arms he found he wasn't ready to let her go. ''Please,'' he choked out. ''Let me hold you till my heart stops pounding.''

She turned her head and rested it on his chest. ''Mine never will as long as you're this close,'' she said.

''Maybe I should hold you forever.''

She lifted her head and gave him a sad little smile. ''We better go back,'' she said.

He nodded and reluctantly let her go. He helped her onto Trooper and swung onto the mare's back, impatiently suffering through her usual antics. They rode back to the ranch in near silence. When they stopped at the stream, he watched her look carefully around as if memorizing every detail. He in turn tried to memorize every detail of her face.

As they came around the barn, Arlen left the house carrying a carpetbag. He stopped, his face the picture of disbelief, then hurried toward them. Christian swung off the mare and helped Lynnette down. He stood, holding both horses, and watched her walk toward Arlen. Her back, and cute little backside, were to him. He should leave them alone to talk. He needed to take care of the horses. He didn't move.

"Where on earth did you get that outfit?"

If she was startled by the rebuke, her voice didn't show it. "Emily found them for me. That was my first time on a horse, Arlen." He imagined her forcing a smile.

"And last, I hope."

"Arlen, I need to talk to you."

"I'm sorry, darling. I need to be going." He walked past her toward the barn.

She followed close behind. "You're leaving again?"

"I'm sorry. Didn't I tell you? There's a city hall dedication and a founder's day celebration I want to take in this weekend. I'll go directly to Topeka from there."

"But Arlen, I need to talk to you."

"I'm sorry, sweetheart." He turned and kissed her cheek. "Change out of that awful outfit before someone sees you looking like...like..."

"Like what, little brother? A rancher?" Christian led the horses past them both and into the barn. He had listened to more than he should. But what had he expected to accomplish with that last remark? Start a fight with his brother?

He led the horses into their stalls. Jake, he noticed, had hitched the buggy for Arlen. Arlen climbed aboard and left the barn without another word to either of them. When he looked, Lynnette was gone.

Chapter Fourteen

It had been a long day. Lynnette had kept to herself as much as possible. The need to escape before Taggart came for her warred with her desire to stay to be near Christian.

But Arlen had taken the decision out of her hands by leaving again. She had to wait until he returned. Calling off a wedding wasn't something she could do in a letter, or so she convinced herself. It was easy to let thoughts of Christian overshadow everything else, even Taggart's threat.

Dressed in her nightgown with her robe wrapped around her, she waited until the house was quiet. She had heard the girls retire to Emily's room and later Hugh's door close behind him. Christian had not come in from the barn.

She opened her door slowly and eased it closed behind her. She walked cautiously down the stairs, through the living room and out the back door.

The barn was a black shape against the deep gray sky. She moved toward it carefully, her eyes gradually adjusting to the dark. She felt along the rough wood for the handle and slid the door open a couple of feet.

If Christian was here doing the evening chores, why was it dark? Had he returned to the house without her knowing? She stepped inside cautiously.

"Christian?" she called softly.

Only the peaceful sounds of insects and shuffling hooves broke the silence. Maybe that was for the best. Maybe she should run back to her room and be grateful she had missed her chance to make a fool of herself.

She had started to turn when a light flared, then grew into the steady glow of a lantern. She could see Christian holding it as he came toward her from the depths of the barn. He wore a pair of denim pants. A white bandage crisscrossed his chest.

"What are you doing here?" he asked as he approached.

"I came looking for you," she whispered.

He hung the lantern on a nail high on a post and reached past her, sliding the door closed. He stood close, watching her.

"What happened?" She reached out to touch the bandage.

"Just a scrape," he said, catching her hand. "Most of this is Martha's way of keeping the bandage on." He let her hand go. Reluctantly, she thought. "You shouldn't be here," he said.

She took a deep breath. "I had to come." This was going to be harder than she realized. She turned and paced, staying just inside the circle of light from the lantern. Her thick braid had swung over her shoulder, and she toyed with the end.

"I love you," she began. "I told you that this morning. I'm going to be leaving soon, and I want..." She swallowed. She hadn't considered the humiliation if he refused. She gathered her courage and turned back to face him, tossing the braid behind her back. "I want to make love to you."

He remained silent, and she added, "I have reason to believe you care for me as well, don't I?"

"Yes, of course." He walked toward her and gathered her into his arms. "It's beyond simple caring. I love you, too. It breaks my heart every time you say you're going to leave."

"But I have to," she murmured against his shoulder.

He stroked her hair. "Can't you leave Arlen without leaving me as well?"

She shook her head. "No. Can't you see what it would do to your family if Arlen knew I left him for you?"

He sighed, and she looked up at him. "We only have until Arlen comes home. Let's spend it together, making love."

"You don't know what you're asking."

She pulled out of his arms. "Of course I do. I've read...lots of things."

She lifted her chin. She was serious.

He pulled her back into his arms. "And to think all I have to go by is *Passion's Secret*."

She tried to struggle free, but he held her tight.

"That's not what I mean, sweetheart. It's hard enough to think of you leaving now. If we made love..."

"But if I go without giving you my love, and experiencing yours, I'll always regret it."

"I know," he whispered, kissing the top of her head. "But what if there's a child? I couldn't do that to you."

She felt her eyes fill with tears. "I wouldn't mind."

He hugged her closer for a moment, then drew her away. "There are ways of loving without risking a child."

She assumed he meant one of the methods women used to prevent pregnancy, but from what she had read they weren't always reliable or even safe. "But I don't have—"

"Do you trust me?"

She nodded.

He let her go and turned to lift the lantern from the nail, muttering, "I hope I can trust myself."

He took her hand and led her farther into the barn. A door stood open, and he drew her into a room. It smelled of leather and was, in fact, filled with saddles and all manner of harnesses and halters. There was also a narrow bunk in one corner, its tangled blanket suggesting a recent occupant.

"You sleep out here?" she asked, watching him place the lantern on a worktable.

He turned to her and nodded. "I called out to you once in my sleep. I couldn't risk doing that with Arlen beside me."

"But tonight," she protested, "Arlen is gone."

"And you would be in the next room. After this

morning, I knew I wouldn't be able to sleep that near you.''

She smiled, and he walked slowly toward her. Nervousness or excitement, she wasn't sure which, produced butterflies in her stomach as he approached. He took her gently by the shoulders and leaned down to kiss her. His lips seemed to quiet the trembling and change it instead to a liquid fire. The heat diffused through her limbs, leaving a hunger that sank lower, pooling at the core of her womanhood.

When Christian raised his head, she stared at him in awe, gasping for breath. Nothing Arlen had done had affected her in any way similar. ''Is this passion?'' she breathed.

The barest smile touched his lips. He ran a cool finger over her fevered cheek. ''This is passion,'' he murmured. ''Or the beginning of it.''

She stood still, reveling in the sensations and his promise, as he slowly loosened the tie that held her robe. He lifted the garment from her shoulder and let it drop to the floor. She trembled though she wasn't cold.

He pulled her flush against his chest as his lips sought hers again. Her nipples sprang to life as the heat from his bare skin penetrated the thin cotton of her gown. His hands cupped her bottom, lifting her firmly against his frame. She knew enough to realize the ridge that pressed against her belly was his manhood. She moaned deep in her throat.

When he ended the kiss, she brought her hands to the fasteners of his pants. Her curiosity was almost as great as her desire. His hands rested on her shoulders, his breath coming fast and shallow in her ear. He was as excited as she was. The knowledge made her hands tremble.

The first button finally slipped free. Her fingers felt the heat of his body as she moved to the next. It gave way more quickly than the first and the third and last made her feel like an expert. Still his white cotton smallclothes provided one last barrier. She groaned her frustration.

With a chuckle he backed up a step, slipping out of the pants and out of the undergarment. He stood before her, his perfection marred only by the strips of white cloth across his chest. Her eyes were drawn to his manhood, and she hoped she would be allowed to test its texture.

He came to her, untied the ribbons at her throat and slid the last barrier off her shoulders. He took a moment to gaze at her as she had at him. "You're even more beautiful than I imagined," he said huskily.

It was the best compliment she had ever heard. "You've imagined me?" she asked, smiling. "Naked?"

He grinned and quirked a brow wickedly. "You'd blush at all the things I've imagined."

"I never blush," she protested, laughing. "Tell me."

He scooped her into his arms. "Better yet, let me show you." He carried her to the bunk and laid her down, stretching out beside her. Propped up on his elbow, he cupped her breast, caressing the hardened nipple.

She threw back her head and groaned. "Did I faint in your imagination?" she whispered.

He chuckled softly. "No, and you won't faint now, either. Think of what you would miss."

As his hand left her breast to caress downward, his mouth took its place. She had thought the touch of his fingers on her sensitive nipple was delicious but his tongue was almost overwhelming. Her whole body was a mass of sensations, spiraling through her loins, flowing through her limbs. And a spot in her privates she had barely been aware of ached to be touched.

He raised his head, and she felt cool air pucker the moist nipple still tighter. He was drawing slow circles on her belly, circles that gradually worked lower until she felt his fingers snag her hair as they passed.

"Look at me," he whispered.

She hadn't realized her eyes were closed. She opened them a crack and saw his face above her, framed by his hair. She smiled and reached up to brush his hair aside so the light would shine on his face. "I love you," she whispered.

His eyes were smoky gray, his smile so gentle and loving it made her heart lurch. "Trust me," he whispered.

She nodded, pulling him down to kiss her. His lips were hungry now, demanding. His tongue plunged into her mouth. But the kiss didn't last long enough to suit her. He drew away and hovered above her, watching.

She started to protest, but at that moment his fingers dipped into the moist folds of her femininity. She gasped. She found herself spreading her legs to allow him better access. She thought perhaps she shouldn't. She had no idea what she was supposed to do, but her head wasn't clear enough to ask.

"Relax," he coaxed. "Ride the feelings, don't fight them."

His fingers found the secret spot and rubbed it, satisfying and tormenting at the same time. She felt her body tense as something undefinable built inside. She heard him whisper her name. Suddenly that something seemed to burst, flooding her with a pulsing energy followed by a warm soothing calm.

She lay relaxed to the point of lethargy, feeling the subsiding pulses against his hand. She wished his fingers were deeper inside, closer to the heart of the pulses. With a flash of insight, she realized why they were not; he had left her, technically at least, a virgin. She was warmed by his thoughtfulness even as she felt a pang of disappointment. She wasn't his as completely as she wished to be.

She opened her eyes to find him smiling down at her. "Was that what you expected, sweetheart?"

She tried to laugh but barely had the energy. "I think you know it wasn't. It was wonderful for me, but what about you?"

He grinned ruefully. "I can take care of myself later."

She rolled toward him, finding her strength was returning quickly. "But let me. I mean, if you can do this for me, surely I can…well…do something for you."

He gave a breathless laugh. "It won't take much."

"Let me," she pleaded. She reached down to touch

his shaft where it rested, stiff and hot against her leg. He groaned, and she thought perhaps she had done the wrong thing. "Please," she whispered, brushing his hair away from his face and pressing a kiss on his cheek. "Let me make you feel as good as you made me feel. Tell me what to do."

He moaned again, letting his head drop to the pillow. "It's hopeless to resist you."

He was lying almost flat on his back, and she knelt beside him. "What should I do?"

He laughed. "Touch anything that looks interesting," he suggested.

"Anything?" She had tried to sound seductive, but it was ruined by the slightest of tremors. "I've always thought your lower lip was interesting." She had meant to trace her tongue over it, but when she tried, he pulled her down for a searing kiss. She rose slowly, stunned that desire was welling inside her again.

She turned her attention lower and found one flat nipple that wasn't covered by Martha's bandage. She bent and kissed it, then sucked it as he had hers, searching with her fingers for the other beneath the soft cloth.

When she raised her head she discovered he had slipped the ribbon from the end of her braid and was carefully running his fingers through her hair, removing the plaits an inch at a time. She expected to find a teasing grin on his face. What she saw instead made her heart pound.

His eyes were dark, almost glazed. His teeth were clinched between parted lips. He took her face in his hands, burrowing his fingers deep in her hair, and pulled her down for another hot, hungry kiss. "Touch me," he pleaded almost against her lips. "I can't take any more."

He released her head and took her hands, guiding them to his swollen member. It was surprisingly hot and hard, yet exquisitely silky at the same time. With his hands guiding her, she stroked the length of him. In only a moment, he uttered a low groan and the member pulsed, then erupted. White cream spattered his belly and ran down her fingers.

She stared in fascination. The once hard shaft softened in her hands, relaxed and spent as her whole body had been only minutes before. She hadn't realized his hands were no longer on hers until he tried to give her a cloth. Reluctantly, and gently, she let him go. She wiped the seed from her fingers and from his belly as well.

"I don't suppose that's something every woman gets to see."

"Did it shock you?" He sounded half-asleep.

She smiled fondly. "It thrilled me," she whispered. She wanted to rest her head on his shoulder, but she wasn't sure which part of the bandage covered the scrape. Instead she stretched out beside him, wrapping his arm around her.

His breathing turned slow and even, and she guessed he was asleep. What if her courage had faltered, and she had denied herself this experience? It had been far more wonderful than anything she had imagined. For the rest of her life she would treasure the memory of tonight. She smiled against his shoulder. And tomorrow night. And the next night. And every night until Arlen came home. She wouldn't think beyond that point.

"You should get dressed soon and go back to the house."

"I thought you were asleep." She made no move to rise.

"Someone will wonder where you are." He nudged her until she reluctantly rolled over, bringing her legs off the bunk. Instead of heading for her nightgown, however, she put out the lantern and made her way back to the bunk in the dark.

He was sitting up waiting for her. He had untangled the blanket, and, as she slipped back in beside him, he covered them both. "You shouldn't stay here all night," he said, even as he pulled her down beside him, cradling her in his arm.

"I'll go back early," she whispered. "If someone catches me I've just made a trip to the outhouse."

"And if you're caught leaving the barn?" She heard the smile in his voice.

"I heard a sound and came to investigate. But it was just Tyrant, I suppose." She yawned and snuggled closer.

He chuckled and stroked her hair until she fell asleep.

Christian woke sometime between midnight and dawn. He didn't want Lynnette to risk being discovered, but he put off waking her for a few minutes, enjoying the feel of her in his arms. She was proof that last night hadn't been another dream.

When he felt himself responding to her nearness, he

threw the blanket off himself and slipped his arm out from under her. He was wedged between her and the wall but managed to climb out by the foot of the bed. Lynnette immediately sighed and stretched out in the space he had vacated.

Moonlight streaming through the small window led him to the pile of clothes on the floor. He dressed quickly, then lit the lantern. Lynnette groaned, pulling the blanket over her face.

He laughed and went to sit beside her. ''You better go back, sweetheart.''

''What time is it?''

''I don't know. A couple hours before dawn, I think.''

''Good. We have a couple hours.'' She rolled over and tried to pull him into bed.

He gave her a quick kiss, then pulled her arms from around his neck. ''Martha gets up before dawn to start breakfast, anyway. This is Sunday, so she'll be even earlier. And I don't know exactly what time it is.''

She frowned but relented. She threw the blanket off, and he stood to let her rise. She seemed unashamed of her nakedness, an observation that pleased him. She bent to retrieve the nightgown from the floor, and he admired her feminine hips and rounded bottom until the gown slid down and hid them.

She struggled to pull her thick hair out of the neckline. As she tied the front of the gown, he found the ribbon he had pulled from her hair the night before. ''Come here,'' he said, holding it toward her. ''Let me fix your hair.''

She turned to him, anticipation evident in her eyes

even in the dim light. She came toward him slowly and knelt on the floor in front of him. He lifted the heavy tresses onto his lap and worked the tangles loose from the bottom upward. Finally, he could rub his fingers over her scalp and slide them down through her hair to where the ends curled around his fingers.

He plaited her hair the same way he did Emily's, but it was a totally different experience. Instead of thinking of a little girl who was growing up too fast, he thought of a woman he wanted as his own. He wanted to do this every night before they slept. He wanted to find a way to make that possible.

"When I watched you braid your sister's hair," she said, breaking into his thoughts. "I pretended it was mine. Even when I was sitting next to Arlen."

"Please don't feel guilty for falling in love with me." His own guilt was hard enough to bear.

"It happened so fast," she said. She made a choking sound, and he suspected she was crying.

"We fell in love because we were meant to be together."

She shook her head, but he was used to Emily's sudden moves and kept from pulling her hair. "I'm grateful to Arlen," he said evenly. "I would never have met you if it wasn't for him. I plan to take whatever you'll give me for however long. And I don't plan to give up on forever."

He tied off the braid and slid to the floor, taking her in his arms. "Don't cry," he whispered. "We can talk about this later. Promise you'll come to me tonight?"

She nodded, swiping at her tears. "Tonight and

every night until I have to—'' She choked, then visibly pulled herself together. ''Leave,'' she finished.

He helped her to her feet and put the robe around her shoulders. When she had tied it securely around her narrow waist he pulled her back into his arms for a lingering kiss. ''Please,'' he whispered, resting his forehead against hers. ''Don't spend the day crying. Spend it looking forward to tonight.''

She gave him a small sad smile and nodded.

Carrying the lantern, he walked with her to the door. He put out the light, afraid someone would see them together, kissed her one more time and opened the door. He stood in the shadows and watched her hurry to the house. She turned once, and he stepped into the moonlight so she could see that he had waited.

Then she was inside, closing the door behind her. He had let her go, but only for today. He would think of a way they could be together.

Lynnette pleaded a headache and asked to be excused from church. She hadn't stayed in her room long after leaving Christian, but had gone down to help Martha with the lunch. As she worked, she imagined Hugh introducing her to the neighbors as Arlen's intended bride. It seemed an even worse prospect now than it had the week before. She had prayed for another road-soaking rain, but to no avail.

Now she stood just inside the balcony doors, watching the party pull out of the yard. Perry was in the wagon with the women. The other three men were on horseback, Christian waiting in the rear. He glanced up at her window before following the others out of the yard.

She left the door open to the morning breeze and moved to her bed, sinking into it. She couldn't regret last night, no matter how much she thought she should. She wished Christian didn't hold out hope for a future together. He was only going to be hurt worse. Still, she had to love him all the more for it.

She rose and crossed to the desk, looking down at the letter she had begun to Amanda. The torn letter from her friend lay beside it, a reminder of Taggart.

She had been filled with panic when she had first read the letters. Now it seemed a little foolish. It was one thing to write a letter, even a threatening one, and quite another to take off across country searching for a ranch hidden in the Flint Hills. Surely when he received no answer to his nasty little letters he would give up.

She had convinced herself that she had overreacted when the sound of hoofbeats on packed earth made her freeze. And made her conscious of how alone she was.

"Taggart?" she breathed. She had to know. She crept to the door, trying to keep herself hidden. She peered out just as the horse and rider came into view below. The horse was dun and the rider was Christian.

She nearly collapsed with relief. She stepped out onto the balcony and hailed him. He reined in the mare and waved.

"What are you doing back?" she called.

"My horse was starting to go lame," he answered.

He was too cheerful for such sorry news. "Really?" she asked.

"No."

She laughed and turned, hurrying from the room. He was just uncinching the saddle when she ran into the barn. He caught her in his arms and swung her around, laughing. When he settled her back on the ground he sobered. "Your headache. I forgot."

She laughed. "I heal as quickly as your horse."

"You're sure? I thought you looked pale at breakfast."

"Martha mentioned it, too," she said. "I was just worried how I would survive my introduction to the neighborhood as Arlen's future wife."

He nodded. "Let me take care of the mare, then we can talk."

She stood back and watched him work, watched the muscles play across his shoulders as he lifted the saddle, watched the grace of his movements as he rubbed down the horse. She would have asked to help him, but she remembered him saying that the mare might bite. Before he left the stall, he wrapped one of the horse's ankles. "Miracle cure," he said, winking.

"I feel so wicked," she said, grinning at him.

"I like the sound of that." He took her hand, and they left the barn. When Lynnette would have gone toward the house, he steered her toward the rock bench under the cottonwood tree. "Sit down," he said. "We need to talk."

She did as he bade her thinking how handsome he looked in his Sunday suit. She hoped she would get a chance to take it off.

"I want you to marry me, Lynnette," he announced.

She sighed. "You know I can't."

He knelt in front of her. "I know no such thing."

She placed one palm against his freshly shaved cheek. He turned his head and kissed her wrist. "Just imagine it," she said. "This is still Arlen's home. How will he feel every time he sees us together?"

"He'll find someone else," Christian insisted.

"Of course. Someone who really is right for him. But by then his relationship with you will be ruined. I know you don't want that. You love your brother."

"I love Arlen, but I love you more."

The anguish on his face tore at her heart. "Please try to understand," she said gently. "I'll hurt Arlen when I tell him I don't love him. But I must do it. To tell him that I love his brother instead, would be too much. There's the election—"

"When it's over?"

"I'll be gone."

He looked at her for a long time, and she felt her heart crumbling. "I'll find you," he whispered.

She shook her head. She couldn't tell anyone where she went because of Taggart. Suddenly she had a vision of Christian trying to protect her from a madman. No, leaving was for the best. She couldn't put him in danger.

"I'll go with you," he said more firmly. "I'll give Arlen my share of the ranch, and we'll leave together."

Lynnette was speechless. He was offering to give up everything for her. It was more than she could ask of him. In time he would regret it. She shook her head. "Let's not talk any more about it. Please."

He looked about to protest but rose instead, pulling her to her feet. "Let's not spend the morning arguing."

She smiled, turning her face up to his. "I'm sure we can think of a better way to spend the time." They started toward the house with their arms around each other.

"I was thinking about a soft bed, large enough for the both of us," he said.

"I know where to find one. See the balcony on the left?"

He frowned. "The one on the right," he suggested. "That's still Arlen's room to me."

"See. It does bother you," she said.

Lynnette was right, of course. Christian couldn't quite get past the notion that he was betraying his brother. He reminded himself that Lynnette did not love Arlen and had no intention of marrying Arlen. But at this moment, while he led Lynnette up the stairs, Arlen didn't know that.

Once inside his room, she came into his arms. Her soft body calling sweetly to his, her lips begging for his kiss, made him forget everything else. After a deep kiss that fed his hunger more than satisfied it, he slowly removed her clothes, peeling away the layers until her beautiful body was exposed to his view.

He stood back to enjoy it, letting his eyes linger on every curve. He saw her tremble and moved to enfold her in his arms. She was warm and pliant, trembling with desire instead of cold.

"My turn," she whispered after another heated kiss. She slid her hands along his shoulders, dislodging his dress coat. He shrugged it off, letting it drop to the floor. He tried to gather her close again, but she moved away enough to reach his tie. "You look very dashing in your Sunday best," she said, slipping the knot loose.

"I consider that a great compliment, coming from such an expert on men's fashion."

She quirked an eyebrow at him. "What gave you that impression?"

He grinned at her. He didn't move to help her with the collar buttons but grazed his hands over the smooth curve of her waist and hips instead. "Your book has quite a few references to your hero's dress."

"Description only," she said, appearing to concentrate on her task.

"I have wondered if you started the little discussion with the girls about men's clothes."

She shook her head. "My main contribution was to defend the close-fitting pants and loose shirts of the cowboy."

He laughed. "And why was that?"

She left the tie hanging loose and started on the button at his throat. "The pants, of course, because of the way they fit," she said.

"How wicked of you ladies. Especially since you hide everything from us." He cupped her bottom and brought her closer against him, pressing his arousal against her flat stomach.

"And the shirt," she murmured, a little breathlessly, "because you leave it open here." Her mouth found the hollow of his throat and trailed downward as she undid each button. He groaned as a new wave of desire washed over him.

When her lips were stopped by the waistline of his pants, he stepped away, divesting himself of the rest of his clothing. He scooped her into his arms and carried her to the bed as he had the night before. This time he nearly flung her onto the larger softer mattress. "Don't try my patience, woman," he growled.

She chuckled deep in her throat, holding her arms out to him. "What patience?"

He slid in beside her, pulling her against him. "Ah, sweet Lynnette. With you I have no patience, no willpower, not even reason." His hands turned gentle, and he stroked her hair. "I feel the most tender love and greediest lust all at once."

She moved to bring her face near his. "I love you, too, Christian. And I want you." Her mouth touched his, and he let her nip and lick at his lips for a moment before turning her to her back and branding her with his kiss.

He loved her slowly, exploring every inch of her precious body and encouraging her to explore his. The sunlight filtering through the curtains made a soft light, casting a dreamlike aura over them. It was at least as wonderful as the night before, but Christian couldn't help but think of what more there could be. If she truly belonged to him, he could lose himself deep inside her softness. But he kept the longing firmly in check.

When their damp, spent bodies began to feel the

chill of the room, Christian rose, found a blanket that had fallen to the floor and spread it over Lynnette.

She gave him a seductive smile, "Do we have to get up?"

He shook his head. "Don't see why." She raised the cover, and he crawled in with her again.

They spent the rest of the morning in bed, touching, loving and resting. It was hunger that finally drove them out. Christian rose first, hung his Sunday clothes away and dressed. He was well aware of Lynnette, lying on his bed, watching every move he made.

"Does this suit your sense of style?" he asked, tucking his favorite shirt into his tightest pants.

She smiled. "Perfect. If you must get dressed at all."

"I need to eat," he said, joining her on the bed. "I need to keep up my strength."

Her eyes twinkled at the promise in his voice. "Martha left a lunch for me. I'll share it with you."

"Up," he said, snatching the blanket off her. "I'll help you get dressed."

He buttoned an occasional button, but mostly he watched the layers go back on, covering her body from his view but not from his memory. She returned to her room to fix her hair, and he went to the kitchen, searching out enough bread and cheese to stretch Martha's lunch to feed them both.

He was setting the kitchen table when Lynnette joined him. He turned to greet her and found her in his arms. They indulged in a long lingering kiss. Too soon the others would return, and they would go back to their roles of soon-to-be brother and sister. But now, as they shared the meal, they pretended they belonged to each other and would share all their tomorrows.

On Tuesday night, Lynnette slipped out to the barn to meet Christian for the fourth night in a row. She didn't know how much longer Arlen would stay away. She vowed to treat each night as if it were the last.

Christian had other ideas. After they had satisfied each other and lay cuddled together in the narrow bunk, he ran a finger across her lips and whispered, "I won't let you go."

She felt tears sting her eyes and turned away from him. "We've talked about this, Christian. We can't do it to Arlen."

"What about what it's doing to me?"

She took a moment to answer. The last thing she wanted was to hurt Christian. But she had known she would since she had declared her love up on the rocky hilltop. "If I stay with you," she began slowly, "Arlen would blame you. It would kill the love I've seen between you. Your father and sister would have to choose. I would be responsible for destroying the family."

"This family's been fractured for some time."

His fingers idly stroking her shoulder made it difficult to concentrate but she had to speak her mind. "Do you think it can handle another blow? Can Emily?"

She heard him sigh. "Then let's both go away. We can leave the family to comfort each other. I'm not vain enough to think I'll be missed for long."

She wondered if he thought she was being vain to

think her defection would wound Arlen so deeply. But how many times had he called her his life? Still, there was Taggart to consider. She wasn't sure how real the threat was to herself, but she knew she couldn't put Christian in danger.

"But you'd miss the ranch," she whispered. "How long before you blamed me for taking you away from it?"

He was silent for a long moment. His hand moved from her shoulder to her breast and he caressed it gently. "Do you know what I've thought about for the past two nights?"

His words were a warm breeze against her ears. She shook her head slightly as silent tears wet her cheeks.

"Loving you. Completely. Giving you the one thing I've held back. If I filled you with my seed, would that bind you to me? Would it make you stay?"

She shook her head, choking back a sob.

"That's what I was afraid of."

She felt his sadness in his touch but knew it couldn't be any greater than her own.

Chapter Fifteen

Midmorning the next day, Lynnette stood on her balcony and watched Christian ride away. Earlier, before she left his arms, he had told her that he would be gone all day checking cattle, but promised to be back by evening.

Even after so many days it seemed incredible. Christian was in love with her. She let the sweetness of that knowledge wash over her for a minute before turning back into the room. Arlen might even now be on his way home. Her time with Christian could already be over.

She looked around the room that had begun to feel like her own. Her trunk stood open against one wall, her writing materials already packed inside. She knew she wouldn't be writing anything but tragedies for a while. Maybe someday the tender feelings she had for Christian would make their way into a book, but she found happy endings hard to imagine.

She decided against any further packing until Arlen had come home. Her need to pack might serve as an excuse to stay one more night. One more night with Christian.

She was becoming too melancholy, she decided. She should go downstairs, see what everyone else was doing, find some way to busy herself.

The girls were using the dining room table to cut out Emily's new dress. Rose seemed to have the task well in hand, and Lynnette left them chattering happily.

Martha wasn't in the kitchen so Lynnette tapped gently on the study door. She and Hugh had shared more than one companionable afternoon reading quietly together. Hugh answered immediately.

"I hope I'm not interrupting," she said as she entered.

"Not at all," he said. "What can I do for you?"

"I thought I might read in here if you don't mind."

"You're more than welcome," he said, offering his well-stocked bookshelves with a gesture.

She stepped to the shelves, and Hugh turned back to his work at the desk. She was reading in a comfortable chair in the corner of the study when a commotion at the back door caught her attention.

"That must be Arlen," Hugh said as he set his pen aside.

Lynnette did her best to smile in return. She took a moment to close the book and return it to the shelf before following him out of the study.

"Felicia!" She heard Hugh's greeting as she stepped into the room. "This is a delightful surprise."

"I'm not sure how delighted you'll be when you've heard me out," she said. "I've been most distressed."

Lynnette barely noticed Felicia, or Arlen for that matter. Julian Taggart stood with the other new arrivals. He looked every inch the city gentleman on a social call. His hair was slicked back, his clothes, despite the journey, were immaculate. His smile reminded her of a snake. Lynnette felt her skin crawl.

She was half-aware of Arlen making the introductions and Hugh's questioning glance. The girls joined them, and Emily ran to hug her mother.

Emily offered to get some lemonade, and Felicia told her to bring it to the living room and wait for them there. She would speak to the others alone.

Lynnette's mind was screaming, *Why is he here?* She wanted nothing so much as to run and hide. Instead, she followed Felicia and the others into the study.

When everyone was in, Felicia closed the door and Hugh moved chairs for everyone's comfort. "What is this about?" he asked.

"Miss Sterling," Felicia began, speaking to Lynnette for the first time. "This young gentleman paid me a visit last week. I can see you're quite shocked to see him. And you should be. You didn't tell Arlen that you had promised to marry Mr. Taggart."

Lynnette gasped. "Marry Julian! But I..."

"Well, my dear, Mr. Taggart has told me something of your misunderstanding. I'm sure you can work it out amicably. He seemed like a reasonable young man. But that's only half of what I came to talk to you about. The rest concerns a book."

Lynnette took a deep breath. "Of course. The book. I should have told everyone about it sooner." She watched Arlen as she spoke, not wanting to dwell on Julian's presence. "I meant to tell you, Arlen."

"Feel free to do so now, my dear," Julian said, clearly enjoying himself.

"I wrote a love story," she offered, "of a somewhat...scandalous nature. It paid some bills, and I had plenty."

"Scandalous may not describe it so much as common," Felicia said.

Hugh laughed. "Does that mean it's popular? Perhaps congratulations are in order."

Lynnette gave her champion a smile. "I'm afraid that's not the point. I kept it a secret, and I shouldn't have."

"My dear," said Felicia. "I quite understand your need to raise funds as well as your need to keep it quiet. But naturally Arlen would never have agreed to marry you had he known."

"Mother," Arlen said, coming to his feet and pacing around the room, "it's not just the book. I've known for some time that things weren't going to work out. I didn't mean to deceive you, Lynnette, but some things have made me wonder about the wisdom of taking you for a wife."

He came to kneel in front of Lynnette's chair. "I'm not putting this at all well. Try to understand. I had serious doubts, but because of your situation, I was determined to hold to my promise. But now Mr. Taggart has come. He'll take care of you."

Lynnette stared at him. She wasn't leaving with Julian! But she would take one thing at a time. "Arlen, I've known, too, that we weren't right for each other.

That's what I wanted to talk to you about before you left this last time.''

He seemed to only now remember that she had asked to speak with him several times. "Yes, well, I was somewhat confused,'' he muttered.

She couldn't help but smile. "I was afraid of hurting you.''

Felicia cleared her throat. "I'm glad that's settled. I don't know about anyone else, but I'm ready for some refreshment.''

She started for the door, but Julian's voice stopped her. "I'd like a word alone with my intended, first.''

"I'm not your intended,'' Lynnette protested. A cold look of warning on Julian's face silenced her.

"We'll only be a few minutes,'' he told the others.

Felicia and Arlen seemed unconcerned as they filed out of the room. Hugh hesitated until Lynnette nodded her consent.

As soon as Hugh had closed the door, Lynnette rounded on Julian, choosing to take the offensive. "How dare you tell Felicia that I had promised to marry you.''

"But you did, darling,'' he said, all innocent smiles. "Don't try to pretend that you aren't Silver Nightingale. I saw the notes in your parlor.''

"That book is a work of fiction. If you see yourself in it, it's your imagination!''

"Come, come, my dear.'' He walked toward her, and she tried not to cringe. "No need to pretend with me. I'm your Julian Robert. So clever of you to use my middle name.''

She thought of the second postscript, of her heroine,

dead in her hero's arms. *Now we will always be together.* The man was mad. She had no idea how to handle him. "What do you want?"

"You, my dear." He reached out a long finger and stroked her cheek. She brushed him off, and he grabbed her shoulders. "Do you think you can abandon me for someone else? That silly politician, maybe? You won't change his mind about not marrying you. No one will vote for a man whose wife writes dirty books."

"You heard me agree to break the engagement." She hoped that would make him turn her loose, but his grip only tightened.

"I can still ruin him, you know. The fact that you were ever associated with him would hurt him. And, of course, there's this." One hand released her and he pulled aside his coat, revealing a pistol in a shoulder holster.

She stared at the gun in horror. Was he capable of murder? She didn't want to trust that he wasn't. She feared for the whole family, and she was the reason he was here. She needed to lead him away before anyone was hurt.

"Please, don't," she said, not expecting her plea to have any effect on him. She would do whatever he said and look for a chance to escape later. She was enormously grateful that Christian was gone. She knew he would try to stop him, and Taggart would kill him. Her own death seemed preferable. "I'll do whatever you say. Don't hurt anyone."

"Now you're being sensible," he said, backing away and straightening his coat as if he had been the one assaulted. ''Go tell the nice folks goodbye. I'll visit with them while you pack your trunk, then we'll be on our way.''

''Where are you taking me?''

''Why, home, of course.''

Christian spurred his horse toward home. In what seemed like record time, he pulled to a stop in front of the barn. An unfamiliar buggy waited near the house. He hoped this unexpected visitor wouldn't keep him from Lynnette.

The living room was full of people. The first to register on his mind after the certain knowledge that Lynnette was not present, was Arlen. He sat in cozy conversation with Emily and Rose in one corner of the room.

In another corner a stranger talked with his father. Between the men sat his stepmother. ''Felicia.'' He stopped in his tracks. He hadn't seen her in years.

''Hello, Christian,'' she said, coming to her feet and gliding toward him. ''You look just like your father did at your age.''

There was a wistful quality to her smile he didn't quite trust. ''You look the same as ever,'' he said, kissing the cheek she offered.

''Oh, I'm sorry. You haven't met Mr. Taggart. Julian, this is our other son, Christian.''

Christian gave the stranger little more than a glance. If Felicia had finally found another husband and had come to ask for a divorce, the less he knew about it the better. Besides, he had other things on his mind.

"Where's Lynnette?" He directed his question toward his father.

It was the stranger who answered. "She's in her room packing to leave."

"Leave?" She had told Arlen, then. But his brother didn't look particularly heartbroken. His laugh mingled with the girls'. He shook his head. Lynnette wasn't leaving.

"With me," Taggart added. Christian studied the stranger for the first time and disliked him instantly.

"She's my fiancée," Taggart went on. "Didn't she tell you?" He straightened a ruffle-trimmed cuff before gloating up at him.

Christian turned away before he was tempted to wipe the smirk off the man's face. He crossed the room and took the steps two at a time. Taggart's voice drifted up to him. "My, my. Everyone seems to fall in love with the chit."

He didn't bother to knock on the door. If it had been locked, he would have kicked it in. As it was, he swung it open hard enough to make it bounce off the wall. She dropped the garment she had been folding and stared at him, one hand on her heart, the other at her lips. He tried to get his breathing under control. His anger was directed at the man downstairs, not at Lynnette. Fiancée, he had called her.

"Are you really leaving?" He walked toward her, pointing back toward the stairs. "With him?"

She turned away and continued her packing. "Yes, it's true. I'm sorry, Christian. I never meant to hurt you. Julian's an old beau. It was his letters that Arlen brought last Friday."

"The day before you slept with me?" Nothing made sense. He felt as if he had been thrown from a horse and hit his head. He couldn't catch his breath and the room seemed to tip.

"I never intended to let you leave," he said. "Arlen will forgive us. And if he doesn't, so what? You're all I care about." He moved closer, but she brushed past him to put a stack of clothes in her trunk.

"Try to understand, Christian. It's over between us, and it has nothing to do with Arlen."

"And everything to do with *him?*" He pointed back over his shoulder toward the door and the odious man downstairs.

She spun around, her face stony white. "I told you. Julian's an old beau. We had broken off, but he came all the way out here to find me. I'm overjoyed to see him again."

He stared at her until she lowered her eyes. "I don't believe you."

She actually laughed, but it wasn't a pleasant sound. "Think, Christian. Can you really imagine me as a rancher's wife? Out here so far from town? I need to go back where I belong."

She turned away again, as if her packing was the only thing that interested her. He sat down on the bed and watched her. After a long moment she spoke again. "You were a fling, Christian, and I enjoyed it. I'm sorry if you thought it was anything more."

"You planned to go back to *him* all along." He was surprised that he could keep his voice even.

She didn't turn around again. When she closed the

trunk's lid and lifted her two small bags, she spoke.
"Would you and Jake carry this down?"

"No." His fingers itched to touch her. He crossed
his arms, tucking his hands safely against his chest.
"Let your precious Julian do it."

He could see part of her profile, but her eyes were
hidden by her lowered lashes. She bit her lip, the only
sign of guilt. "Please trust me that this is for the best,"
she said before she left the room.

Christian didn't move. What had he been to her? A
character for a book? An education? *He* was certainly
wiser now.

He was still sitting on the bed when Jake and Arlen
came for the trunk. They were obviously curious why
he was there. Not wanting to talk to anyone, he rose
and walked onto the balcony. He braced his arms
against the railing and hung his head. He had offered
to give up this ranch, his home, his family for her. She
had offered him nothing but a lie.

His own bitter laugh sounded foreign to him. He
had held back, denied himself to protect her. Had she
manipulated that somehow? It didn't seem likely. She
must have had a good laugh over it, though.

He heard voices below him and watched Arlen and
Jake load the trunk into the boot of the buggy. Emily
was there to hug Lynnette goodbye. He heard her
thank Hugh for his hospitality and nearly laughed
again.

As she walked to the buggy, Taggart at her side,
she looked up. He met her gaze coldly, and she
stopped. Taggart turned as well, but Christian ignored

him. He stared Lynnette down until she looked away. It wasn't nearly as satisfying as he had hoped.

Soon the buggy rattled out of the yard. He heard the door below close and assumed his family had gone back inside. Still he stood where he was. He remembered back to the first day he had met her, barely two weeks before. He relived every glance, every word, looking for hints of her deception but found none. She had seemed more genuine than any other woman he had known. And he had loved her. If the pain he felt was any indication, he still did.

When his arms and shoulders began to ache, he straightened and stretched. He was as bewildered as ever. He left the balcony and crossed the room. He caught a hint of her perfume and held his breath until he was on the landing and her door was closed behind him.

He went slowly down the stairs. Hugh and Felicia were together in the living room, and they watched him descend, the very picture of concern. He wished he could think of something glib to say to end the tension and allow him an escape. His mind seemed too dull, too numb.

"Christian," Felicia said, coming to her feet. "I had no idea. When Arlen took the news so well, I thought the worst was over, but now you act as if you love her, too."

Christian shrugged. "She fooled us all, I guess."

Hugh spoke up. "I'm not so sure about that."

Christian looked at his father sharply. He was amazed to find a tiny spark of hope still survived in his heart. Foolish. He should snuff it out, not fan it to life to cause him additional pain. He turned away.

Felicia said, "I can't see how she could prefer Mr. Taggart to either one of my sons."

Christian's response was automatic. "I'm not your son." He saw the pain on her face and sighed. "I'm sorry. I shouldn't have said that."

She came to him and wrapped her arms around his waist. "I left you too, didn't I?"

"Shhh," he said, stroking her narrow back. "It was a long time ago."

Over the top of Felicia's head he watched his father stand and walk toward them. "I don't think we misjudged her," he said.

Christian clinched his jaw. Why did his father insist on torturing him?

Felicia raised her head, half turning but remaining in his arms. "You mean she didn't really want to leave with him?"

"I think she's being blackmailed somehow."

"But he already told everyone about the book," Felicia insisted. "What else would there be?"

Christian gave a mirthless laugh. He waved away his parents' questioning gazes, unable to explain. When she confided in Taggart, had she flattered *him* into thinking he was the only one who knew? God! She had made him feel special.

Hugh continued, evidently undaunted by the pain he was causing. "Before Taggart arrived, I would have sworn the girl was in love with you." This news startled Felicia, but Christian was beyond any more surprises.

"Felicia." Hugh turned to her. "Remember her first reaction upon seeing Taggart? She was frightened. She denied that she was promised to him. It was only after they were alone that she changed her story."

Christian eyed his father, trying to decide what he meant. He gently set Felicia away from him and stepped toward the older man. "You think she left here against her will?" He shook his head. "Upstairs she told me I was nothing to her."

Hugh shook his head sadly. "I don't know, son. I just don't want to see you make the same mistake I did. You shouldn't let her go."

Christian didn't stay to see what Felicia's reaction might be to that confession. He started for the door, hurrying faster with each step until he left the house at a run.

Lynnette chewed her lip to keep the tears at bay. She had a feeling Taggart would enjoy seeing them. He had laughed and gloated over Christian's broken heart all the way to town.

She had tried to block out his voice and think. Now that she had led him away from Christian and his family, she needed to find a law officer, someone trained with guns. She didn't know how much law there was in Cottonwood Station, if any. She would have to wait until they got to Topeka and talk to the police. But what could she tell them? She had destroyed the letters with their veiled threats. Julian would deny that he was taking her against her will. He could be very charming if he wanted to.

The idea that she might have to stay with him horrified her. She would escape. But to where? She couldn't seek protection from Amanda or any other acquaintance without endangering someone else. She would have to take her chances with the police and hope they believed her.

She pictured herself running and hiding from Taggart all her life. The desolation she felt reminded her of Christian's face, and a new wave of tears threatened. She had hurt him beyond forgiving, but perhaps she had saved his life.

"Here we are," Taggart said, pulling the buggy to a stop near the train station. "Come with me while I buy our tickets."

"I'll wait with the buggy," she offered, uncertain if her legs would hold her if she tried to stand.

He laughed. "I'm not that stupid." He took her arm, dragging her from the buggy. "You'll come with me."

He bought the tickets, directed the porter to the trunk and paid a boy to return the buggy to the livery, all with one hand firmly gripping Lynnette's arm. Taggart was eager to board and moved to a few feet from the edge of the platform where he could watch for the train. There they stood side by side, as close as lovers, and waited.

It was a surprisingly short wait. If Lynnette had realized, she might have stalled in her packing, making them miss this train. That would have made little difference, though, she supposed. He would have simply bought a room in town for the night. She shuddered at the thought.

The train was coming into view when she felt Taggart stiffen. She turned to see what had caught his attention and gasped. Christian was galloping toward the station. He looked magnificent. But Lord, he shouldn't be here!

"Let's discourage your rancher friend," Taggart said, swinging her around to face him. "Kiss me."

His mouth came down hard on hers. She feared for Christian and knew she needed to make him leave. Still, she couldn't pretend to enjoy Taggart's assault. She tried to struggle, but he held her too tightly.

One hand left her arm, and she hoped for a chance, trying to wrench away. The next horrifying second she realized he was reaching for the pistol under his coat.

Time seemed to hang suspended. Events happened in quick succession, even overlapped, but she saw them each clearly, helplessly. Christian dismounted and ran toward them. She screamed a warning, but it was drowned in the shrill whistle of the train. Taggart had the pistol out, hidden from Christian by her body, which he clutched as a shield. He raised the pistol to aim it, and she shoved with all her might, knocking him off balance. He stumbled back, one step, two. The pistol discharged, and she felt a burn near her throat.

If she was shot, Christian was safe, she told herself even as she felt herself falling. But she was falling forward, falling with Taggart. He was going over the edge of the platform into the path of the oncoming train. And he was taking her with him!

She thought she screamed, but it might have been the train whistle again. Strong arms encircled her waist, pulling her back, wrenching her arm free of

Taggart. The train screeched past in front of her, coming to a stop.

She turned and buried her face in the strong chest, grateful for the arms that held her up. She was shaking, but, she realized, so was he. She would have pulled back to see his face, but one callused hand pinned her head against his chest.

"I couldn't let you go," he whispered.

She couldn't speak. There was too much to say to know where to begin. All that mattered now, anyway, was that Christian was safe, and so was she.

It was dark by the time they returned to the ranch. They had told their story to a young deputy, who found plenty of witnesses to Taggart's final minutes. Lynnette buried her face in Christian's shoulder as what was left of his body was removed from under the train. Christian rented the same buggy, reloaded Lynnette's trunk and, with his horse tied on behind, took her home.

Jake came to meet them. "Take care of the horse," Christian said. "We'll unload the trunk in the morning."

Lynnette let him help her down. He grabbed the valises and escorted her to the door as Jake jumped into the buggy and turned it toward the barn.

She had told him everything on the way home. He had said so little she didn't know what he was thinking. He had come after her and now had brought her home. She clung to that and prayed.

Everyone was waiting for them in the living room. Hugh and Arlen stood when they entered and Hugh greeted her with a kiss on the cheek. "I'm delighted to see you've come back to us," he said.

She smiled her thanks. Christian led her toward a chair and deposited the bags at the foot of the stairs, taking a seat across the room from her. She tried to look at everyone except Christian, but they all seemed a bit of a blur.

"Has Mr. Taggart left, then?" Felicia asked.

Christian supplied the answer. "He's dead," he said simply.

Felicia paled, but Emily looked at her brother with admiration. "You killed him for her?" she asked.

Christian left it to Lynnette to answer. "I killed him," she said. She told the whole story again, starting with her brief relationship with Taggart. Hugh and Felicia seemed to have pieced much of it together in her absence, but Emily listened enthralled. When she told of falling in love with Christian, the girl sighed dreamily.

She couldn't explain the terrifying letters from Taggart without explaining about the book. Emily sat up, her eyes wide. "You wrote *Passion's*—I mean, a book called *Passion's Secret?* That's wonderful." She and Rose exchanged a look.

"Can you keep that a secret, Muffin? Rose?" Christian asked. Lynnette could see a certain speculation in the gaze he leveled on his sister and her friend.

"Swear to God," she breathed, her hand on her heart.

"Rose can keep a secret, too," Arlen said, smiling at the girl. "Can't you, dear?"

The girl blushed furiously.

"I doubt if it will hurt Arlen now that you're no longer engaged," Felicia ventured.

"Unless she's engaged to Arlen's brother," Hugh suggested.

"We should keep it quiet then, I suppose," she said.

"I need to check the horses," Christian said, rising. Lynnette watched him sadly. The talk of his possible engagement to her had made him uncomfortable. It was not as sure a thing as the elder Prescotts assumed.

He was almost to the door before he turned and addressed her. "Come with me," he said.

She was startled. What explanation would they give the family? Christian evidently felt they needed none. He took her hand as she rose and led her from the room without another word.

Inside the barn, he lit a lantern, then turned toward her. She had hoped he would pull her into his arms, but he kept his distance. She had explained everything twice. What more could she say? Was he angry that she hadn't trusted him to protect her?

It was on the tip of her tongue to ask his forgiveness when he spoke. "Can you forgive me?"

She laughed in surprise. "For what? For coming after me? For saving my life?"

"For letting you go. I should have known you didn't want to leave with him."

"I intended to be convincing," she said. "I was scared for your whole family. Especially for you." She walked toward him, hoping he would welcome her into his arms. "I knew about the pistol under his coat. I was afraid if you tried to stop me he would kill you."

"He almost killed you instead." One gentle finger touched the powder burn at her throat.

He opened his arms, and she stepped into them, pressing her body flush against his. "We're both safe now." She looked up at him and smiled. "Help me forget it ever happened."

"I think I can do that." His voice was so seductive it made her tremble. Keeping one arm around her, he took down the lantern and started toward the back of the barn. "No more excuses. You're going to marry me."

It wasn't a question, but she murmured, "Yes."

He kissed her then, tenderly at first then fiercely. When he lifted his head, he chuckled. "I shouldn't do that while I'm holding the lantern. I'm liable to burn the place down."

Inside the tack room, he set it on the worktable. She didn't wait for him to come to her but moved into his arms as soon as he turned around. Her fingers sought his buttons as she kissed him eagerly.

"No more secrets?" he asked as he raised his head.

"None," she murmured, pressing upward to await another kiss.

He grinned again, that heart-stopping dimpled grin she loved. "I just have one more secret to share with you."

His lips found hers, as filled with promise as his words. She felt the familiar passion rise inside her along with anticipation.

He carried her to the bunk and laid her down gently, bracing himself above her. She looked up into his dear face and felt emotion bubble up inside her. It came out a throaty laugh.

"What?" he asked, smiling fondly.

"I thought each time we made love it was special because it could have been the last. Now, I discover that knowing we will always be together fills me with such joy I can't contain myself."

"Don't try," he said, brushing his cheek against hers. "We deserve a little joy."

He loved her then, with kisses and caresses and whispered promises of more to come until she thought she would go mad. How could this final fulfillment be better than what they had already shared? But it was. Feeling him fill her body as he did her senses brought her to a peak higher than she could have imagined. He followed less than a second behind.

When their pulses had returned to normal, he rolled off her, cuddling her against his shoulder. "Now you belong to me completely," he said.

She turned to look at him, amused by the arrogance in his voice. "And you belong to me," she said.

He grinned down at her. "That sounds wonderful from your lips." He turned to kiss them again.

"If I marry you," she began, drawing circles in the fine hairs on his chest.

"When," he corrected. "When you marry me."

She laughed. "When I marry you, can I continue to write?"

"Of course."

"Even if I have to publish them as Silver Nightingale?"

He laughed, rolling over to look down at her. "Have

I told you I'm very proud of Silver Nightingale? And don't think I haven't noticed the little silver nightingale feather you like to wear.'' His fingers teased her collarbone where the pin usually rode her bodice.

She laughed. "You won't be jealous of my heroes?"

"Oh, absolutely. I'll be insanely jealous. You'll have to work hard to prove that I'm your real hero."

She wrapped her arms around his neck, pulling him closer. "I think I can do that," she whispered.

* * * * *

Take 4 bestselling love stories FREE

Plus get a FREE surprise gift!

Special Limited-time Offer

Mail to Harlequin Reader Service®

3010 Walden Avenue
P.O. Box 1867
Buffalo, N.Y. 14240-1867

YES! Please send me 4 free Harlequin Historical™ novels and my free surprise gift. Then send me 4 brand-new novels every month, which I will receive before they appear in bookstores. Bill me at the low price of $3.69 each plus 25¢ delivery and applicable sales tax, if any.* That's the complete price and a savings of over 10% off the cover prices—quite a bargain! I understand that accepting the books and gift places me under no obligation ever to buy any books. I can always return a shipment and cancel at any time. Even if I never buy another book from Harlequin, the 4 free books and the surprise gift are mine to keep forever.

247 BPA A3UR

Name	(PLEASE PRINT)	
Address	Apt. No.	
City	State	Zip

This offer is limited to one order per household and not valid to present Harlequin Historical™ subscribers. *Terms and prices are subject to change without notice. Sales tax applicable in N.Y.

UHIS-696   ©1990 Harlequin Enterprises Limited

Harlequin® Historical

"One of the top five historical trilogies
of the nineties." —*Affaire de Coeur*

Bestselling Harlequin Historical author

THERESA MICHAELS

presents the story of the second widow
in her heartwarming series

THE MERRY WIDOWS
Catherine

"Sensitivity, sensuality and a sense of humor are
hallmarks of Theresa Michaels' captivating storytelling."
—*Romantic Times*

Don't miss reading about Catherine in the second book in the
Merry Widows trilogy, coming to you in February 1998.

KEY TO MY HEART

Unlock the secrets of romance just in time for the most romantic day of the year— Valentine's Day!

Key to My Heart
features three of your favorite authors,

**Kasey Michaels,
Rebecca York
and Muriel Jensen,**

to bring you wonderful tales of romance and Valentine's Day dreams come true.

As an added bonus you can receive Harlequin's special Valentine's Day necklace. FREE with the purchase of every *Key to My Heart* collection.

Available in January,
wherever Harlequin books are sold.

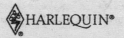

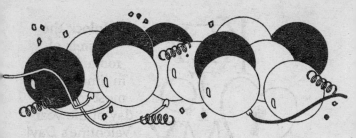

Ring in the New Year with

New Year's Resolution:
FAMILY

**This heartwarming collection of three
contemporary stories rings in the
New Year with babies, families and
the best of holiday romance.**

Add a dash of romance to your holiday celebrations
with this exciting new collection, featuring bestselling
authors **Barbara Bretton, Anne McAllister** and
Leandra Logan.

Available in December,
wherever Harlequin books are sold.

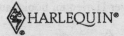

HARLEQUIN WOMEN KNOW ROMANCE WHEN THEY SEE IT.

And they'll see it on **ROMANCE CLASSICS**, the new 24-hour TV channel devoted to romantic movies and original programs like the special **Romantically Speaking—Harlequin™ Goes Prime Time.**

Romantically Speaking—Harlequin™ Goes Prime Time introduces you to many of your favorite romance authors in a program developed exclusively for Harlequin® readers.

Watch for **Romantically Speaking—Harlequin™ Goes Prime Time** beginning in the summer of 1997.

If you're not receiving ROMANCE CLASSICS, call your local cable operator or satellite provider and ask for it today!

Escape to the network of your dreams.

See Ingrid Bergman and Gregory Peck in *Spellbound* on Romance Classics.

Free Gift Offer

With a Free Gift proof-of-purchase
from any Harlequin® book, you can receive
a beautiful cubic zirconia pendant.

This stunning marquise-shaped stone is a genuine cubic
zirconia—accented by an 18" gold tone necklace.
(Approximate retail value $19.95)

Send for yours today...
compliments of  HARLEQUIN®

To receive your free gift, a cubic zirconia pendant, send us one original proof-of-purchase, photocopies not accepted, from the back of any Harlequin Romance®, Harlequin Presents®, Harlequin Temptation®, Harlequin Superromance®, Harlequin Love & Laughter®, Harlequin Intrigue®, Harlequin American Romance®, or Harlequin Historicals® title available at your favorite retail outlet, together with the Free Gift Certificate, plus a check or money order for $1.65 U.S./$2.15 CAN. (do not send cash) to cover postage and handling, payable to Harlequin Free Gift Offer. We will send you the specified gift. Allow 6 to 8 weeks for delivery. Offer good until March 31, 1998, or while quantities last. Offer valid in the U.S. and Canada only.

Free Gift Certificate

Name: _____

Address: _____

City: _____ State/Province: _____ Zip/Postal Code: _____

Mail this certificate, one proof-of-purchase and a check or money order for postage and handling to: HARLEQUIN FREE GIFT OFFER 1998. In the U.S.: 3010 Walden Avenue, P.O. Box 9071, Buffalo NY 14269-9057. In Canada: P.O. Box 604, Fort Erie, Ontario L2Z 5X3.

FREE GIFT OFFER   084-KEZ

ONE PROOF-OF-PURCHASE
To collect your fabulous FREE GIFT, a cubic zirconia pendant, you must include this original proof-of-purchase for each gift with the properly completed Free Gift Certificate.

084-KEZR2